WEATHER AND

BEASTS AND

GROWING THINGS

# WEATHER
## AND
# BEASTS
## AND
# GROWING
# THINGS

### CHARLOTTE SUTTEE

LETHE PRESS

# WEATHER AND BEASTS AND GROWING THINGS

Cover design by TK
Interior design by Inkspiral Design

ISBN: 9781590217580

"There is time enough to gather plenty of wild oats and sow them too, and sing to little Oom, and listen to Ool's joke, and watch newts, and still the story isn't over."

Ursula K. Le Guin

"Have you reckoned the earth much?"

Walt Whitman

ELI DREAMS INTO GENTLE GRAY dawn, dreams, ocean and sky oranging Apartment. Morning sun gauzes skin, gently unfolds shadows from three breathing bodies.

Elinose flares softly. Black hair strands tickle eyes open.

They smile at Stevven, friend, lying long awake beside them on mattress.

Big storm, Stevven replies without noise.

Eli mimes thunder between lips and hands. Boom!

Snickering.

Eli peeks behind them. On second mattress, Mary sleeps like dying.

Hungry? Stevven asks.

Eli nods.

Stevven slides off mattress, gathers blood into head. Bare feet slippery on crop carpet, they cross to furthest window, squat and pee in cold toilet bowl. Eli goes next. Stevven tosses urine out window into ocean five stories below. Yesterday rainwater trickles from spicket into plastic washing bowl, froths leftover soap scum. They wash hands.

What do you want to eat? Stevven whispers.

Beans.

Eli moves into kitchen, residual night, limbing wide and familiar to doorless cupboard, collects beancan, spoon.

They sit across from each other using light on floor as table. Stevven reaches, cranks window open completely. Morning marsh tides gnaw on Apartment building. Galling birds stir over barrier islands where pioneering thicket sniff into blowout, chewup places, roots and rhizomes slow, callusing in air, complicating water.

Lone person walks pallet bridge through old financial district, passes saltwater reeds blooming out tumbler doors, mud caking yellow road lines. Eli balances lone person on fingertip until they disappear behind beach dune, broomsedge.

Stevven turns bean can in hand. *Pecan Acres Organic Maple and Onion Baked Beans*, wooden spoon lifting beans from dishpan, farmland rolling into horizon, cows, red clapboard barn.

Lies, Stevven says, works dull pocketknife around can circumference.

Eli spoons out one bean from syrup bath then sucks spoon dry, passes can to Stevven.

You can eat more, Stevven says.

I want them to last.

Stevven fills spoon with beans, heavy, grainy, sweet. Beans fall apart on tongue. They pass spoon between them, eating and watching ocean life. Apartment stirs awake, noises and rumblings, flyswat sounds that steal eye and ear briefly.

Time for Garden, Stevven says.

I want to play jungle.

I have to go see BluBerry. To see if the storm hurt them. It's important. Then we'll play jungle.

Can I come?

Okay.

Stevven slips on shoes, makes note to resole them later. Eli does not wear shoes.

They step out into hallway, pale and dark, into stairwell, darker. One flight up to rooftop, Garden.

GARDEN TEEMS, EARLY INSECT AND bird.

Stevven rushes past everyone, garlic and rutabaga, greenbean blossoms, gourds. They settle in cool dark shadow before BluBerry shrub.

BluBerry swells, bold bluegreen, robust. Heaviest leaves droop with storm, some breaking from stems, leaves round and redrim as purslane, full and fleshy as sedum succulent.

Stevven hands leaf to Eli. They bite in.

This one's sour spicy, Eli says.

They must be in conversation with the garlic, Stevven says, tests soil. I'm worried we still don't have enough drainage.

Ginohead lifts head from amaranth and eggplant as if he, too, beard foresting moss and field mouse, roots there. He rises, walks slow through rows and potato barrels, settles slow and heavy beside Stevven and Eli.

Good morning, Gino says.

Good morning, Eli says.

Gino smiles eyes at Stevven, then hangs long fingers crawling with mites on planter bed edge, works other hand into wet compost layer. He sighs, sits back, brushes soil off lizardskin grafts on wrists, forearms.

I think we are doing everything we can, Gino says, gently scratches underarm, redgreen mosses. But they don't seem to mind the water.

It looks like you mind the water, Stevven says. The new moss still bothering you?

It will all balance out, he says.

You're already a multispecies assemblage without armpit moss, Stevven says.

Gino smiles. What did June say about BluBerry and water?

Stevven shies from earthing gaze, looks to atomic tomato respiring in headless bleach jugs, to lemongraz springing out old life buoy like living champaign.

Life is celebration, June echos in Stevven.

The lab was shut down before she could determine ideal conditions, Stevven says, picks fallen BluBerryleaf. I'm scared of getting it wrong. Hurting BluBerry.

Gino lays deep hand on Stevvenshoulder. Conglomerates, dirt and microorganisms texture skin.

Greenmaking is a difficult process, he says.

Stevven glances at Gino, lichen bright, red moss tips probing like small mammalian teeth.

And a two-way process, he adds.

Gino prays over BluBerry. Then he stands, returns to tall Garden bed. He lifts rain gutter heavy with young pole beans, works slow, breaks frequently, and then completely by sun up. Ginomind, greening from outside in.

Stevven eats BluBerry leaf, closes eyes on tang, acids, allicins. Miracle plant.

Plant doesn't cover it, June echoes in Stevven. BluBerry is BluBerry.

Eli, what does a monkey sound like? Stevven asks. A happy one?

Ooo ooah.

Ooouah ooah!

Oooahah oooa!

Roof door squawks open. Ms. Jones steps tentative slipper out, gaze swiveling through eye fog.

My screen's broke again, she says.

Ooooahah! Oooooooo!

Eli circles Ms. Jones. She holds tablet high and away from swatting Elihands.

Why don't you discipline this child? she says. They need a good spanking, is what they need. And a haircut. Their mama's too soft on them. Now what's going on? You a monkey too?

Ooooahah! Stevven replies.

Are you gonna fix my screen or not? Ms. Jones retreats one step.

You hear that? Stevven asks.

Eli cups ear. Ms. Jones frowns.

Heartbeat, drumbeat. Beat, beat, beat. Hunting party. Stevven drums steadily on barrel, closes eyes, inhales jungle, frivolous birds, mist dewing, sliding down colocasia leaves, dragonflies.

What are you making all that racket for? Ms. Jones says.

Before we can eat you—Beat—we got to fatten you up with these!

Stevven extends hand alive with grub and beetles, elytra glistening like rubies.

Yeah! Eat them, Eli says, beat, beat, beat.

And then we'll squeeze her.—Beat—Wring her. —Beat—Juice her like a mango!—Beat, beat, beat. Squeeze her, wring her, juice her like a mango. Squeeze her, wring her, juice her like a mango!

Oh, not this again, Ms. Jones says, makes slow retreat to apartment one story below.

Jungle canopy critters quiet. Frogs pause song. Salivating breeze touches neck. Stevven stops beating drum, feels for eyes training on back.

Someone's watching us, Stevven says. Someone big, hungry.

Jaguar! Eli cries.

We're not safe yet. Here's a cave!

Big dark swallows them. Down, down they go, adrenaline pumping. Down, down, wet green leaves stamping skin as they churn through darkening understory. Then lighter, sparkling blue waves. They burst into light, seashore. Stevven collapses before growling water.

We're almost to the boat! Eli says, points.

They tug Stevvenarms, but adrenaline flickers out, last salts dripping from nose.

Stevvenneck swells, pricklings, deathfingers.

Jaguar leaps from cave, heels churning, rosettes spinning. Jaguar flies, laserlining emerald eyes. Moist teeth puncture, stretch and break Stevvenneck. One life.

Bang!

Stevveneyes open. Eli stands sentry over them, cocking imaginary gun. Pooling blood evaporates, play time over.

Did you just shoot Jaguar? Stevven asks, sits up onto hands. That's bad. Even if they are pretend.

But they were going to eat you!

That's part of it. We don't always escape.

I don't want them to eat you!

It's okay.

No, it's not! Eli says, stomps once, squats, back to Stevven.

Water laps consolingly on makeshift dock Eli and Stevven share in silence. Stevven looks up steep Apartment face, up to BluBerryleaves shining in rooftop Garden, now five stories above them. Sun heats fast, molds feet to deck, wax. Stevven lies down on side, kickstands head in arm. Elitoes roil on planks as breeze gathers hairs onto right shoulder. Eli begins to pick at some soft disintegrating wood, elemental.

Ocean water undulates between Apartment and mainland, Mollusk Beach, birthing mangrove. Water clicks against concrete, feeding barnacles, algae families.

Stevven echolocates new arrival bobbing in shallow pool against dock. They handknee to edge and look.

Seagull reeks scavenger fish and fly, dredge spoil clinging like cape. Gases turn seagull inside out, plastics big and bright as wildflowers blooming from intestines. Green grocery bag parachutes from abdomen, flickers in small breeze.

Eli points over Stevvenshoulder. Babies, they say.

Dark wormy bodies swirl in seagullstomach.

Neat, Stevven says.

Airboat drifts through narrow sound, rocks water. Ripples touch composting seagull.

Stevven! Ms. Jonesvoice dives from fourth story balcony.

Stevven looks up.

My screen's broke, she says.

Okay, I'm coming up, but only if you promise to stay off Reddit, Stevven says.

What? I can't hear you.

I'm coming up.

And don't bring any of that monkey business with you.

Stevven shakes head, pokes Eli. Let's get you back to your mama, they say.

Eli pouts. But today's bath day! I want to go with you to Ms. Jones.
Come on.

They step into building slow, eyes adjusting for subtler shadows. Apartment lobby sinks underfeet, viscous, granite tiles becoming sand, sleepy portal to rooms and nests, rodent, insect, human.

We need to make you some new shoes, Stevven says in acoustic dark. Those storms wash up needles and who knows what.

Okay.

Last week you stepped on a sharp seashell and Mary nearly passed out. She worries a lot.

Do you worry about me? Eli asks, voice like vapor.

That's a parent's job, not mine.

Does BluBerry worry about me?

Probably not. I wouldn't know.

Reeeeakk, stairwell door. They scale first flight, clunk, clunk, clunk. Stevven stops at landing, tastes stale air.

Waaaaaaa, they speak humpback whale.

Eli giggles, replies in lightsaber woomp.

Who are you today? Stevven asks.

Darth Vader.

Not Obi-wan?

Eli spins, saber crashing into Stevvensaber, crssshshs.

Only a Sith deals in absolutes, Stevven says.

Wooomp. Wump. Womp. They battle up next two flights.

THEY TUMBLE INTO FOURTH FLOOR hallway. Light shreds through broken window, draws rainbows around footwork.

Eli coughs, coughing.

Stevven sheathes lightsaber, puts hand to Eli.

Eli coughing.

You okay?

Eli coughs, swallows mucus, then stills.

Mold consumes beige walls like shadow, eclipses Apartment mycotoxin by mycotoxin, always working, even before rashes on arms, working up through lobby, old plumbing, bust air supply ducts, shooting out spores by billions that stick to mattresses, bathtubs, Elilungs.

Eli finds crayon on floor and draws creatures on soft, rotting walls. Stevven clocks dripping and bubbling from inside wall, something always leaking. They consider precarious ceiling, considers what to repair and what to abandon.

Click, apartment door handle turns. Mary pokes head out into hallway, smiles, plastic sticking in hair.

Good morning, you two! she says, voice sucrose, small, eyes warm charcoals, small. I didn't even hear you leave the room this morning. Sorry I slept in so late!

Are those... Stevven says, squints, recalls.

Curlers! Ha, I'm trying something new, she says, pats head, rounds eyes. How is BluBerry? she says. Did the storm hurt them?

No, they're fine. BluBerry is the most resilient creature I've ever known.

I'm sure June would be happy—

I've got a lot to do today, Stevven says, searches for itch on head. I'm just here to drop this dirtball off.

Hey! Eli squints at Stevven, forces frown.

Thanks for playing with Eli, Mary says. I have been so bad at waking up!

It's fine. Hey, don't forget to replace your flume pipe today.

How do I do that again?

She can't, Eli says. You have to help her.

The section that's scorched through, Stevven says. You pull it out from each side. Out of the joints. Put the new one in. A little twisty motion always helps. Mm, maybe I'm not explaining it right.

Mary blinks. Do I need any tools?

Just your hands, Stevven says, shakes head. Never mind. I'll do it later.

Mary squats down next to Eli. Ready for bath, little monkey?

Eli frowns up to Stevven, pleads, then sighs, dips under Maryarm into room.

Bye, Stevven says, wags fingers.

Door closes on Marysmile, soft cheeks.

Stevven listens at door. Small shufflings, complaints, birdsong.

STEVVEN CROSSES TO WEST SIDE, knocks on apartment door.

Metal slides, falls, clanks, rattles. Ms. Jonesface hangs in open door like twisty brass chain lock.

I would put in a noise complaint if you weren't the only one to complain at, she says.

May I come in?

Stevven slips shoes onto rack inside apartment. Soft carpets dread and pill. Print photos sweat in plastic frames across dozen shelves and tables.

I like the table cloth, Stevven says. Is it new?

I change them out when Coco tears em up bad, Ms. Jones says, sets tablet in Stevvenhands. It ain't letting me log on.

Something wrong with facerec?

White text dances under camera, winky face. *We don't recognize you. Enter pin.*

Stevven angles camera on Ms. Jones.

Hey, do you think you can get me any more—

No more lag, Stevven says, adjusts angle of camera. And no more Reddit, please. Huh. It doesn't recognize you.

I didn't wake up with a different face all of the sudden, she says.

Maybe to the robot, you did.

Stevven avoids Ms. Joneseyes, hard pupils in milk. Coco arches against Stevvencalf, meows.

What's your pin? Stevven asks.

I don't know, she says, wilts over Stevven like flower cutting, meaty scent.

We set it to your birthday last time, Stevven says. Remember?

Oh, ninety eight. Eight of August, nineteen ninety eight.

Stevven inputs pin and reelhalo springs up around Stevvenhead.

*Stevven's headline picks provided by BUBBL3.*

*OpEd: SpaceX's Trying to Sell the Unsellable: Vacations to Venus During Hurricane Season*

*MASS SHOOTING INSURANCE CLAIMS BANKRUPTS LOCAL PROVIDER IN MIAMI*

*Pleasure Implant CEO Found Guilty of Sporing Rival, Stocks Plummet*

*The last 3 planes took off from the Seattle-Tacoma International Airport (SEA) yesterday as Chinese forces take Emerald City*

Stevven hands over tablet and reelhalo adjusts algorithm around Ms. Jones, plays jingles for hardhearing.

Soft whirs, whirring outside window.

Turn that down, Stevven says, crosses to window.

Huh?

Mute it now, please, they say, crane ear to window.

Whirrrrr, black drone rises from Apartment base, flutters up to window, drifts up to Garden.

Shit!

Stevven rushes past Ms. Jones, snags shoes, fumbles with locks. Drop bolt, chainlock, click, clack, rattle. Ms. Jones mumbles something about forgetting as Stevven turns last bolt, cranks door open, out.

They run up stairwell. Gino feet thunder down, fast as Earther feet can go. Stevven and Gino meet at middle landing.

Drone, Gino says, pants.

I know, Stevven says. It will see BluBerry. Shit. I'll distract it. Get Skeeter.

STEVVEN SCRAMBLES UPSTAIRS TO ROOF, bursts into Garden. Hand blocks hot sun. Drone wings buzz. It sights Stevven, hovers nearer, slowly, as if Stevven is flighty horse.

Hello, Stevven Pane. I have been commissioned by Charleston County offices to discuss options with users not utilizing traditional comm services as required by the state of South Carolina since 2078. I am here to inform you that you are in violation of two federal homestead laws, two state homestead laws, and twenty state identity laws. It does not look like you are enrolled in an e-colony program or demonstrate any intention to. If you wish to update your citizen status, please say so now. Great. I will proceed with Charleston County's expectations for you, Stevven. In accordance with—

What local homestead laws?

Code section 354 amended under the South Carolina GreenRoof™ Act of 2080 states that persons may only engage in urban gardening at 10 square feet or less without express permission from their local GreenRoof™ representative. Section 354.3 states that participating gardeners must undergo bimonthly checkups to ensure that nonhuman life propagation is in accordance with GloboCrop standard.

This is my home.

Yes, but this is irrelevant information. Code section 354 applies to all nonbusiness, private green operations.

Just tell me what's going to happen.

Stevven Pane, you are expected to vacate the premises immediately—Drone projects holo eviction, official seal in blue laser—That is, six hours from you receiving this message. Gather your belongings. If you fail to comply, you will be forcibly removed by on-the-ground personnel. Would you like to address your identity violations now?

Stevven clocks small scurrying sound inside stairwell behind them: Skeeter.

They cross arms, clear throat. See that old waste-to-power plant across the water? Stevven says.

Yes. I do not see the relevance—

I used to work there. We'd scoop up trash and power homes out of it. Trash just like you.

I'm sorry, I don't understand—

How do you feel knowing you are built to break down before the new year?

A GreenRoof™ representative wishes to speak to you directly.

Or any minute now, Stevven says. Tech is so flimsy these days.

Drone sputters and drops onto Marigolds.

Skeeter slinks out stairwell clutching hacking interface. He avoids touching eyes, quickly recovers prize, drone propellers still spinning.

Thanks, Skeeter, Stevven says, deflates, kneels to support bruising flower heads. Fuck.

Stevven drops Marigold stem, stands, blood spiking.

So, y'all leaving? Skeeter asks.

He breaks open drone panel with tool from chain, crushes chip inside hand, scatters parts to sea.

Stevven looks at Skeeter. Remember that pathway I gave you a few months ago?

Skeeter nods.

I need you to send a message. Highest priority.

What's the message?

Junebug.

Skeeter nods, tucks drone underarm and meanders towards stairwell, eyes flicking like harddrive LEDs.

Don't tell them my name, he says, looking back.

You're safe, Stevven says. Thanks for all your help.

Skeeter whispers away into dark building. Stevven runs hands over head, grapples for calm, calm, calm. They cross to BluBerry, startle pigeon from nearby bed. Stevven runs hand down woody alcove, across hollow at base where Eli, just small enough, curls up to rest sometimes.

Jumping spider leaps onto shaky hand. Stevven raises finger to face.

Time to get packing, they say. Enjoy Garden while you can.

Spider lingers on finger, pedals hairy pedipalps, black eyes unblinking. They turn, leap onto leaf, bring death onto unsuspecting aphid.

AT WORKBENCH, STEVVEN SIFTS NOISILY through plastic, glass, carbonate containers. They pick out Nalgene waterbottle, screw lid hanging by nylon chord.

Stevven returns to BluBerry, sets waterbottle aside. They curl fingers into loose claws, sink into good soil, turn humus over forearms, bathing. They bring soil under nose, inhale, then carry earth to waterbottle.

Stevven sorts through BluBerry new growth, clipper in hand. Rust springs from clipper joints. Crunch, BluBerry splits into two, Stevven nearly. They inspect cut, cambiums and phloems dewing life waters.

Stevven pulls off young leaves, slow, ritual. They lower BluBerry cutting into waterbottle, gently, then gentler, pack in soils.

Ginofeet climb stairs like heavy bearpaws. Stevven turns, smiles sadly at him in doorway. He walks to Stevven, settles hand like wet river soot on Stevvenshoulder. They present waterbottle.

Gino takes BluBerry in both hands. Most of the lichens of my forest body originate from the Northwest of this continent, he says. Where I once spent much time as a young person. There I learned how to be a tree, and then I had to unlearn.

Gino quiets for some moments, rotates BluBerry in hands.

We are living in the age of Metal and Fire so we must be Water, moving swiftly around the axeblade, unharmed. In our fluidity, we are a vessel for other creatures trying to escape the great Fire.

He hands BluBerry to Stevven. What can I do to help you? he asks.

You can take care of Eli and Mary.

You're going alone?

I need to get BluBerry to the lab in Sewanee as soon as possible. That's where BluBerry began, and that is where BluBerry's friends are. Where my friends are, I hope.

Stevven rises.

Freshen up that first aid kit, maybe, they say, massage temples. But don't strain yourself. I already saw you lose a colony of acrocarpous running down the stairs.

Gino drifts to apothecary locker, organizes jars on workbench. I will get things together if you go explain the situation to the others, he says.

Stevven crosses to plastic storage bins in rain barrel shade. They shake out old pack, breaking nest and scattering two mice.

Stevven? Gino says, voice quietloud like sycamore.

He stops working, watches.

Stevven retrieves sewing and sealing kit in rusting Altoids box. They thread fabric stapler with brown string and close gaps on pack, twice over, click, click. Pack reflectors twinkle like blue morpho butterfly scales. Stevven covers them with sticky camouflage patches.

Spend this time with Eli, Gino says.

Stevven drops pack. Why don't you? they say.

Stevven moves wet sleeping mat into full sun. They inspect rain jacket, core fabrics still adjustable for humidity and temperature, hood permanently exposing black.

The University may still have the labs, people who worked with BluBerry and June in the early stages of development, Stevven says. They're the last people we can trust with BluBerry. Shit, where did I put the filter?

Stevven digs out featherstitch breathable pants, three sock pairs, four underwear, solar lamp, infinimatch, sawtooth knife, pocket knife, cord blanket, binoculars, bladder, purifier.

Gino crosses to Stevven, hands them medicines, carrot seed oil, marigold oil, flowers, hips, cured garlic, mustard, aloe.

We do not have any more clove, he says.

That all went to Eli's tooth ache last month, Stevven says. You forgot the pharmaceuticals.

Those are not good for the body and soul, Gino says.

No, it's good.

Stevven crosses to locker, collects pain pills, loratadine, capsule vitamins, mineral sunscreen. They draw string bag. Ginoeyes hit Stevven like boulders.

I believe it would be wisest if we all went together, he says. With Eli, Mary, and Ms. Jones. Barbara could help us, too.

Stevven scoffs. Barbara, glad to never see her again.

Stevven folds pack flap in and over, fills water bladder from rain barrel faucet.

You know in your heart—

Mary's probably at Al's party by now. I'll go explain the situation to her. She can explain to Eli. That I'm leaving with BluBerry.

Stevven—

I have to focus, Stevven says, slips BluBerry into mesh waterbottle holder on pack.

They shoulder pack and cross to stairwell door, stops inside entrance. They look back at Gino.

Al owes me a favor, Stevven says. I'm going to cash it to get you all out of here safely.

They start down stairwell, dark, slippery. Door clams behind them.

Stevvenhands caution flaking paint on railings, shellack junk that sometimes cuts hands in hurry. They descend to second floor, wince into blistering bright hallway, stale trash and Fritos.

Stevven stops before open door, body cramping, adapting to gasoline generator, speakers, factory perfumes, religious fervor, Sunday football in full force.

Mostly people ignore Stevven. Woman at door flicks eyes up and down Stevven, taps red claw on margarita glass, turns away. Three pink men in polo shirts waft to buffalo dip. In center room, Al swivels captain seat recliner, waves at Stevven.

Stevven! Al bellows, shirt peeling up, Dorito crumbs surfing white hairless flesh.

Stevven crosses to, catches frigid beer can in hands midway.

Sit, take a load off, Al says, eyes tracking jumbo screen.

Speed boat roars through room, hauling people in swim trunks, bikinis, brand names. Women laugh at Stevven flinching away from advertisement, blue light emulating ocean waves. Stevven ices forehead and neck with beer can.

Where's Mary? they ask.

Somewhere or other, Al says.

He twiddles fingers through air, shrinks life size game to coffee table size, examines player line up. Two dimensional streaming continues on Southern wall, scrolls through screaming stadium crowds.

Did Skeeter tell you? Stevven asks.

Course he did, Al says, swigs beer. So you're goin then? Hold your hogs, Bama's going for a field goal.

Woman starts rattling plastic maracas emblemizing Alabama *A*, hunches as if to pounce, ligaments coiling, pupils swelling.

Stevven leans in to talk to Al. I have a favor—

Hush now, he says, inches forward.

Maraca woman leaps from seat as kicker meets ball. Leather spins through giant yellow roaster fork. Room explodes. Stevven ducks under open firing high fives.

Al, I need your help, Stevven says. When they come searching for me, don't let them find anyone else. Gino, Mary, or Eli. They can all fit on any of your guys' boats parked out there. Just ride them out for a couple hours, bring them back, or something.

I figured you'd ask me for somethin kin, Al says, squints up at Stevven, shovels chips into mouth. And what about you?

I'm leaving soon, Stevven says. I got a ride.

Al chuckles, potato morsels springtailing out. Why don't you just take your folks over with you then?

They're not my folks. And I'm asking you to do this as a favor.

Alright, I'll get Skeeter to take them out at half time.

Stevveneyes touch Maryeyes as she steps into main room, hand tender on curly hair, glancing around.

So where you goin? Al asks Stevven, eyes on game. You kiddin me? Boy, pick up that ball. Get it, god damn it! There you go. 29's got it. First down—Al finishes beer, crunches can—Anyways, it's been one hell of a few months. I'll probably miss you bitchin about sortin my trash.

Everything you throw out is useful, Stevven says.

Al grins. Whatcha use Skeeter's diaper for, he says, kicks up wetwheeze laugh. Catchin flies? Aw, now, *Stev*ven. Loosen up. Hell, we're sinkin. We're sinkin, and it's your last day, and you're telling me that you ain't gonna raid the cellar? Come on, son, drink up!

Thanks for looking out for them, Stevven says, drops beer can back into ice.

Stevven steps through white yard lines reeling out over floor and furniture like road painters over roadkill, crosses to Mary and woman with margarita.

Excuse me, Stevven says. Can I talk with Mary for a minute?

Woman takes margarita and paper plate sagging sauces to main room without second look at Stevven.

Sorry to interrupt, Stevven says to Mary.

Oh, no, it's okay, Mary says, foot slightly pigeontoeing over other, bat shy. How are you?

Player takes ball twenty yards. Man leaning on bar slaps ass hanging off seat next to him.

GreenRoof™ evicting me, Stevven says. That means they're coming to search the building. They might find BluBerry and will probably destroy Garden.

Mary brings hand over mouth.

Don't panic, Stevven says. Listen to me. Al's going to take you, Eli, and Gino to a temporary hiding place tonight. He's good for it. Just take your emergency packs we prepared together. Remember where they are?

I can't believe it, she says, forms tears.

I know this is a lot at once, but it is very important that you do this. For your safety, and Eli's.

Stevven risks hand on Mary shoulder.

Do you understand that in the eyes of the state, Eli is a nonperson? Stevven asks. They will take them, maybe arrest you.

I don't understand. Why will they destroy Garden? We worked so hard to build it. Why do they want Eli?

Stevven sighs, clocks space around them, no obvious listeners. They step closer.

If it's any consolation, I'm taking BluBerry with me. See the bottle on my pack?

Mary looks at Stevvenside. Oh! Where are their leaves?

They'll grow new ones. I'm bringing them to Sewanee, in Tennessee.

Maryeyes flicker, wet. Big tear. Some vowels dribble out mouth.

Look, go tell Eli what's going on, Stevven says. Okay?

Stevven squeezes Maryshoulder, slips away from Marybody collapsing for embrace. They close door behind them, muffling, like diving underwater without taking breath.

REEEAK, STAIRWELL DOOR OPENS.

Barbara enters hallway gowning latest pearldrip suit, ready to parse out soul through plastic wrap pesto dip.

You're suited up, she says, accent shapeless cosmopolitan. Going somewhere?

Something's come up, excuse me, Stevven says, swerves around Barbara.

So Donna's coming to get you?

Stevven freezes at stairwell door, looks back at Barbara.

What do you know about Donna? Stevven asks.

I do research on all my subjects, Barbara says, waves remark away. Have a minute? I wanted to ask you about the water quotas you enforce on the apartment residents.

We just ration water according to the weather. I don't see how that's relevant.

Well, you haven't seen the story, have you? she says, square teeth glinting.

When will I be able to see this working *story* you've been writing about us?

I would show you, but we have a one-way relationship with our sources, sorry.

Stevven massages temples.

Barbara ticks eyes around digieye. Wow, Donna's already on her way, she says. You're tracking her?

You really have been living under a rock, Barbara says, switches pesto dip to opposite hand. Anyone with a legal presence has location enabled. For safety reasons.

When's she going to be here?

Half an hour, Barbara says, clocks onto some shoe advertisements. I'm going to drop this dip off and we can chit-chat some more.

She enters football party.

Stevven retreats into stairwell, awaying Barbara.

Stevven! Elivoice ricochets down stairwell.

Stevven backpedals into hallway, jogs past football party, dives into furthest room at hallway end. They click door quietly behind them, clenching body, breath.

LASTPICK MATTRESSES PILE IN room corner. Extra clothes unsuitable for Garden projects hang in closet behind limp sliding door. Spores and dust marinate in sappy yellow light. Floor sags.

Stevven steps over molding goose feather coat on floor, slides pack off. They inspect BluBerry, sad but sound in waterbottle.

The hardest part is almost done, Stevven says.

BluBerry respires quietly.

Fishbowl air forces calm. Stevven wrestles tank top off, shoes, shorts. They stand naked in room center then step to window that opens ten inches from floor. They lie on stomach, fit face into cool metal frame. Steely plastic carpet pinches chest as they fit arm out window, dangle, read burning Apartment face with fingers, collect salt grains, calcites.

World splits laterally into sea and sky. Edges salivate, tickle each other, tendril and entwine until unseparate, one fluid blue. Stevven tries to untangle sea from sky, erase, redraw boundaries, breathe.

Klonk klonk on door.

Stevven, Eli says, now inside room.

I can't talk right now, Stevven says, words falling out window, plip plopping into waking blue.

I can't hear you, Eli says giggling, vibrations nearing.

Blood takes hard turn in Stevvenchest as Eli plops down, hard kid angles jabbing into ribs. Stevven reels head inside Apartment, groans.

I want to play go fish, Eli says into face.

Ugh.

They punch Stevvenbutt, try to start chase around room.

Eli, quit.

Stevven rises and puts shorts back on, wipes humidity from face with shirt.

I want to play!

Your mama is looking for you. Go find her.

Let's play in Garden, Eli says. With BluBerry.

I can't.

Why?

It's too hot for that today.

But it's hotter in here.

Go play with Gino.

Gino said to find you.

Gino, Stevven sighs. Shit.

Eli kicks styrofoam wedge against wall, impatience elaborating.

Stop that, Stevven says.

Eli kicks again. You have to catch me, they say.

Come here.

Eli somersaults over mattress, rebounds on wall.

Stevven leaps up, snatches Eli by waist, tickles them down.

I said come here!

Eli laughter fills room, birdsong. They roll belly to floor as laughter putters out. Eli handknees to North window. They walk fingerperson along open frame.

Stevven joins Eli, plants fingerperson along coastline, crosses Mollusk Beach in one small step, skips along Shipyard, Casino, other drowning apartment buildings, stepping stones in great unfathomable pond. Elifingerperson jumps onto financial building further inland, blows smithereens. Stevven kicks powerlines down, punches gaping fisheye windows on Casino, leaps into blue and pops distant sunsoaking cloud like yolk. Fiery juices flood entire district, trickle off docks into sea, hissssss. They destroy city twice over, mime distant explosions inside cheeks. Shhhpow!

It's all coming down now, Stevven says as fingerperson dives into high rise.

Eli? Stevven? Eli! Mary voice scurries like mouse down hallway.

Go, Stevven says, helps Eli to feet.

Come! Eli motions.

Stevven shakes head. You go, they say. I have to do some things.

Eli? Mary calls.

We will play later if you go help your mom.

Promise?

Stevven croaks. Of course, they say.

Eli smiles, disappears out door.

Maryvoice soft, always brinking. She asks to brush Elihair and talk.

Stevven rises, body remembering blood, wump, wump, wump. They roll tank top over sweaty skin, step into shoes, shoulder pack. They wait until stairwell absorbs Mary and Eli, slip out room.

STEVVEN SITS ON DOCK, BLUBERRY in lap, watches boats rock. Pallid water glugs against pontoons, slugs from ropes, sea sickness. Life simmers in old financial district across water, red brick buildings reddening, green overgrowth greening. Further North, skyscrapers blink, construction cranes cranking, playing jenga.

Stevven searches for Donna boat.

Rummagings, people descending stairwell, approaching dock. Stevven tucks BluBerry in pack, stands, squints into dark Apartmentmaw. Eli bursts from shadow, pack jogging, shoe laces galloping.

Yay! Eli says. We're going to the city!

Mary crosses into Stevven, smiles drying tears, drops two evac packs to dock.

May I hug you? she asks.

Stevven gapes as Maryarms fold around them. Breath shallows, muscles clicking, rattling.

Barbara explained everything at the party after you left, Mary says, clings tight. I just know that if we stick together we can get through this.

What did she say, exactly?

Gino eases from shadow, dons leather travel tunic. Field mouse scurries up arm, nests under long beard. He smiles, foliose forests bleaching in direct light.

Can I see what's in your pack? Eli asks.

Not right now, Stevven says.

I'm bringing Winky, Eli says, holds up plush walrus.

Stevven holds Winky with both hands, squeezes.

Barbara says that Donna is coming to pick us up, Mary says. Is she an old friend of yours?

More feet descend stairs, clumsy, foreign. Barbara grunts into lobby, wheels heavy suitcase. Gino meets her, carries luggage to dock.

Oh thank god, Barbara says. You're such a gentleman. I have one more at the top of the landing, please.

Gino kindly lumbers to stairs. Barbara dares high heel onto dock, steps back onto vinyl floor in lobby. Her face cringes at saltiness, high sun, at Stevven. She smacks blue gum.

Your suitcases are so beautiful, Mary says.

Hey there, Barbara says, shows teeth at Mary. Thank you. This one is the pop-up bar, blenders, shakers, everything. Unfortunately, I won't be setting it up today.

Wow, Mary says, touches sleek casing. It must be expensive.

I got it on sale, actually.

What's in the other one?

A few changes of clothes, of course, Barbara says. Are those the shoes you're wearing to the city? I liked the ones you had on earlier.

Oh, thank you. Those weren't very comfortable, and I can only take the necessities, so, I left them upstairs.

So, this is everything you have? A girl can't live on this—Barbara puts weight to one hip, blinks—How do you feel about leaving so suddenly?

Well, haha, um, I know that it would be harder without Stevven's help.

Oh, tell me more, Barbara says, smacks gum.

Stevven looks away to water.

When Eli and I first came here almost a year ago, Stevven showed us how to prepare for emergencies like this.

Barbara turns to Stevven. Yet, Stevven, you invested so much into the GreenRoof™, as if you were going to stay for a long time, she says. What do you think?

Stevven runs fingers over BluBerrybottle in pack, forces hand down. On the off chance we could stay, Stevven says.

I see. Do you feel that you may have been planting a false sense of hope for all the people living in the condemned building?

Stevven turns to look at Barbara completely, red underglare. I'm not responsible for anyone but myself and—

And who? Barbara says.

Stevven returns eyes to odd currents in water swirling underfeet. Myself, Stevven says.

Engine tears into soundscape. Purple boat skips into view, decorative beads bouncing on bow rails. Boat chops, slows, drifts towards dock.

One hand on tiller, Donna fans greeting. Sunglasses, chewing gum, brilliant white teeth.

Hey doll, she calls, throws rope to dock. You call?

Stevven catches rope, docks boat. Donnahand extends, smooth caramel. Stevven helps her off boat quickly, then pockets dirty hands in pack straps.

Thanks for coming, they say.

I'm glad you reached out, Donna says, hand to Stevvenside. I'm sorry about all this. Fuck GreenRoof™. You got something you can wear tonight?

What's tonight?

Just a little get together, Donna says, shrugs, eyebrow sequins glimmering. With some old friends and some new ones. It will take your mind off this bullshit.

It's only the biggest party in Charleston this week, Barbara adds. Hi, I'm Barbara. Barbara Betner, with Buzz News.

Donnaeyes flash behind sunglasses. She shakes Barbarahand like dozen journalist hands before. What brings you out here? Donna asks.

I'm writing a story about the marginalized people of Charleston, Barbara says. Giving a voice to the people the city has left behind since the riots.

Uh huh, I see, Donna says. And you've been able to shake some emotions from Stevven?

Barbara laughs. She's starting to open up, I can tell.

They.

Sorry?

Stevven's pronouns are they/them.

Right.

Could you help clarify some things for me, about your relationship to Stevven? Barbara asks. I don't quite understand the extent of your connection since your professional one ended during the riots.

If I could put it into words for you, I would, Donna says, turning to Stevven. Got everything?

What we can carry on our backs, Stevven says.

Then let's hit it.

Donna brushes close, steps aboard. Earrings swing and chime. Rose scent.

Gino moves to help Barbara with matching luggage set.

Gino, take a rest, Stevven says. You're earthing for Harvest's sake. I'll get the bags.

Stevven loads luggage, helps Mary aboard. Eli climbs up next, giggling like rain. Barbara shoos away Stevven hand, stumbles into boat. She sits down, sanitizes hands and tidies hair, sunglasses.

Stevven wipes hands on shorts. They untie docking rope. Look around, feeling as though forgetting. They hop on.

Motor kicks, pulls boat back into water. Donna watches over shoulder, back arching. Purple bralette ties into bow behind neck.

Here we go! she says into breeze, intoning like gems.

Gino sits on low seat next to Donna, somber as stone.

She didn't want to come, he says to Stevven.

Who?

Agh! Barbara plasters hair down with one hand, strangles purse with other. Boat rips forward and she deathgrips rail, grimaces. Eli pulls away from Mary, leans from bow. She reels them back.

Passengers, we may experience a little turbulence, Donna says, winks at Eli.

Boat roars up one gear. Stevven wraps arm around pack, BluBerry. Eli squeals delight. Maryface recycles anxiety and cheer.

Stevven turns to tell Donna to slow—freezes in pale face hovering behind her. Ms. Jones stands on fourth floor Apartment balcony, robe and slippers, curly white dandelion hair, tablet blinking in sun. She ghosts with distance, spirit clinging to world by clothespin.


BANK LEFT, RIGHT. BOAT SLOWS, approaches thick barrier islands before North docks. Styrofoam toss in frothy trail behind boat, reshape, break apart. Stevven looks at Donna again, sees Juneeyes. They cruise faces, Gino, Eli, Mary. Speculations haunt Stevvenmind, bruise bodily nowness, knowing.

They refocus on sprawling dock matrix creeping, twisting over water like roots, moving with tide. Further North, big export processing docks stand high above water, frigid and defiant.

Boat shifts from buzzing to drumming, wake rocking buoy. Buoy blinks slowdown red light Eli recognizes from Apartment at night, but Stevven avoids eye conversation.

They drift into boat parking docks, some boats sheen, others as if fresh from ocean beds. Donna drifts into parking spot, cuts engine. Stevven hops off and steadies hull.

Barbara climbs out, loses curses to slopping water and boat traffic horns. She props herself on dock post and scrunches nose, scolds contaminate air. Gino hands luggage down to Stevven, slow.

Thank you for the lovely boat ride, Barbara says, recomposes as Donna steps down. I love how you've decorated it.

Donna looks Barbara up, down. Sure, she says. So, what's next for you?

I just have a few more questions for Stevven, and then I return to Nashville, home base.

Stevven throws Barbara bag from boat onto dock.

Barbarasmile falters. She kneels, sets bag upright, draws out handle, click click click.

I mean—Barbara huffs as Stevven throws next bag—I'm so curious. You two are from different worlds.

Wasn't always like that, Donna says, draws out suitcase handle. Here, let me help you with that.

You're so kind. Are there no attendants at the dock?

Stevven shoulders pack. Eli drops Winky. Walrus at sea. Stevven unshoulders pack and reaches down before current pulls stuffy too far.

Careful, Stevven says, wrings out water.

Eli unzips pack, stuffs Winky on crayolas, two bean cans, little gift box rattling with rocks and fingersize trinkets.

Where's all your stuff? Stevven asks. The stuff we packed together?

Eli points to Mary sweeping tentative foot outside boat. Gino helps her down. Stevven can almost hear crustose patches tearing under tunic, blood beading.

We made a pack for each of you, Stevven says to Eli.

It was too heavy.

That's a lie, Stevven says.

Eli looks down, shakes zipper where Winky catches.

Okay, everyone got all their parts and pieces? Donna says.

They follow her forward, inland. Barbara fusses with suitcases, wheels tumbling, grating, purse perpetually sliding off shoulder. Gino stops for Barbara, collapses suitcase bars, click click, picks one up in each hand.

Gino, don't, you'll stress your forest, Stevven says.

You are *such* a gentleman, Barbara says to Gino.

She fishes spray bottle from purse, swats away some insects, mists repellent.

I got immunizations last year, she says. And the bugs are *still* biting. I'm cursed!

Path merges onto main dock, more foot traffic, strangers pinching gray sea eyes. They step from dock onto old coastal highway, asphalt beach. Cinder block storefronts boast neon food menus, gadget repair, boating services. Boats shore behind metal patchwork fences, kids and birds playing between them. Stevvenfingers brush runic fish carving in street post that signals forager landing.

They walk to road intersection prowling with taxis and rideshares. Donna waves to driver. Driver crushes cig under bigtoe boots, claps long paddle hands together, laughing smartly.

I knew you were going to come back to me baby girl, he says.

You call me baby girl one more time and you'll have one less customer, Donna says.

Can't have that in this economy, no ma'am, he says, turns to Stevven. Hey man, let me help you with that bag.

Stevven steps back. I got it, they say.

I ain't going to do you dirty, he says, widens eyes on Barbaraluggage. Damn, girl. Miss Donna, she with you? There ain't no way we gonna fit all that in the car.

Donna points to next taxi. You know them?

Yeah, that's Michol, driver says, waves him over. He good.

I can check his profile, Barbara says, taps on phone. I can get us a five star driver.

With all due respect ma'am, those ratings don't mean nothin, driver says, takes Barbaraluggage. Anyone can black hat their way to five stars. Me n Michol get you where you need to go safe *and* sound.

He smiles iridescent teeth tattoos. One bag, two, into trunk. He claps hands again, looks at Eli. Hey little man, can I get that bag from you? he says. I bet you can hold onto that walrus for the *dur*ation.

Driver closes trunk on bags, opens passenger door for Donna. She slides in. Stevven climbs into back seat, sits pack on knees. They lift BluBerry away from cold air stream pushing out center console. Eli and Mary sandwich them in.

Stevven turns, stares through rear window. Barbara slips into passenger seat in second taxi, frantic texting. Gino winks at Stevven.

Car doors snap shut, kill breeze.

CAR PEELS AWAY FROM CURB. Traffic elaborates, torque and rush, car brakes, industrial whinnying. Road becomes bridge over lagoon, over people and plants in plastic garments choring in water. Taxi slows at crest like corrosive dawn over city, four wheels plummeting hill into viscous grey, concrete umbras, electric advertisements vocalizing, eating all organic soundspace. Giant toothy walls with small square windows consume them. Security checkpoint.

Stevven drapes travel scarf over Eliface as driver rolls car window down.

Donna reaches over driver, displays phone to robot guard. This ride and next one, she says.

Guard waves passage.

That's new, Stevven says.

Can't get anywhere without ID or money, she says.

What about the train, the station?

That's the first place they locked up, she says. You were still around for that.

Donna licks lips, thinking, swivels seat. You tryna get on a train, doll? she asks.

Car dips into pothole, chiming Donnaearrings.

Stevven nods.

I hear you, she says. Let me look into it for you.

Hey y'all stressin for a snack? Driver says. Check this out.

He taps button on front panel. Cylindrical rack with bottle water and vinyl snack bags spins out center console.

Elieyes swell at buffet.

Fucking dumbfuck, stopped right up in the middle o here, driver says, leans out window.

He jabs horn, jolts Stevven from seat. Car brakes, rocks characters and bobble heads on dash. Fingersize Hello Kitty hologram walks to dashboard window, flips traffic off. Cortana hologram lounging in cupholder tilts head, waves at Stevven, then looks up to driver, breasts sensitive to car jostling.

Bass music throbs, hammers pores. Car flashing suspension creeps into left lane, passengers milling around console hookah. One points at Stevven, bugs eyes, flicks tongue on glass.

Stevven pinks, stares at seatback.

Eli grabs cookie pack from snack rack. Vinyl squeaks open.

Can I take a peek at those ingredients, sweetie? Mary says.

Eli steals thin cookie lumpy with chocolate chips before Mary takes bag. Eli breaks cookie, hands half to Stevven.

One second, sweetie, Mary says. I can't pronounce most of the ingredients on here.

Stevven eats cookie. Sweeter than maple beans, almost bitter, petroleum.

I don't want you to eat that, Mary says to Eli.

But Stevven—

Stevven is an adult and can make their own choices, Mary says.

Please? Eli bounces miserably.

Mary sighs. Just this one half, she says.

Eli bites into cookie, eyes swirling out windows.

Look at that! Eli says, cookie chunk flying from mouth.

Stevven follows Eligaze to giant cupcake three times as large as car, pink frosting and ripe cherry top. VRcades and shopping, sleek gold arches dipping in and out retail like nightmare serpent, McDonalds.

What's that? Eli asks about highrise.

Some E-state headquarters, Donna says. Stardew, I think.

Buildings warp tighter, taller, flashier. Downtown explodes for attention, windows outshining day, fast, gastric colors, spewing dying words. Sounds rob depths, set fire to wind, birds. Algorithms overcomplicate street corners, wash living textures into planes, swallows people into nameless distances.

Sensory fuzz trenches Stevven. They press hands to ears, shutter eyes, legs dense, aching cold, scream. Pressure chrome ocean welling up, brinking, smacking down. Swim up, they must swim out. Now! Out!

Donna spins seat. What's going on, doll?

Out, Stevven says. I want out of this car.

Are you feeling sick? Maryface loud, green.

Donna nods to driver. Pull off up here, she says.

Aw shit, they ain't gonna throw up or nothin?

Horns blare. Driver curses. Donna out, rounding. Stevven, pavement.

We're only a couple blocks from our place, she says.

BluBerry. Stevven reaches into car, pulls cool pack onto body, presses BluBerry to eyes, flames. Fingers pulse road, grain. Drum, imagining straw, green shelter. Stevven exhales, opens eyes. Donna face dark inside buildings, brick fingers closing into fist. Recognition, then standing.

That's it, Donna says, coaxes, balances. Hey, you see where we are? Remember this street?

Yes, Stevven says, sensing aniseed, hanging planters, cafe.

Woah, hey, where are you going? Donnavoice.

Stevven? Maryvoice.

Muscles unfurl, push forward.

Stevven! Donna snags arm, eyes sparking for connection. Where are you going? My place is the other way.

I need place. Space. I need to breathe.

Listen, I got you a private room in the apartment. All the space you need. Just simmer down for a second.

I'll meet you later, Stevven says, aways.

How we gonna make that happen, Stevven? Donna says. You ain't got a fucking phone.

Stevvenfeet go.

Listen, I moved during the renovations, Donna calls. Serendipity sixteenth floor. Room four. Party's next door. I'll see you there tonight. Shit. Don't you go far! Stay out of trouble!

INNARDS STEW GUNNING THROUGH CITY bustle. Stevven walks old gum trail and pavement, unquilling nerves step by step. They turn into wide strip mall, slide through drug store alleyway, consignment, hissing steampipes, trash bags puttering glass and critters.

We're almost there, Blu.

Forceful yellow green Ginkgo, fifty feet tall. Bird flurry erupts from nook, soars from green penumbra. Dense ocean air squeezes through boulevards, paddles Ginkgoleaf, harp string. Ginkgo, blazing noontime gold.

Stevven stops four strides from trunk, feet venturing onto torrential, callusing roots, stinking fruits. Stevven invites BluBerry from pack, seats them at Ginkgo base below carving *M + J*, scar, heart. Stevven sits against trunk. Sweet stomach acid scents tickle nose.

People recline on benches facing walkways, lap up Ginkgoshade. Small grass patches effort inside concrete curbs. Stevven places hand on bark. Ants dance through arrows, fucks, and initials cutting into Ginkgoflesh seasons ago. Above, branches reach up and out, fan photosynthesizers, circle.

Stevven looks out from Ginkgo island at humans. At multipurpose tower base, revolving doors chew people up, spit them out.

Human in nylon hoodie staggers. They try to stop others, begging hands, body concave, hollow, hungry. Most swim past, eyeing other horizons, unbodily. Hoodie pulls over small bubble cheek secretary, smiles apologetically, convinces them to swipe money. Secretary taps phone, wishes them good day, pulls away from prayerhands, hymnals, thanks.

Ginkgo frees leaf onto Stevventhigh. Stevven gently pinches slim stalk and lifts closer to eyes, traces parallel veins, veins like young strong rivers.

Blood balances, cools.

CAN I HELP YOU?

Police officer, inflame fingers pinching hips. Gray eyes, steely eyebrows.

No, Stevven says.

Can I see some ID?

I'm taking a rest in the shade. I used to come here a lot.

I need to see some ID.

Can I see what you got stuck up your ass?

Officer shifts feet. I'm going to ask you one more time or I'll facerec you. Facerecs by officers go on your record. Don't want to have that. Now, let me see some ID.

This is public space.

This is a public space for United States or affiliated e-colony citizens only, officer says. Face me.

Stevven hides face inside hands.

Stand up, officer says.

Officerhand goes for Stevvenwrist. Stevven swivels, scoops up BluBerry between belly and tree, hides face in Ginkgo.

Another move like that and I'll arrest you.

Fuck you fuck you fuck you fuck you.

Officer grabs Stevvenshoulders, wrestles them from Ginkgo. Bystanders stream video. Stevven thrashes.

Yeah, I bet this gets you off, they spit at crowd.

Fucking retard, officer says, jingles cuffs.

Stevven! Barbara calls, trots into scene. Oh officer, thank you so much for finding them!

Barbaraheels struggle on Ginkgoroots.

You know her? Officer asks.

She's a distant cousin, Barbara says, refixes purse on arm. My sister and I have been looking after her since her mom passed away.

Is she special or something? officer asks, lifts Stevven to feet.

Yes, Barbara sighs, poorme smile.

Alright, take her and clear out. She's disturbing the peace.

Fuck you fuck you fuck you.

Go on! Officer shouts, shoves Stevven.

Ginkgo groans, waking, stretching open. Ants pour from belly like shadow, black sesame, roll over Stevvenfeet, flowing fast. They storm, weigh down officerleg like chain, drag him back to earth. Barbara, too slow in heels to escape, trips into digestive vat, hand reaching for invisible help. Soil laps up blood, Ginkgorhyzomes blinking red delight.

What are you staring at? Barbara says. Let's go.

Stevven collects pack and BluBerry, follows Barbara onto sidewalk, glares back at officer. Bystander phones return to pockets, some linger, salivating for more outbursts. Digieyes blink to refresh entertainment, move on.

Did you follow me? Stevven asks.

That's a sad way to say 'thank you,' Barbara says, heading North towards Serendipity Apartments. What were you doing there? Just trying to get arrested?

I wasn't doing anything.

Hm. No wonder then.

What do you mean?

It's the people who aren't doing anything for society that are causing all the trouble. The officer was just trying to protect the interests of civilized society.

Will the fact that you think I'm a threat to civilization appear in the story you're writing?

Barbara chuckles sadly.

Look—Stevven jogs up to Barbara, intercepts her speedwalk—I don't get why you're so obsessed with this operation but it's time—

Operation?

—it's time to wrap things up. Just tell me what you need from me right now, for your story or whatever, and we'll split.

Traffic ruffles Barbara and Stevven, jostles pack, BluBerry. Stevven refrains from biting off noses. Barbaraeyes snare something unpleasant in crowd.

Shit, she says through teeth. Don't look.

Stevven looks.

Stevven, I swear—

Barb? Barb! Baaaarb!

Woman bobs in crowd, hands overhead, squeezing like extra mouths, swallows Barbara in hug.

My goodness, how *are* you, sorority sister!

Hi! Genny, hi! I'm doing well, Barbara says, face like pink minutemade. How are you?

George and I bought the house, Genny says. Of course you saw on insta. He's on the phone with them now. See him over there? Oh, so serious, ha! Hi George! And look at this—Ginny shakes box from plastic bag, inflatable flamingo pool toy—I just couldn't help myself, we're so excited. Hey now, I thought you were living in Nashville?

Work is sending me everywhere these days, but I'm going home soon. My dry sauna calls!

I just can't *wait* to read your story! Sounds so *dang*erous, involving yourself with all those *crazy* people—Gennyeyes widen on Stevven—Oh I'm sorry, I don't think we've been introduced.

Hi, I'm Stevven, and today I'm Barbara's niece with complications—Stevven extends hand—Nice to meet you.

Oh, I had no idea, Barb!

Oh, I'm just helping her—

Ooouah ooah!

Ginny and Barbara recoil, some shoppers slow.

Ooouah! Stevven monkeys, long vowel vibrations lighting up body.

Oh dear, are you okay? Genny says.

When I hear someone spouting petroleum, I like to clear the air, Stevven says. Oooooo. Ooouah!

Ginny steps back, nearly falls. Hey Barb I think, I got to get back to George, she says.

Oooooah. AAAAoooooAh!

Ginny slips into crowd, calls for hubby. Streamers laugh and point phones, blink digieyes. Stevven smiles after Genny, then turns to Barbara. Barbaradigieye flickers, bluered fury, blistering. Stevven freezes before new Barbara, brutal, unpolitical. She cocks head. Pursing lips finally bubble over.

Do you not have any respect? she says.

No, Stevven says.

After your first episode running out of the taxi, Donna asked me to keep an eye on you, she says, scoffs. You run around like a child. Have you ever thought about taking some responsibility for yourself?

Barbarajaw twists. She turns head to other side as if to step off one hot burner onto other.

Here's what's going to happen, she says. I'm going to go pick up some lunch at that salad bar over there. If you have to freak out again before we get to Donna's place, get it out now.

Are you sure you can film me from all the way over there?

You think you're the center of everything, don't you?

Stevven grinds grimy hands into each other, air stiffening. I'm not going to wait for you, they say.

Barbara wags phone. I have authorization to the apartments, she says. You just have a stinky backpack and a bad attitude. Think about your options.

Barbara turns, crosses traffic. She passes under cursive letters, *Salata*, purple light rouging produce assembly. Machines portion ingredients into bowls that slide onto conveyor to *order pick up*.

Stevventhroat clogs. Guts storm. They sink down against wall, scrape pack on bricks. They watch Barbaraback through window as she points and builds salads. Indoor seating lies empty in green plastic plant forest.

Stevven interrogates storefronts, harshness compounding, denying entropy and being.

Could you do it again?

Stevven looks up at kid. Fake snot bungeechords from hoodie. Shoe screens throw ninja stars. Digieyes blink, recording.

Do what? Stevven asks.

Go bananas.

I don't feel like it.

C'mon just do it.

No.

Fuck you, man.

What's your name? Stevven asks.

Fuck you bitch freak monkey ass bitch, kid says.

You're doing it just fine without me.

I ain't doin shit you stanky monkey ass bitch, croner ass.

Save it for the man.

Kid kicks gravel into Stevvenface, bolts, glares back muttering monkey sounds.

BARBARA HOVERS SALAD CONTAINER OVER Stevven.

I thought you might be hungry, she says.

Stevven takes crinkly plastic, utensils in cellophane. *Salata—our story*, container advertises in lumi letters.

You didn't have to do that, Stevven says.

Click, click, Stevven opens container. Spinach, green apple slices, sweaty grapes, protein blocks. Cheese crumble, walnuts. Stevvenfinger catches oil vinaigrette smear from bowl edge. They suck finger dry.

I got it to go, so let's go, Barbara says.

What's the rush?

I don't have time for this.

What do you have time for?

Fine, eat, Barbara says, clocks phone. Let's just pause the world for you.

She answers call, laughs, talks headlines, placeless, dying things. She crosses to shade under awning one shop downwind to talk apart from Stevven.

Stevven skewers thick spinach, walnut buttoning leaves like bow tie, brings forkful to mouth. Tang, crunch, sweet, stinging lips. Dressing dribbles down chin. Walnut catches in molars. Stevven moans, closes eyes around next bite.

Almost done? Barbara asks, looms. It's way too hot out here.

Stevven fastens Salata container, licks lips, stands.

I can take the rest of this, they say.

They walk North, surge, becoming traffic. Stevven dizzies tracking white dashes, cross walks, but trips when they look away, body too cerebral, anxious and forgetting.

Barbara drops salad into trash bin. Stevven stops, fishes salad out. Barbaraeyebrows raise, digieye glinting.

You still have a few bites left, Stevven says. I'll save it.

Stevven brushes off sticky wrapper, falls back into precarious stride behind Barbara.

Serendipity Apartments rises into view, bulk commanding atmosphere, shadowing entire street. Sleek dorsalfin balconies jut out from block, drapes sensuous lines, silver and seaglass. Cruise ship windows adamant, eloquent, sparkle like sea life.

What are you going to wear to the party? Barbara asks.

She scans into apartment building. Touchless doors part into jarring cold lobby. Metal plates on walls shine, float turquoise light halos. Vents pump air with deadly consistency. Grey faux leather armchairs harden in corner. Stevven frowns at glass flowers in wicker vase.

Where's Eli? Stevven says.

They're all probably waiting in the room, Barbara says, smacks gum.

They step into elevator. Barbara presses button sixteen. Doors rumble shut.

Stevven turns inward, spiraling, intellectualizing, trying to transcend sprocket clicks, metal ropes hauling them higher.

Soft chiming reawakens skin. Doors slide away to hallway bending like coasts. Stevven turns left. Floor remembers footsteps like water, forgets them like water. Walls reflect amorphous phantoms, doors twice as tall as average human.

Wait, you know where we are? Barbara asks, following.

I used to live here. When it looked very different.

But your profile—

Unofficially.

Like, at the same time as Donna?

With Donna, and others.

Oh my god. How did you—

Here we are.

Large security square beckons. Barbara hovers phone over scanner.

It's for hands, Stevven says, squeezes fists at side.

Barbara places hand on scanner. Red flashes. She tries again, same red flash. She flicks eyes up and down Stevven as they place hand on scanner. Red flash. They wipe hand on shorts and try again.

Turquoise light.

You're kidding me, Barbara says.

More to this story than you thought, Stevven says.

Silver washes over scanner like koi in moon pond. Door hushes open, whispering rememberings, salty ghosts. Windchime welcome. Barbara steps into suite, jaw dragging.

Stevven stands opaque in windless threshold.

STEVVEN, COME LOOK!

Elihand tugboats Stevven through doorway.

Hall feeds into kitchen, corrugate metal rippling up to ceiling, opposite wall all window, balcony. Eli rebounds off clamflesh couch cushions, rouses Mary from stupor, hauls Stevven towards patio door.

I was so worried, Mary says, tails.

We just needed a breather, Stevven says, pats BluBerrybottle.

Something smells really good, Mary says.

Cool rocks this way! Eli says, presses through door.

Stevven hands over Salata boxes. Ingredients you'd mostly agree with, they say. Courtesy of Barbara.

Eli fizzes, impatient. Stevven follows Eli through door. Glass rails guard round balcony. In center, rock pond absorbs LED lights, swells and sinks blues. Gino sits legs square in chair, meditates. Maryhand gently alights on Stevvenshoulder.

Stevven, I know you told me not to worry, but I had a bad thought that you wouldn't come back. It doesn't make sense, I know. But I was worried. So I am really glad you're here. Everything changes so fast, and I'm so grateful for Donna but, but I thought we had a home at the Apartment finally, and, I don't know. I'm sorry.

Tears edge Maryeyes. Stevven removes Maryhand, concentrates on rocks, gritty.

All of this is really sudden, really stressful, they say. So we're going to talk about what's next, okay? Gino?

Ginobreath remains steady. He extends arm out, pats chair.

I don't have time to meditate right now, Stevven says.

Gino pats chair again. Always time, he says.

Stevven groans. They set pack and BluBerry beside chair, drop down next to Gino. Mary settles down on other side, fidgets with fraying ruffles on shirt waist.

Do you know anyone at the party besides Donna? Mary whispers to Stevven across Gino.

What? No. I don't know. I'm not going.

I want to play oilman hunters, Eli says, bounces on Stevvenknee.

Where did Barbara go? Mary asks. I thought I saw her come in with you.

Probably taking a shower, Stevven says. You know what I think about Barbara—

Shhhhhhh, Gino hushes like great tall waterfall. Everyone takes silence.

Sky circulates through perpetual gray sheen, sorts out yellows and blues, oranges, reds. Building lights battle dusk, windows, patios, street lights flickering on like living, corpuscular things. Cheers and splashes break, opposite balcony divider, Donnaparty gathering momentum next door. Stevven feathers BluBerrybottle rim.

Ooooommmm, Gino hums, starting deep, low, on exhales.

Stevven closes eyes, releases BluBerry, dives deeper. Turquoise shadows, breeze like water. Swimming, suspending. Toothy predators swim in and out briny fog, circle Stevven. Shark lunges, drowns Stevven.

Snap! Eyes open. Eliteeth smile two inches away from Stevven.

I thought you were a shark coming to eat me, Stevven whispers.

Gino continues bee breath, Mary too.

I want to play, Eli says.

Sharks?

Elihands clap into dorsal fin. Stevven matches, closes eyes, inhales deeply. Lungs push through ribs, stitch gills. Body sways, swimming, shark. They are off, circle enchanting underwater volcano. Fish schools dart away when they drift too close. Entire body one muscle, accelerating, catching food.

Look out!

Net tills sea floor, grinds corals, inflate sand and debris. They swim fast, faster. Sharp rope snags Eliside, tears in.

Stevven, help!

Stevventeeth snap through threads. They swim away together. Hunger drives them to strike small fish too quick. They divert course, tasting seal bleeding in current. Eli leaps from water and crashes down on meal.

Gentle there, little one, Gino says, peels Eli from side. I am many.

Oops, sorry, Eli whispers into mouse nest in beardforest.

Gino squeezes Elishoulder, mighty exhale. Can I see that quartz you were playing with a minute ago? he asks.

Eli fetches crystal from rock pond.

Oh, you found a good one, he says, turns rock over in hand. For the compostists, and also in our ancestral and sister cultures, minerals are sacred. Quartz is for purity. To lead us to right intention. To bring us back to our self-knowledge. Quartz does this. It is often represented by a circle.

Elifoot twists around, politely listening.

Intention, motivation. Our will to do good, Gino says, switches rock to other hand. When I was young and living in the mountains, we held ceremonies, using quartz, and others. I was training to be a priest. The priest's job is to generate this energy of right intention, will to do good, from the crystal. We are trained to do this since children, younger than you. I ate a specific diet to train my nervous system to be sensitive enough to the crystal's energy. From this sensitivity we can generate light. Not like starlight or dawnlight but the whole light of becoming.

Wow! Like this light? Eli points.

No, the light you see here in the rock pond is from bulbs underneath. The light I speak of emanates from within the crystal. I do not know the terms to explain well. Everything you see in this world has a vibrational network that responds to everything else, temperature, pressure, sound. But the specific vibration is a bit of a mystery, so you have to work hard to detect it among all the other matter on earth. Priests perceive the molecular matrix of the crystal as they would their own mind, reading it, activating it through energy pathways. When you do see the light— Gino traces line from crystal to Eliforehead—your confusion goes away, like fog lifting from a mountain. You see clear again.

The rock has superpowers? Eli asks.

All laugh. This hurts Eli some.

There is a lot I have failed to explain, but yes, Gino says, winks, places crystal back in Elihand.

Eli, can I braid your hair? Mary asks.

No, I want to play.

Let your mama braid your hair, Stevven says. We'll play another time.

Eli groans and crosses to Mary. Stevven kneels next to Gino.

Gino, Stevven whispers. Can you help Mary get to her sister in Charlotte?

Ginoeyes blink slowly. I know less and less the routes to places as they all become nonplaces. Here's why I cultivate place in myself.

Just tell me you can help them.

Gino blinks. They aim to go to Sewanee, with you and BluBerry. Just as I do.

We can't travel like this, Stevven says, stands. All of us criminals in one light or another. Too slow, too risky. It's just impossible. I have to get BluBerry to Sewanee. I have to get BluBerry—

Barbara steps out onto balcony wearing evening party gown. Donna's asking for you next door, she says.

How exciting, Mary says.

I want to come, Eli says.

No, I'll be right back, Stevven says, picks up pack, BluBerry.

You're taking that to the party? Barbara says. What, you think you'll need your first aid kit?

Gino lays hand on Stevvenwrist. Let us watch BluBerry, he says gently.

BluBerry? Barbara asks.

It's what we call my pack, Stevven says.

They will not be disturbed, Gino says, closes eyes, returns to breath. I will pray over them.

Stevven levels pack against Ginochair. I will be right back, they say again, cross to Barbara irritating doorway.

Please? Eli says, braid unravelling as they bound over to Stevven.

No.

Please!

I need you to stay back and take care of BluBerry, Stevven says. It's really important to me.

Eli turns and stomps away to patio edge, presses frown into glass pane. Mary whispers after them. They shoulder her away.

NOT EVEN DEODORANT, BARBARA MUMBLES as Stevven passes inside. Hold on, I got to fix my lips.

She bends towards complexion in standing mirror, coral beading crowding frame. She unscrews deep purple lipstick, stretches mouth in oblong mirror. Bitter tongue presses behind white teeth, corkscrew cheeks.

Could you not stare at me? she says. It's a little creepy.

Stevven turns, faces kitchen. I thought Donna was calling, they say, peek back at Barbara in silence.

She drags lips, spreads stain. Plastic cap, snap makeup bag closed.

Let's go, she says, leads into hallway. But don't stand so close.

Stevven catches themselves in coral mirror, patchy tank, soily shoes, round trashmonger eyes. Small mouth, shoulder muscles ropey with acid and strain, shame.

Apartment door hushes, closes after them, but Stevven lingers in on themselves. They walk across glossy hallway behind Barbara, thirst for something dry.

STEVVEN STEPS THROUGH PORTAL, BLUE, orange, red, purple, licorice vapor. Bass. Lights and sounds swallow, barge into pores, mix fibers. Purple horses thunder, splash. Arms, heads, neon parts writhe. Sequin shoulder scrapes Stevvenskin pushing through, what hurry, energy. Black leather fringe tickles Stevvencalf. They retreat, where, sticky skins, breath. Waxy sugar air washes Stevven against spaceship wall. Stevvenhands grapple walls as if on cliff, rockface untrappable as boiling copper kettle, dimply, sliding down.

It's always easy to find you in a crowd, Donna says.

Stevven opens eyes. Cateyes. Cuffs. Knit lingerie.

Donna leans into Stevvenear. Let me guess, you need a drink? she asks.

Where's Barbara? Stevven blubbers.

I put her onto a journalist friend, she says, eases back. C'mon, doll, let's loosen you up.

She takes Stevvenarm carefully, steers them hip to hip through bioluminescent flesh.

Moscow mule still your favorite? she asks.

I haven't drank since June.

Whatcha say?

Yes, Stevven rephrases. Mule's good.

She passes orders to bartender, massages Stevvenhand on bar.

You're tight, she says. We can't get you a drink fast enough.

I'm not here to party.

Oh?

Bartender pours, hooks lime wedge on rim, sets glass on granite top before Stevven. Stevven takes glass, looks left, right, before speaking.

So, will you help me with BluBerry?

Of course, Donna says, smirks. But you're not getting it til tomorrow morning. Tonight the only business is party business. Trust me, it's for your own good.

Stevven looks up to ceiling, brain ebbing, music summoning migraine. Donna—

One drink with me, Donna says, holds up finger. All I ask in return for my help.

Stevven exhales, joins hand to cold glass. Donna kickstands arm on bar, watches Stevven, cateyes. Stevven sips drink. Yow.

Remember that night, here, Donna says, when you went off on Antwon's cyborg, got us all eager to start crocheting coral reefs?

Yeah, and then you called him a colonizer.

Oh shit, I did? Donna says, perks. Probably called him an insinuated enlightened penis. We were all surprised how long Djenny stayed with him.

Stevven chuckles, brings glass to lips. Ice bites. They drain glass, rattle icecubes.

That was a sipper, doll, Donna laughs. Let's get you another.

Stevven receives second mule. Light ice in glass revolves through green, turquoise, yellow light, witchbrew.

Ready to meet some people? Donna asks, hangs arm over Stevven.

Can't promise to be on my best behavior.

Donna smiles gemstones, guides Stevven into sea, swimming.

Decompressions, she muses.

Manes, lionfish, stripes, arms, orifices, squid. They drift around pearly pillar, couple massaging orange lips together, smudging reflections, hooking fingers on straps, rings.

XiXi, I love the look tonight, Donna says to snakeskin person. XiXi, this is Stevven.

Oh! Nice to meet you Stevven, XiXi says, blemishless. Can I just say, June was always raving about you.

You knew June?

I was receptionist for Agrigen, started there a few weeks before the incident. Oh, I just know Daryl would love to meet you. Daryl?

Daryl, Stevven says, looks around. Is he the one dressed like the tetradactyl?

Donna nearly spits drink, laughs with Stevven. Let's go find you some manners in the lounge, she says. We'll catch you later XiXi.

No probs! I'll see you two around.

They weave to couches, hookah fumes. Look out for the tails, Donna says, steps Stevven over to empty couchspace.

Tails! They've gotten longer over the years, Stevven says. You could never get me to wear one.

I know someone who could.

Woah, here we are, Stevven says, plops down on cushions. Oh creature, comfort!

Stevven touches fingers to chest, looks around, gathering, opening. Eyes sore, heavy party ambience, dehydration.

Donna, I'm having a good time, they say. But I'm here for BluBerry. You know June would—

My sister, Donna says, would want you to be happy.

This plant she helped create at Agrigen, they're not just a plant. June died for BluBerry.

That's an oversimplification, Donna says.

You know it's not. She believed she was working on something to topple the food poverty industry, from inside the labs of Agrigen itself. Superplant. All parts edible, totally resilient, self-propagating. When they found out that BluBerry could not be contained, she stood up to BluBerry's termination, and Agrigen terminated her.

And when it was time to confront them, what did you do? Donna says. Dove undercover, holed up in that trash heap I just rescued you from.

I had to protect BluBerry.

We needed your support. You never showed up for a Justice for June rally.

Those politics and emotions did nothing.

Not even the funeral, Stevven? Donna says, sits straight up. I know we all grieve in our own ways, but you couldn't even make an appearance to your own partner's funeral.

Look, I just couldn't do all that performance bullshit, protests, funerals, crying in front of cameras.

It's called activism. And at it's core, it's community. Remember this? Your whole life before all this BluBerry business?

I see your pleasure activism campaign is doing just fine, Stevven says, looks around.

What the fuck do you mean by that?

Cashing in on the grief, Stevven says. All the profits packed into champaign bottles. Great work. The death of your sister at the hands of grandchild Monsanto generated a lot of sympathy. The wine overfloweth, all while BluBerry's still being hunted, Agrigen bigger than ever.

Donnajaw stiffens. You can't say shit about what I do. You haven't been here for any of it.

I can see it from all the way over there, Stevven points directionlessly to Apartment.

Donnahead tics away, flames chin to brow.

Stevvenhead aches, bass rattling like death behind ears. They bring fingers to temple.

Look, Donna says, I'm going to give this to you now while I still got the heart to.

Stevvenstomach flips, ears ring in, out. They refocus on Donna. She takes small clear square one-inch case from hidden breast pocket. Stevven accepts chip in hand, looks around at loud party fish, peeks inside sweaty palm.

What is this? Stevven asks.

A temp eID, with a train ticket and some cash. Though you're not high profile enough to have been arrested already, if you showed up to the station trying to get on a train as Stevven Pane, they would take you—Music changes, Donna leans in, speaks up—This temp chip will get you on the train to Nashville. A friend living there is going to tell the university to expect you, with a 'package.' If any of June's colleagues are still there, they will understand and be ready to help with BluBerry.

Wow. This is, this is great, Stevven says, meets Donnaeyes. Exactly what we need.

Donnalips swallow smile. She recrosses legs. So, what are your friends going to do? she asks.

I don't know, Stevven says, laughs, pockets chip deep into velcro pocket.

Tough thing to laugh about. The kid… Stevven, Eli's completely blank. No birth certificate, no online presence. The most at-risk kind of person. Did you know this?

Stevven shrugs.

The best thing to do for Eli is to keep them hidden until they can acquire personhood from the Underground. Their mother is crazy to bring them out here, to not register them in the first place. And then there's Gino, a fucking *Earther*, I couldn't get someone like that a bus ticket, much less a train ticket.

You can't get them fake eIDs?

What, use more of my dirty campaign money for your friends that you don't even seem to care about?

Stevven drops head, struggles, figures. I do care, Stevven says. But I'm committed to BluBerry.

They rest for two beats. Potions and drugs stack on coffee table like buildings on silver lake, little city diorama. Urge to knock them down, crashshshsh.

Don't let Barbara know any of this, Donna says. Any more than she already knows.

I'm shaking Barbara tonight, Stevven says.

She's a journalist for a gossip magazine, but a journalist nonetheless.

I know, Stevven says, hurting, twisting. I didn't mean what I said, earlier.

I think you did. And it is what it is. I'm used to working with assholes like you. Especially assholes that meant a lot to my sister. Now, if you'll excuse me.

Donna rises. She blends into low light and sound, away.

Seat next to Stevven hollow, hurting, then changing, white lips, pink teeth. XiXi.

So what is your favorite hobby? XiXi asks, aluminum cheek amplifying voice. What?

I thought it might be gardening. Donna mentioned your GreenRoof™. My sister has a GreenRoof™ but her virtual one is much nicer. I visit every other weekend. The eFood they serve in some colonies is really out-competing Charleston. What do you grow in yours?

I'm retiring from roofs on gardens actually, Stevven says, browses drinks on coffee table.

They pick up champaign glass from table, swirl liquid.

Is that your drink? XiXi asks.

Fire down throat. Cough.

No, Stevven says.

Empty glass twinkles in Stevvenhand. Glass twinkles in Stevven, dissolves.

I got to go to the bathroom, they say.

Blood thins to Stevvenhead, light, standing up. They shuffle sideways through dancers, dodge flying hand gestures, feet shifting in talk circles. Neon Chinese dragon glides overhead, projection, screen, costume, eyes rolling like wild compasses, claws poising to grab. Stevven ducks, sidesteps into rubber, inflatable dress. They collect scolds, keep swimming forward. Fish schools pass, life so aquatic in drowning society.

They stumble into bathroom queue, right into face dangling giant modnose.

Sorry, Stevven says, steps back, locks gaze into long hairy nostrils.

No apologies necessary, modnose says, steps to Stevven, nostrils livelier than eyes. You have a *very* interesting scent. May I sniff?

Woah! Stevven stumbles back.

You smell like the old levee, and chamomile! modnose says, lingers, lifts finger, sniffs again. And you are agitated. Fearful.

How'd you guess? Stevven says with edge. Now I really got to—

Eli. Eli inside glass, behind glass, on balcony. Masonjar eyes. Stevven stares through floor to ceiling window at Eli watching people cannonball into pool.

Guilt is more of a fruity oriental than floral, modnose says. You have a dark citrus accord, dusted with pepper, a suggestion of dirtiness. But your top notes have a promising glow, the heart of the fragrance is flowery. Green.

Get out of my way, Stevven says.

Stevven apologizes to no one, everyone, room tilting, falling forward. They reach glass, rap, rap. Eli jumps, turns, smiles at Stevven.

What are you doing? Stevven asks.

Elilips move. They point to pool.

What? Stevven says. Stay there. I'm coming.

Elilips move again. They point.

No, stay there.

Stevven snakes along glass towards door. Excuse me, excuse me. Partygoer with hair like raspberry leads laughing party inside from balcony, impassable. Stevven stops, head swimming, waits. They glance back to Eli, only smeary light and glass.

Outside, people busy pink lawn below giant projector screen. Screen cycles famous little black girl empowerment collage, pleasure activism city art installments, fertility festival highlights, and bursting brandstandard purplegreen, *earth is lover - liberate each other!*

Stevven swivels to pool side, scans heads. Towel dryer exhaust pushes steam into Stevvenface, noodles limbs. They break fall on lawnchair, disturbs martini onto zebra. Hooves jump back, little rabbits. Stevven becomes two hands, two feet, grounding. They sink lower.

Barbara. Barbara grins through crowd, fangs, blue digieye.

Stevven crawls, scratches up veranda pillar. They frown down down, down, ground.

Primal, someone says. Whistle, hoot. Are they okay? They must have taken a lopper. Get them on the chair. Stevven growls, moans, shakes sweat, sinuous lines. All hard surfaces soft, bending under fingers. They're going to fall in the pool!

Gentle arms hook under, pull Stevven up. Stranger. XiXi. White. Ghost. Cyborg.

What are you? Stevven says, face wet.

Hush, poor thing, XiXi says. I'm taking you back to rest.

Did Donna ask you to babysit me, too? Stevven says, consonants lulling.

XiXi slings Stevvenarm over shoulders, lifts them from ground.

Yes, she says, carries Stevven.

Here we are, XiXi says.

Red. Lava. Blood, swelling cushion.

Remember Donna's room? she asks.

Orange and red swim around fingers, little guppies. Stevven lies against giant lava lamp, XiXi hand supporting them upright.

I need to leave, now, Stevven says.

There's no way we're sticking you in a taxi tonight, XiXi says. You're staying here.

No, Stevven says, points through wall. BluBerry.

Doorway beads clack, clack clack, crystal sunsets. Donna arrives.

What's going on? Stevven?

They drank a lopper. XiXi says.

On top of everything else, Donna says, shakes head. Fuck, Stevven.

BluBerry. Rain. Stevvenjaw stretches open, rolls around, loose, rocks in socks.

Should I call someone? XiXi asks.

How much did they take?

I don't know. It was just the bottom of a champaign glass.

Stevven melts onto bed. Donna sits them upwrong.

If you're going to stay here we need to get you cleaned up first, Donna says.

Stevven chortles, smelly, dirty stinky, no good crawler. Soap, soap, soap.

I'm going to set you up in the washer, Donna says.

Ah, me and my clothes? Stevven laughcries.

Donna and XiXi move, Stevven sliding between them like wet tomato seed.

Lean against this, Donna says, helps Stevven into white purgatory. Let's get you undressed.

Arm hooks around Stevven waist. Water gushes.

Donna, um, can't this wait? I think they just need to lie down, XiXi says.

In my bed? After today? After all the opportunities to wash up and be decent company? No, no space for compost here.

Stevven sobs. June.

Hush, Donna says, runs hand through bath water. Steady now. You still got your socks on. Whew. These stink.

You think I'm gross, Stevven says.

Donnaeyes, teacups, serious. She stops washing.

You work real hard to give yourself an excuse to be, she says.

Water turns on, stings. White tiles with little red room, little red lava lamp inside. Light needles. Stevven slips down enamel walls, soapy. Water splashes neck, runs down breasts, dark crotch, hairy. Water hums on skin. Brown marbles on feet.

You got to put in a little effort to take care of yourself now, Donna says in steam. Use that soap.

Hands scrub. Scrubadub. Scrubadub, weak. Stevven drinks in hot, scratchy water. Hot.

Don't lie down. No drowning. Whoa whoa! Shit, you're getting me wet.

Water shuts off.

Blotch tones, voices, hands. Drip, drop, water. Murky water, choke, choking drain. Towel, fuzzy warm.

World turns vertical, upside ways, lava rising, sinking. Bed, red, red, red.

B RIGHT HURT. GIANT LAVA LAMP looms, blobs. Head fuzzes, furs on bed. Bare skin, alone, bedroom. White light cracks blackout curtain, daylight.

Stevven lifts head, rests. They twiddle fingers, let blanket fall. They sit up. Cruel air conditioner air. They cross to clothes on chair. Shirt to nose, sickening. They must dress, so they dress.

Socks missing, shoes missing. Stevvenfeet clam up. They pass through beads hanging in bedroom doorway, click, clack, click. Shrink against electric squalling ricocheting down hallway. Stevven braces sound into main room, full day streaming in from windows. Robot vacuuming sofa pauses machine. Stevven crosses to closet next to apartment entry, sifts through urbanite clothes, shoes two sizes too clean.

Stevven looks up to robot. Where are the guest shoes? they ask.

Good afternoon, Stevven, I have notified Donna that you are awake.

Just need the shoes.

I am sorry, I cannot help you with this task. Is there something else I can do for you?

Stevven leaves apartment.

CUTLERY DRAWER CLANKS AS STEVVEN enters neighboring apartment, approaches kitchen in barefoot silence. BluBerry glistens on countertop in rich yellowing light. White roots tickle bottle edges, primary growth, tentacular, feeling, reaching. Three leaves beginning.

Stevven exhales tension noisily.

Mary startles, wheels from pantry. Saltine crackers skittle on floor tiles, break.

Stevven, you're back! I thought, well, I was worried because Barbara—

Eli rounds corner offering saltine with nut butter spread. Try this! they say.

Stevven frowns at Eli. I saw you last night at the party, they say. What do you think you were doing there?

Eli shrugs.

Oh, Eli! Mary gasps.

You didn't know they were gone? Stevven asks, looks up to Mary.

I was asleep, she says, toes turning inward.

Stevven crosses to BluBerry, brings them close to face. What's this? Stevven says, unscrews bottlecap.

Quartz, Eli says, smacking cracker.

You put a piece of quartz in here?

Eli nods.

Why?

Because it has powers.

Where's Gino?

Rap rap at apartment door jumps Stevven.

I think that might be Barbara, Mary says, wipes cracker hands on hand towel.

She scurries to front door, whitehush opening. Barbara enters room with brown bags, savory yeasty sandwich shop bags. She drapes black summer suit with vinyl accents on barstool, pulls sunglasses to head.

Hi Stevven, she says. Have fun at the party?

What the *fuck* are you still doing here?

Maryhand jumps to mouth. Oh Stevven, she says. Did something happen?

Barbara sets bags down on counter, feigns pitiful offense. Maryhands frantically dust air to keep animosity from settling. Eli mixes nut butter bowl with knife, dresses saltine cracker, eyes on Stevven.

I'm not done with the story, Barbara says.

Stevven reels BluBerry in, plays with screw top lid, finds breath. You're not welcome here anymore, they say.

From what I saw last night, I wouldn't think you were either, Barbara says, roams through purse.

And what did you see? Stevven stands up.

Oh, Stevven, please be nice, Mary says, prayer hands. Barbara brought us lunch. Let's eat!

And you think it's from the goodness of her heart, don't you Mary?

Of course.

Barbara looks up from texting, returns smile to Mary, then answers call, crosses to lounge. Stevven sits back down, pockets hands. They turn over plastic square, chip, ticket, sharp remembering.

One ticket West. For BluBerry.

Are you okay? Mary asks. What happened last night? What happened to your shoes?

I don't know.

The cleaning bot probably thought they were garbage, Barbara says, returns from call. Realistically speaking. Like, they were made of trash anyways, right?

I repurposed some plastic, yeah. Also, go away.

Oh, Stevven, you're going to need shoes! Mary says.

Looks like we need to go shopping, Barbara says. Want to go in-store? I know a place.

Shopping! Mary says, claps hands. I'll go get Gino.

Mary exits onto balcony. Stevven ruminates on bar stool, steadies on BluBerry.

Eli slows munching on cracker. What's that? they ask.

Barbara smiles. Food for you, she says, passes bag. Do you like grilled sandwiches?

I don't know, Eli says.

Did you get enough to eat at the apartment? Barbara asks.

Sometimes I get hungry.

Oh, that's not good. Growing boys like you should always have enough to eat. Go ahead, pick out whichever one you like. I've got ham, turkey, and tuna in there. Sorry, Stevven, I would have grabbed you something—

Eli, you always tell us when you're hungry and we feed you, yeah? Stevven says, taps fingers along countertop.

Eli nods, tips toes, dives two hands into bag, retrieves sandwich.

Barbara raises eyebrows. Looking pretty hungry to me, she says. I'll get you a napkin sweetie.

Eli owleyes Stevven, unwraps sandwich. Patio doors open.

What are you eating, monkey? Mary says, hurries to Eli. Oh, we don't eat meat, remember?—Mary folds up sandwich paper—I don't mean to sound ungrateful, Barbara, she says. But did you get a vegetarian option?

I didn't, she apologizes. We can get something along the way to the shoe store.

Oh no, you've already done so much, Mary says. We can eat some more crackers, can't we, monkey?

But it tasted so good, Eli says.

It's no problem, Barbara says. There should be plenty of vegetarian options around town.

Mary, this is good food, don't waste it, Stevven says, scoots sandwich back towards Eli. No one should go hungry.

What's this? Gino settles big earthing hands on countertop, sniffs air.

Here's a tuna sandwich for you, Barbara says.

You are very kind, Gino says, bows to Barbara.

Gino, can you eat that on the go? Stevven asks.

No, Gino says, unwraps paper.

What?

No. I cannot eat and walk. That is impossible.

So you're going to sit here and eat this while we watch you?

No trouble, no trouble at all, Mary says, quakes air with anxious hands. Eli, can you make me another cracker with sun butter, please?

Gino breaks off sandwich pieces with fingers, chews slowly. Mary scrambles for broom and dust pan.

It looks like I do have a sandwich for you, afterall, Barbara says.

Stevven picks up sandwich, hunger knocking. Wheat dust rolls under fingers. They bite into plush, savory bread, close on oily turkey, young arugula, salty. They slurp stray onion piece, suck grease from fingers.

I missed you at meditation this morning, Gino says after chewing.

Good Harvest, please just eat your sandwich, Stevven says. Too much of the day is gone.

Long windows tint afternoon sun turquoise, paint stripes across North wall. Coal power electricity undercurrent silence.

Have all your things together? Stevven asks Eli, Mary, finishes sandwich.

Yes, Eli says, clears out sun butter jar with finger.

Stevven picks up BluBerry, secures them in pack.

Gino, how's that sandwich coming?

Gino chews, swallows. Sucks juices from fingers.

I would prefer time to settle the sandwich, but if we must go—

We must, Stevven says.

Where do we put empty containers? Mary asks.

Anywhere is fine.

Where are we going? Eli asks.

Stevven blinks. West, they say.

There's a trash can right there, Barbara says, points.

Just leave it on the counter, Stevven says. Someone will use it for something.

I should wash it out, Mary says.

Mary, just leave it.

Stevven takes jar from Maryhand, places it clumsily on countertop. They violently avoid standing mirror as they lead out apartment, trudge to elevator, adjust pack straps.

Elevator dings as others catch up. Stevven holds arm over elevator door. They stack in, descend. Sleek elevator walls warp them into one large smear, cold, drowsy, seasick.

Eli swims Winky through reflection.

DING, DOORS PART. THEY FILE out elevator, walk cold lobby floors, step out Serendipity onto hot gritty sidewalk. Stevven hops into shade peeling from neighboring cafe. People lounge in chairs and computers. Human face awash with mega reelhalo grimaces, glares through interface at Stevvenfeet.

Dirty Earthers, they spit.

Teenagers huddle next to charging bar wearing sunbreakers, glossy makeup, insignia loyal to various ecologies, meshing together in blue light cloud. Stevven looks out to street. People blur, assimilate into efficient streams through in points, out points, unity by velocity. People line up to access vending machine wall. Bundles roll out machine mouth, plastic with handles. They take groceries, walk into traffic flow.

Complainings build up nearby, Gino clogging traffic flow.

Barbara points East. The boutique is this way, she says.

Stevven points Northwest. The station is this way, they say. I can find shoes on the way.

Maybe someone has extra, Eli says, tracks flashy kid in green soles.

I'm not sure people carry more than one pair with them, Stevven says.

But Barbara does.

Her shoes aren't for walking, Stevven says, tests feet in sun, adapts.

Barbara mumbles, complains, something about heat, luggage.

Stevvenfeet grease and blacken and thicken as they walk, wary for sparkling sharp edges on ground, but too hot to hesitate. Sidewalk runs long, passes restaurants and business fronts, opens to park exercising finicky, non sticky fake grass. Stevventoes dig in, sniff earth burying deep below.

Sput tut tut, splash, water claps pavement, elephant. Small splash park draws exotic animals around children. Stevven gapes at water drops stringing down from pipes, animating zebra, stripes and legs, disappearing on squealing human heads, grates.

Sorry, sweetie, Mary says to Eli. I don't think we have time.

I want to play in the water more than anything in my whole life, Eli says.

Tiger pours from air, paws kids into excitement. Stevven taps Elishoulder.

I'll hold your pack and you can run through, Stevven says. Don't stay under the water. It isn't fun to walk while wet.

Yay! Eli says, scurries on, bright.

Stevven shoulders Elipack, follows along park edge, steps in soothing, shallow puddles.

They probably think I am an evil villain, Mary says, follows dry trail.

My fault, Stevven says. Look at them play.

Eli waits, watches one complete cycle of animals, then leaps through tiger maw with other children, wet, ecstatic. They run back to group walking parallel to park.

Did you see me?

Yes, Stevven says. Looks refreshing.

How was it? Mary asks, hand on Eli.

I want to stay here forever! Can I go again?

If you're in such a rush, maybe we just get a taxi? Barbara says to Stevven.

Gino lingers over pansies in planter midway through park. He resumes walking, slowing for criss crossing children, slower than breeze.

I can go to the water and back before Gino gets here, Eli says, bounces. Watch!

You're wet enough already, Stevven says, catches Eli. Gino, there are more flowers this way. Let's go.

Stevven steps from grass to brick path, outdoor strip mall, feet relishing shady walk. Above, large chromium beams rig like stitches between retail buildings, bear blue fabric tarps, shading shoppers. Stevven spies birdnest in beam, steps forward. Foot pinches, ouch. They pull foot to face, watch watery red swim down arch.

Oh no, what happened? Mary says.

The inevitable. I'll be fine.

Stevven eyes sharp culprits hiding in grout, sticking from brick divots. They collect small carboplastic blade, hobbles to garbage bin, chucks piece in. They continue walking. Stevven rebalances, cut baking shut on bricks.

Speakers speak future garage music, AC units hiss, milk frothers squeal. Sound presses in.

Maybe we should slow down for Gino, Mary says.

What's that? Eli points to windows, cut meats sweating red.

That's a butcher's shop, Stevven says. Where they sell animal parts.

Where are the heads?

They don't put those on display.

Why?

Because most people only eat some parts of the animal.

Why?

Because they're silly, Stevven says, hand on Eliback, urges movement.

How is it red?

They pump oxygen and nitrates through the glass to keep it looking freshly cut.

Why?

A marketing trick. Before the American grocery store, the butcher would go into the locker where the meat was dry aged, the same way we save our pigeon at Apartment.

Stevven sidesteps massive drainage grate on path, watches butcher hand out waxpaper tenderloin to customer.

Are you sure your foot is okay? Mary says. Can we put a bandage on it?

I have to find some shoes first, or else I'd clean it and patch it up for nothing.

Is it still bleeding?

I don't think so.

I hope we can find a store soon, she says.

What do they do with the heads? Eli asks.

Sausages, probably, Stevven says. Most people eat all parts of the animal thinking they don't.

I didn't need to hear that, Barbara says.

Blue tarps give way to great glass arch, escalators and second story retail. Wood and iron railings stick out old brick warehouse wall, neorustic barnstyle, sleek, spacious.

Pseudosterility, Stevven mumbles.

What? Mary asks, stepping closer.

This block has been completely paved over since the riots, Stevven says. I almost didn't recognize it. Hm, that's a new smell.

It smells delicious! Mary says.

They float along yeasty trail to shop, doors generously wide. Inside, flour dusts metal countertops, woodfire oven incongruously homely against steel plate kitchen. Small crowd gathers, watches spectacle, bread maker kneading dough with bare hands. Baker smiles, mustache curling up, bids regulars and newcomers carameleye hellos.

Now that I have it the shape I want, I only knead to leave it in the window here for an hour, Baker says.

They drop dough on large hanging shelf in concave window where other doughs breathe and billow, yeasty, eukaryotic, living. Bakerhands clap, dusting off, feed long paddle into oven.

Out comes glossy brown, perfect round loaf. Sell price for bread blinks blue digits above checkout, jumps twelve bits. All around, babyskin fingers swipe at devices. Blink, blink, bread auctions off, fifteen, twenty, thirty bits, sweet fungal labor coaxing invisible dollars from cloud banks.

I just love real bread, Barbara says, records scene.

Stevven backs away from shop, leads everyone deeper into promenade.

I didn't know you knew the city, Mary says. Has a lot changed since the riots?

Not as much as we hoped.

Synth sugars in candy store buzz air, sizzle nose. Bubblegum globes float around entrance, magically untethering, blink soft fairy lights.

What are those? Eli points.

I don't know, Stevven says. Decorations.

Eli jogs ahead, pack zippers skipping. They stand under one pink orb, like happy dream. Eli reaches, touches.

It's soft!

Maps says there should be a shoe store up on the left, Barbara says.

Oh, good! Mary says.

Eli catches up, eyes still stroking candy shop.

Stevven squints up at monolith shoestore front, letters steeping in billionaire gray: *Fitters ~ practical minimalist footwear*. Dark slate steps lead up to modernist store front.

You think they have a no-shoe policy? Stevven says.

No one catches joke, Stevven not one for jokes.

I'll be right back, they say.

Are you going in there? Eli asks. Can I come?

Okay, Stevven says.

What's inside?

Place I can buy shoes, hopefully.

Eli takes Stevvenhand. They rise stairs. Clack, clack, clack, Barbaraheels follow.

You don't have to come in with us, Stevven says.

Maybe I want some shoes, too, she says, smacks gum.

Anyone else coming in? Stevven turns to Mary, Gino. They probably have AC.

They'll kick me out, Gino says, settles down onto shady steps.

Police are just as likely to harass you sitting here, Stevven says, sneaks glance at Barbara.

I'll stay with Gino, Mary says. So no one bothers him.

Stevven looks between Mary and Gino, one anxious and one calm, both aging, too collectivist, too punishable by states to travel.

I won't be long, Stevven says.

Stevven checks BluBerry secure in pack pocket, pet, pet. They push tall doors in.


WELCOME TO FITTERS, SAYS ROBOT attendant. I'm Shawn. Are you here to pick up an order?

No. I am looking for shoes that I can walk long distances in.

Great, Shawn says. Let's look at our trekker models.

Shoe shelf islands twist from cool concrete sea, mirrors elaborating all sides. Hexagonal basalt columns make fitting stools, designer shoe displays. Eli laughs, jumps up and down, plays with reflection in enormous mirrors.

Your child is adorable, Shawn says, rolls towards far island.

They're not my child.

Here we are, Shawn says. Our trekker collection, like all of our shoes, is inspired by less is more. 100% durable carbon fiber makes our product simple and sustainable.

100% durable? How about that one—Stevven points—unsupported sole?

Shawn extends metal claw arm, silicone padded fingers, picks up shoe. Would you like to try them on? they ask.

Yes.

What size would you like to try? If I may, it looks like you may need a size 40.

You probably know best. Stevven says, shifts feet, cut stinging. Do you have a bathroom?

I'm sorry, Shawn says. We do not.

Where is the nearest sink?

According to Maps, all public restrooms are closed, Shawn says, forklifts shoebox from lower racks, parts tissue.

Barbara, what do your maps say? Stevven says. About bathrooms.

Barbara parks suitcases in corner, mists herself from spray bottle, checks phone. McDonalds is across the street, she says. But you'd have to buy something.

Stevven sets pack on ground, sit on cold stool. They scrub soles with forearm.

Is your foot okay? Eli asks.

It's fine, thanks. Just cleaning off what I can.

Stevven lifts shoe from box, pulls toe and heel apart, small give, strong. Shoe fits on foot, snug. They wiggle toes, flex, stand and walk once around shoe shelf.

Those shoes are weird, Eli says.

Yeah, but I think they'll do the trick, Stevven says. You got socks for these, Shawn?

They are designed to be worn without them, but we have some liners if you prefer those.

Yeah, we got a lot of friction ahead.

Of course. Are you happy with your selection?

Yes. I'd like to check out.

Great, please scan eID here. Shawntorso morphs into payment receptacle.

Five hundred dollars? Is this the cheapest option?

Outside of our sandal collection, yes. Would you like to see your total in a different currency?

No.

Stevven fishes fake eID from pocket, hovers chip over Shawn.

Thank you. You still owe one hundredfifty dollars. Is there another way you'd like to pay?

I have some dollars, Eli says.

They drop bag on ground, open single zipper pocket, pick out green roll secure with elastic. They present money to Stevven.

For emergencies, Eli says.

Your mama gave you this?

She said only if we really, really needed it and we got separated.

You all are going to need this money. Put it away.

Eli shoves wad at Stevven.

Stop it. Put it away.

Shawn blinks. I read anxiety, they say. Please do not attempt to steal these shoes. You will be arrested.

I'm not stealing, Stevven says.

Would you like to try a different pair of shoes, maybe?

Yes. Something cheaper.

All of our trekkers are five hundred dollars. We have more affordable options in our sandals section.

Stevven curls feet inside shoes. Fuck it all, they say, accept cash roll from Eli.

Eli smiles. Fuck it all, they echo.

Stevven wraps elastic band on wrist, counts out one hundredfifty.

Okay Shawn, where do I insert cash? they ask.

I'm sorry, we do not accept cash.

Is there a human I can talk to?

I am sorry if I am not meeting your needs. Could you please describe the problem so I can perform better upon next revision?

You're great, Shawn, but I need a human.

I have invited Fitter's manager to come speak with you.

Thanks.

Second robot rolls up to Barbara, asks if she needs assistance. Barbara says no thank you, crosses to flats section. Stevven folds and unfolds cash over thumb, feathery, metallic scent. They hand remaining wad to Eli.

Can you count how much is left? they ask.

Eli removes each bill from stack, creates new stack on floor, counts aloud. Ten, Twenty, Twenty one, uh.

Twenty one plus fifty is... seventy two.

Seventy two, Eli repeats.

Good job, Stevven says. Now pack it up and don't lose it.

Eli ties and stows cash. Why doesn't Shawn like dollars?

They're silly, that's why.

You always say that.

It's the reason for everything.

Am I silly?

Not like them.

Can we go now? Eli asks. It's really cold in here.

We have to pay for these shoes.

Eli looks at Shawn. Do you have movies? Eli asks.

Yes, Shawn replies. I can stream a number of shows.

Play Samurai Jack!

Payment interface snaps to cartoon, fire and blood, magic sword. Eli sings along to opening sequence, *gotta get back, back to the past.*

Mirror panel wall next to sandals slides open. Manager steps onto retail floor, eyes hesitating between Stevven, Eli.

Hello, manager says, rubs hands together, manicure purple. Shawn says there is an issue regarding your purchase?

I need to pay in cash, Stevven says.

I'm afraid that's not possible, manager says. Where are the shoes you came in with?

I have none.

Managereyes comb out Barbara, smile. Are you with them?

Barbara shakes head.

Sorry to bother you, manager says, turns back to Stevven. I'm going to have to ask you two to leave.

Stevven frowns at Barbara, manager. It's not even my money, they say.

Excuse me? manager says.

This kid here, Eli. It's their money. And they've given this to me so I can have shoes. I feel bad enough taking it from them, but we can't keep going without some shoes—Stevven stands, holds out money—It's just the last one-hundred fifty that I owe.

Manager crosses arms, looks down, up. There's only so many places I can deposit this, they say. I can't even verify that it's real without going to an ATM. What's your name?

Stevven.

Digieye glimmers. The ID attached to the payment you authorized says Katreen, manager says. Give me a reason I shouldn't call the cops.

Stevven opens mouth, shutters, drops shoulders. I don't know what to say.

Manager fear tics back one inch. They juggle eyes between Eli, Stevven.

They take cash, step back, fan through, count. This smells like shit, they say. Tell me your real ID, in case this stuff turns out to be fake.

Samurai Jack snaps back to payment interface. Eli blinks heavy, exiting trance. They pout.

Shawn will take your fingerprint, manager says.

Stevven hesitates, lays finger on Shawn.

Stevven Pane, Shawn says. What is your birthdate?

January 19, 2057.

Who is your emergency contact?

What?

In order to verify your identity, it is important that you answer this question.

I thought that was what the finger scan was for. What do you need my emergency contact for. Isn't that an invasion of privacy?

Who is your emergency contact?

I don't see how this is relevant. June. Juniper Ariana-Álvarez. Deceased.

Processing icons make rounds on interface. Green verification mark.

Shawn, override payment, manager says, slips cash into plastic baggie, sanitizes hands. I'm sorry for your loss. Thanks for shopping at Fitters.

Stevven stands, shoulders BluBerry.

I want Samurai Jack, Eli says.

Another time, Stevven says, takes Elishoulder.

Would you like us to send you a receipt? Shawn asks.

No.

Anything else I can help you with today?

No, Stevven says, crosses to door. Eli, I'll pay you back.

Why?

I just will.

Okay.

Barbaradigieye flickers.

MARY SMILES. WOW, SHE SAYS. Those look great!

Stevven looks down at shoes. They don't feel too bad, they say.

Where's Barbara?

She's chosen not to associate with us anymore. We're good to go.

Stevven helps Gino to feet. He squints at Stevvenshoes. So white, he says.

Maybe we can stop for food, Mary says. I'm getting pretty hungry.

What happened to the food in your pack?

We ate it last night, she says.

You mean you didn't eat what was in Donna's apartment?

I wasn't sure, I'm sorry.

I have to pee, Eli says.

Stevven sighs. Okay, let's take a food and bathroom break. Maybe McDonald's has some vegan stuff.

Is Barbara still in there? Gino asks.

Yeah. She pretended not to know us when we were trying to check out. Let's go.

Gino touches hand to heart. We should wait for Barbara, he says.

I disagree.

Leaving her just doesn't feel right, Mary says, turtle shy.

Nothing about Barbara feels right. You think she cares about any of us? We need to ditch her now while we can.

Here she comes, Mary says.

Barbara steps from shop, drags suitcases, sneaks wave to manager behind closing doors. She poses with new shoes, slides sunglasses on. What do you think?

Very cute! Mary says.

We're going to McDonalds, Stevven says. But you probably don't want to be seen with us in there, Harvest forbid.

What are you talking about? she says. Gino, can you help me with the suitcases? I have enough struggle breaking in new shoes.

Don't drag those around for her, Stevven says.

Gino's a gentleman, Barbara says. So kind.

You're an Earther, Stevven says to Gino. You'll kill yourself.

I am not some weak old man, Gino says, locks eyes.

Stevven shakes head, turns forward, tags animosities onto passing cars. Across street, golden arches stack up building corner like notebook binding, exterior walls sleek and cycling advertisements, interactive games.

A bear! Eli says, bubbles.

That's a chow chow, Stevven says. A big dog.

Human leashing chow chow sits on bench, smiles at Eli. You can pet him if you want, they say.

Can I pet you? Eli asks chow chow.

Dogtongue explores Eliface. They laugh, disappear into dogfur. Dogtail rolls side to side.

COLD SALTY WIND BLOWS HAIRS back. They enter McDonalds through red sliding doors, ground floor like hospital cafeteria, double story, elevator. Grease hangs in air like nets. Asses sit on glossy, unforgiving booths. Cartoonish, flimsy tables toothpick cold floor. Room busy, stinky, shellac.

Menu reel sneaks over Stevvenhead. They touch $x$, close hologram. Eli spins McMerch reel, fast and fast, doom carousel, merch blurring, little flags with red and yellow stripes, golden arches where stars would be on American flag. Barbara orders for herself, Mary, and Eli. Gino declines food, pats tunic folds bulging with earthing snacks.

Stevven, you want food? Barbara asks.

I'm going to find the bathroom, they say.

You'll need the order number, Barbara says. 781.

Gold arch ceiling opens to red hallway, flushing water sounds, consumer traffic. They stop before great slash between universal white figures for man and woman, types 781 on digipad. Bathroom door slides open.

Someone in McDonalds uniform fixes heavy eyelashes with glue in wall mirror. Big eye slides to Stevven, doubletake. Long fingernails drop from face, wrinkles accelerating into question marks. Stevven heads for wide stall at end, hurries from someone they once knew.

Hey, you, Chassy says, I almost didn't recognize ya.

Stevven pauses at stall door.

Remember Blue Bird? she says. Ya got the Midsummer Nights' tea, and bagel on the regular every Saturday since I started workin the afternoon shift.

I remember, Stevven says, turns to mirror. Hi, Chassy.

How've you been?—Chassy smiles, bats lashes over headlight eyes, adjusts— You gettin enough to eat? You look worse for wear. Now I ain't in top form neither, all goin to my hips. I'd give some to ya if I could. Hoo, I'll tell ya, after the café got torn to pieces I couldn't hardly find a place to put myself 'cept here. I'm customer service when the bots are actin up or someone's makin a special order, though we don't get many of those. At least they don't have me moppin vomit yet. It ain't bad here but it ain't no Blue Bird. Poor Niko, the manager, ya know him. Well, I just felt so sorry for him, to lose a business like that. Lost more than any of us in the riots, I reckon.

Chassy props freckly hand on counter, gazes long at Stevven, clicks nails. Charms jingle on wrist, conjuring café afternoons in Stevven too good to remember. Stevven looks at wall tiles.

Get yarself a burger?

Stevven shakes head.

Come on then, let's get ya some food.

Stevven forfeits big stall to someone else. I'm not hungry, they say. I already ate.

Ya ain't gonna come sit with me then? Catch up a minute?

Sorry Chassy, I'm in a hurry.

No wonder I didn't recognize ya right away, she says, finishes up eyelashes. Not often I see a face from beforetimes. Y'all move so fast, ya young ones, when somethin burns down y'all run off and don't come back. This city's all strangers now. I'm stickin 'round, I'm workin on makin somethin. This is my home cause I'm here now. And got knees good enough to go no where else, anyhow.

Chassy snaps makeup bag shut, strings floppy purse on shoulder.

Take care of yarself, hun, she says, leaves bathroom.

Stevven startles Stevven, skeletal. They look down into sink, wash hands, wash feet. Brown small gash clears with water. They rub in pink soap from pump, grab silicone med bag from pack, fight off looks from mirror. They dry foot with paper towel, lightly douse gauze in disinfectant, peel apart thin protective layers on patch.

Cool plant, someone says.

Stevven meets brown eyes, warm, geode earrings, wasp nest necklace.

What species are they? Geode asks.

Oh, um, murus cultivar, Stevven says. Dwarf.

Very cool, she says, raises fingers to v. Peace on your journey.

Geode exits bathroom, dreads swinging.

Stevven patches foot, slips on shoe. They shoulder pack, brace mirror, eye contact.

We are taking care of ourselves, they say.


GINOHAIR DRAPES OVER BOOTH BACK. Mary sits dimly before burger. Eli munches on fries, waves at Stevven.

Stevven slides pack into booth, hides BluBerry against leg. Barbaraphone hovers over charging stand center table, Barbara busy inside digieye.

Hey, Barbara, can you look up how to get to the station from here? Stevven asks.

Yeah, she says. We take a car.

No, on foot.

What? That's not possible.

Barbara picks up phone from charger, shows Stevven three branching blue lines enslaving digital map.

Here are the routes if we get a car, she says, taps button, vanishing blue lines, graying map. And these are options for walking. None.

Can I look? Stevven asks, reaches.

Barbara withdraws phone. It needs to charge, she says.

Stevven churns hands, looks around. Gino snacks from oats in tunic pocket, closes eyes, ruminates. Eli eats fries like regular, swabs limp crisps in ketchup, pops them in mouth.

How's your vegan burger? Stevven asks Mary.

It's tasty, but it isn't organic.

But you already ate half of it.

I know, Mary says, puts hands to head. I wasn't thinking. I asked Barbara and she looked it up, and their vegan burgers aren't organic.

Mary, you won't make it two miles more if you don't eat.

Would you like some oats? Gino asks.

You already ate half the burger, Stevven says. Eat the rest of it.

I don't know what to do, Mary says.

A little nonorganic stuff is definitely going to trump an empty stomach. Not eating is going to make this harder for everyone. And in case you're worried about it, eating this vegan burger instead of the beef one is not making you any less complicit in the destruction of the Amazon rainforest.

What did you say about the Amazon? Mary asks.

Little Ronald McDonald hologram bounces onto table, clowns with cricket dexterity. Eli laughs. Hologram climbs atop burger and waves to Mary. She giggles. Big red lips face Stevven and mimic frown. Barbara waves hand, shoos Ronald to next table.

Stevven stands.

Where are you going? Barbara asks.

I'm going to ask around for directions.

Everyone has the same maps, she says.

No, they don't.

Someone with mighty orange hair makes quick pass over Stevven, looks back down at phone. Stevven crosses to them.

Hey, do you know how to get to the station from here on foot?

Do I look like a GPS?

No, you look like a flaming hot Cheeto.

They exchange middle fingers.

Stevven stands center aisle, scans room. Loner deeptethers to laptop, burger paper intercepting screen, meta living. Happy Meals break onto floor around six children, two droopeye parents.

Stevven walks into arcade room. Geode sits on red stool in dark alcove, idly shoving away McMerch ads, observes child playing game.

Stevven crosses to them, smiles. Hey, I meant to say back there that I like your jewelry, Stevven says.

Geodehands flash to ears. Oh, thanks, they say. My sister's a jeweler here in town.

Cool. I don't wear much jewelry myself, but I think it's cool. Um, I was wondering if you knew how to get to the station without a car. I've been away from the city a while and don't remember the best way.

Sure, I'll have to look at my Maps. See this street here? Maple? they say, point to gray line on map.

Yeah.

Maps says it ends up here, but it just ends for cars. I remember when they blocked it off because of the flooding. It's not safe, but I think it's possible to cross through the old suburbs there in Roman's district. I doubt they connect directly, but maybe. I don't know if that helps.

It does. Thank you.

Yeah, they say, fiddle with earrings.

Arcade game music speeds up. Little burger avatar leaps across platforms, collects coins.

Wow, you're good at this game, Stevven says to kid.

I'm only on level 10 but I can go to level 100.

That's something.

I'm babysitting for my aunt, Geode says. He loves the McArcade. He earns xp to redeem for food and prizes.

I have lots of prizes. I have the biggest prize, kid says, pale fingers smearing light. The biggest prize is plush Donald. I have three.

Working on your fourth?

Yeah. I have more than all my friends.

Geode shakes head, smiles at Stevven.

Thanks again, Stevven says. Have a good one.

Good luck. I hope you and your plant get to where you need to go safely.

Stevven crosses to table, drops down next to BluBerry. They reach across table, grab burger, bite in, salt gush, bitter soybean, sweet ketchup, crackly pickle. Mary watches.

I thought you didn't want anything, Barbara says.

Better to not let these calories go to waste. Lots of walking ahead.

Do you have to make those sounds when you eat? Barbara asks.

Stevven runs tongue around lips, laps noisily. They swipe grease on pants, stand.

The light is going, they say, so we better get moving.

BARBARASUNGLASSES CATCH FOUR SETTING SUNS. Gino lugs suitcases outside McDonalds, opposes foot traffic. Mary apologizes to edgy people shoving through her. Eli collects candy wrapper from ground and feeds Winky.

Stevven leads towards Maple Street, sidewalk baking, sweating feet in shoes. They keep one direction, pass parking garages, restaurants, last stickerless street signs. Shadows take them under buildings three stories high.

Blue collar workers turn out onto street, towards cars, bars, home to screens. Sidewalk narrows, huddles up against red brick buildings with cement feet, old obscure services become expensive housing. Cars shove by, electric engines tuning up and down, occasional combustion growl.

Sidewalk and street narrow, traffic gooseeye women with wounds, families hauling laundry bags like week old snow, children silent and brown or thin and white. Buildings cavity, chimneys turning green in last light. Person dragging shorts begs for money.

God bless, God bless. Please.

Mary stops. Beggar swarms her.

Eli, can you please give me the money? Mary asks. We need to help this poor man.

Eli sets Winky on sidewalk, unzips pack.

No, you need that, Stevven says.

But I never use money, Mary says.

It's different outside Apartment. Put that away. I owe you some, besides.

What?

I had to use some to buy the shoes.

Aw please, please, God bless, Beggar says.

Gino offers oats.

Beggar rolls bag in all directions. Na, na, they say, give oats back to Gino. Please. Just a few dollars. All I need.

A police drone can be here in thirty seconds, Barbara says, voice buzzing.

Beggar lifts hands, aways, mumbles like dark water into gutter.

That was unnecessary, Stevven says, turns to Barbara.

Where are they going? Eli asks.

Don't worry. They won't bother us anymore, Barbara says.

Where do they sleep? Eli asks.

Mary tilts, stumbles. Stevven catches her.

Oh, stood up a little too fast, she says, chuckles sadly.

Time for water and food break, Stevven says, supports Mary to palisade fence, dog yapping from near balcony.

Gino uncaps water bladder, offers fruit and seed to Mary.

I don't want to be here after dark, Barbara says, works hands into biceps, inventing cold climate.

Then don't be, Stevven says.

Eli holds Winky to Stevven.

Winky smells bad, Eli says.

We will wash them when we get to some better water. Are we ready to keep moving?

Perhaps we should stop for the day, Gino says.

We can get to the station, Stevven says. It's less than two miles from here. See the light trains?

Wow! They're like satellites! Eli says.

Mary caps water bladder. I can keep going, she says.


SUN MARRIES HORIZON, HONEYMOONS. WRAPPERS flit about in shifting air. Cigarettes butt from half inch crevasses. Barbarasuitcases jump and fuss.

Eli points. What's that?

That's a neon sign of a cocktail drink, Stevven says.

What's a cocktail drink?

A mixed alcohol drink.

Loud men cross ahead, barrel into swinging bar doors, snapping pool balls. Stevven watches yellow stripe ball sink into pocket. Doors yawn shut on game.

Stevven slows steps, accommodates Gino, Mary, Barbara.

Cars fewer now. Street lights diversify, bluewhite, warmwhite, ultraviolet in apartments feeding plants in neat little pots. Electric wires string on lines across road like loose stitching over giant gnash. Pipes gurgle in alleyway where people piss and skittle like crabs. Stevven runs hand along bricks, moisture and heat chapping infrastructure. Elements and ruins, harmony, tragedy.

Train tracks lie ahead, oxidizing, feeding grasses, life unabandoning.

I'm getting a car, Barbara says.

Good for you, Stevven says.

There's only one more hotel this far out of downtown, Barbara says, holds phone close to face. And it's super sketch.

Mary, how are you holding up? Stevven asks.

I'm pretty tired, she says. We've gone really far. I don't think I can walk much longer.

You can do it! Eli says.

Light train shoots across bridge four blocks ahead, starspeed. Something glows below bridge, orange, flickering.

Oh my god, oh my god, Barbara says, turns full circle, sits on breaking bench, stands back up. This is ridiculous. Ubers don't even come this far out.

Our next checkpoint and water break will be over there, Stevven says. Under the light train bridge. I think it might be a camp, since the city road ends up here. We must be on Maple Street. We need to cross this creek. Huh, the maps didn't show a creek here.

We're not even on the map, Barbara says.

Stevven rounds cement barricades closing bank from street. Swamp reed, frog, cicada, sewage, methane, sludge cakes in unofficial dump site.

I'm not going over there, Barbara says.

Stevven whirls. Then shut the fuck up and pack out, they say. I will hurl your suitcases into the water if you don't shut up.

Barbara blinks.

Stevven waits for protest.

Spaciness draws over Barabara, digieyes sparkling blue.

Yeah, take your fucking picture, Stevven says.

Stevven follows creekbank North, searches for dry foot places. Suitcase wheels chop chop, drop from crumbling pavement onto gravely path, scrape up beer glass. Suitcases, Eli, Mary, Gino, and Barbara keep safe distance behind Stevven.

Patchwork mound rises from swamp, bridging banks like beaching leviathan, pluming industrial feathers. Stevven puts weight onto rusty car door finning out one side, other foot onto burlap sacks, plastic crates, chain link and rubber tire.

What is it? Eli says.

This is our way across.

This is literally garbage, Barbara says.

And literally a bridge, Stevven says, climbs up, cattails kissing ankles.

Critters groan, croak, clap in murky understory. Stevven turns, helps Mary and Eli onto bridge. They cross, step down onto asphalt road before great orange maw, encampment under light train bridge. Silhouettes shift in lowlight, barrel fire. Light train speeds along bridge, brights space overhead. Sky bleeds back to dark, darker.

Barbara squeals crossing bridge, face spinning horror. She loses feet, stumbles, shovels sludge onto asphalt. Ew ew ew ah! She runs hands down arms, legs, then doubles down on bug spray, wobbles around uselessly. Mary catches panic two tentative steps from Barbara.

Are you okay? What happened? Oh, your poor shoes! I think I have some paper in here somewhere.

Stevven hikes to underbridge.


THREE HUMAN FIGURES LOOK INTO barrel fire like single eye. Every size solar lanterns expand visibility circle. Sleeping bags, packs, plastic mats slope against pillars. Something drips on South side, knotnose smells, fish, human manure, dampness. Acid and brine. Train rushes overhead, shakes rust from ceiling rebar.

Ain't you a band, person says, stirs phlegmy, tomatoey soup over fire, matchstick fingers and plastic ladle glowing red.

Hi, Stevven says. Can we join you?

Ain't a bother, they say.

Gino drifts into circle beside Stevven, bows greeting to each person, sits on block. Eli takes Stevvenhand. Mary and Barbara tease outskirts.

Old bearding human with cherry nose and few teeth smiles from lawn chair Northside. They rattle cardboard box, crackers, like show and tell. Air behind them shimmers, dollar store fairy wings, pink elastic tying tight into shoulder skin.

Cheese monkeys, they say. Mine!— They yank crackers away from nobody, hug them close—Mine.

Ain't no one after your cheese monkeys, Morty, pot stirrer says. Now come get some soup.

Mine! Morty says, flits eyes greedily from person to person.

There ain't enough soup for y'all, brooder sitting South side says, accepts bowl from pot stirrer.

That's okay, we already ate, Stevven says. We're just resting up before heading to the station.

I can tell it's been a long journey, pot stirrer says.

Hey kid, brooder says to Eli. Tell me what you think of this.

Brooder balances soup in one hand, reaches inside jacket with other. Barbara sidesteps behind Gino, phone glowing emergency red. Brooder lifts hip from chair, digs deeper, pulls out something small enough to hide inside hand bulk. He slowly opens hand palm up before Eli. Eli takes two steps forward. Mary leashes to Elishoulders, paralyzing. Eli picks object from palm, looks from all angles in low light.

Oh, it is so beautiful, Mary says. Not at all what I was expecting.

What the fuck were you expecting, brooder says. I pull out a gun and shoot the kid?

Mary squeaks, smiles nervously. No, I—I didn't know what to expect.

Eli hands small thing to Gino. He makes approving sound, opens hand like flower to Stevven.

Wood bunny, ears slick along rounding back. Stevven runs two fingers over flower etches.

Brooder stands, towers close to Stevven, points to small creature. See I'm putting daisies on each side of his little belly but I only got one side done yet, he says. I'm making it for my baby girl. She had a pet bunny like that.

He packs bunny away, sits, ages fast, resumes soup.

Aw man that needs something. Y'all don't got Tabasco in one of them bags, do you?

No, but I have habanero, Stevven says.

That will do even better.

Stevven squats, digs under pack brain for vegetables. They hand pepper to brooder.

I used to make all sorts of things out of wood back at the shop, he says. Went Vincent van Gogh on all the bed posts and things, always delivered the best pieces myself to make sure they'd be appreciated and all that. I was proud of my business. Proud of the crib I built for my baby girl, proud of the apartment I could afford my family.

What happened? Mary asks.

What you think happened? The riots are what happened. Lost it all. Lost it all in the fire.

And your daughter? Gino asks.

My baby girl's aright, missing her daddy for sure. She up North with her mama. They ran out of here when those riots came. I stayed to protect our business. I said I could protect them but they didn't believe that and so they went and run off to inlaws up there. But I stayed to protect our business. It was a good business. Now I gotta get me a trainride—Brooderhand charges air, mimicking bullet train—But trouble is the feds tagged me for a rioter and I can't get on no train.

Train shoots overhead, South.

Pot stirrer manages soup cup into Mortyhands.

Hmmmmhmmm! Morty dribbles excitement and soup on lap.

Eli looks up to Stevven. I want to introduce BluBerry, they say.

How about you show them the walrus instead? Stevven says.

Winky, Eli says.

Yeah, show them Winky.

But Blu—

No. Not now.

Stevven retrieves Winky from Elipack.

Eli turns other cheek, crosses arms. I don't want them, they say.

Hey Morty, want some habanero? Brooder asks, rocks to stand.

Habanero! Morty howls, crackly fairywing vinyl glinting green.

Brooder crushes habanero in fingers, cascades seeds in low light. Hold still, I'm gonna miss the bowl, he says. Now, let's see if you can handle this.

Hot! Hot hot! Morty says, fairywings flapping.

Yeah—Brooder says, settles back—I been homeless before, before the business, and now I got to be this way again, but some folks, like Morty here, they've always been living this way. Inter-generational. Ain't that right?

Hmmhmm! Hot soup—Morty sets soup down for cheese monkeys, adds crackers in soup, stashes box away quickly—Mine!

But no more, Brooder says, huffing between soup swallows. We breakin the cycle together. He's coming up north with me. Ain't you, Morty? You're family now.

Family, Morty echoes.

That's right. Brooder leans back, drains soup, exhales aah.

How did you meet? Mary asks.

This brave man here, shit, I couldn't believe it, hit the cop trying to cuff me out at the park. He was like my guardian angel, haha. You messed that guy up didn't you?

Morty grimaces, tomato slop on beard, raises skin and bone fist over head, slams fist down to chair arm, maintaining eye contact with Stevven. Barbara shifts noisily behind, hyper focuses between phone light and precarious life in low light. Mortyeyes simmer down. They slurp soup from bowl rim.

We make a good team out here, Brooder says.

Out here, Morty echos.

Y'all ain't trying to get to the station tonight, yeah? Brooder asks.

Is it possible? Stevven asks, adjusts sweaty shoulder straps.

Yeah, but it ain't too friendly past here. All them killings you hear about in the city, well, double that amount right out the other side of this bridge. We call it the Borderlands, where anything and everything goes down. Cops don't play any game out here—Brooder lingers eyes on Gino, Mary, breaks into smile—I'm just playing with you. It's not all bad, but still better in the daytime.

So how are you going to get on the train, being tagged as a rioter? Stevven asks.

You just got to know the right people, is all. I got a buddy that can get me in the building. I got a piece that messes with facerec. Silicone, strap it right on my chin. Works good if you don't look too close. But then we got this man here, who is always trying to make a scene when he don't got no reason to.

Make a scene! Morty says.

Yeah I know you'd be on your best behavior at the station cuz you want to stick with me now, don't you?

Yeah.

Morty sets soup bowl down by feet, picks up cracker box, crosses to moonlight streaming in from West. Pee streams.

It's heavy around here, Brooder says. Everything's sinking, you feel me? Slowly going under again. More riots comin. People been talkin. I can feel it. We're getting out of here, Morty and me, before things get too rough.

It's better up north, where your daughter is? Stevven asks.

That's what I hear. Hey, little lady, fancy shoes hiding back there. You're going to the station too? Hey, I'm talkin to you.

Not open for questions right now, thank you, Barbaravoice crackles.

She focuses on phone, adrenaline audible.

She just lookin to get killed? Rollin in here with all this shit?

I know what I'm doing, thank you.

You paying for all their tickets? Brooder asks. You look like you're good for it. Think you can help a brother out? Spot us a passage. We can help you get over there in the morning.

I will call the police.

Whoa whoa, I ain't tryin anything with you. We chill. We chill—Brooder shifts attention to Stevven—Look, you all want to get there tonight, it's just like mile and half straight that way. You're gonna hit a fence, and then you got to follow that up to a big ass tree. You'll see it. You can climb over the fence there and it will drop you in the employee lot full of vans. You can walk to whatever entrance you want from there. But if you tagged, they gonna snatch you.

Tagged for any offense? Stevven asks.

Tier two or higher.

Morty returns sticking penis in shorts, buttons up. Don't go, Morty says. Don't go.

If they want to go tonight we ain't gon stop them, Brooder says.

Sharks. Sharks everywhere, Morty says, crouches down, shies from imaginary predator.

Eli glances up at Stevven, eyebrows asking into shark habits.

You. You. You!—Morty points finger at Mary—Shark bait!

I'd like to go now, Mary says.

Yes, me too, Barbara says.

Stevven turns plastic square in pocket, one ticket only, for two persons, Stevven and BluBerry.

Sounds like you're headed out, Brooder says, stands. Give me some skin.

Brooder leans in, Eli meets knuckles.

I hope you get to your daughter soon, Mary says, chihuahua.

Preciate you. Don't let go of that child. Don't do what I done.

I won't, Mary says, squeezes Eli, shuffles small feet forward, around fire, opposite Morty rattling cracker box.

Small breeze drifts under bridge, picks up barrel flame. Morty grins, canines chipping into blackness. Stevven shakes sleep, deceit from eyes, wakes, walks. They hesitate at bridge end.

Shadows swell in shrinking moonlight, quiver street edges, strangle roads and firebomb buildings. Cicadas scream into night ahead.

THEY WALK. LONG TELEPHONE POLES lean, lines free, reach for ground like snakes in trees. Barbara suitcases jump at every asphalt mole, roar into deadness. Cloud passes over moon, gray and old, sky like skin receding eye. Scuttling sounds, some cutthroat silences.

Barbaraphone juts angry red light, Barbarahands triggery. She stops as bicyclist pumps across street, bags swinging from handlebars, spokes hitting plastic. They disappear, gear and chain sinking into whisper, then nothing.

They walk two blocks, cryptic letters talking at them from walls. Laughter runs through street like wild dogs. They walk.

Look, Gino says.

Lone figure flickers inside dark clothes, two blocks ahead, face aiming straight at them. Barbara moans terror.

We're fine, Stevven says, grinds teeth at suitcases, squawking wheel.

Stranger walks at slant, bow step, sheathing something on hip.

What do we do we do? Mary whispers.

Look ahead. Mary, stop looking at them.

He's looking at me, she says.

Stranger passes on opposite sidewalk, green eyes already far away. They vanish down alleyway.

No trouble, see? Stevven says, laps at humid air.

Can we stop for a second? Mary says, crumbles. I need to sit down.

Light train crosses over bridge downslope from them, rolls into dark, taillights steady red like Barbaraphone. Stevven turns to Gino huffing uphill, Barbaraluggage dragging heavier than before.

Leave her shit, Stevven says. It's only incline from here.

This is my stuff, Barbara says.

Then put your phone down and carry it yourself.

I can almost see the station from here, Gino says. It's no trouble.

Yeah, we're almost there, Mary says. I just need to rest a minute and I can help with a suitcase.

No, Mary, you can't, Stevven says. You can barely carry your own pack.

If you're so strong then why don't you offer to help out? Barbara asks.

Stevven stares up at stars, bright and furious. We've wasted enough time—Stevven looks at Gino—You do what you want, killing yourself over this petroleum blooded bitch—they stab finger at Barbara—but I'm done. I'm not waiting up for anyone.

Stevven, what are you saying? Mary squeaks.

I'm saying I'm getting on a train with BluBerry tonight. I have my ticket—Stevven digs in pocket, holds up plastic square.

What about us? Eli says.

Stevvenmouth hangs, air stinging.

Gino catches breath. Stevven—Gino coughs, coughs and coughs.

Stevvenwords break inside throat, everything wrong. Eyes catch on Barbaraphone blinking red.

Stevven swallows bile. Why is it blinking? they ask.

Barbara steps back, fearful. Phone blinks red.

Stevven takes two steps back. What did you do? they ask.

Gino cranes ear. Drone, he says, coughs.

Barbara trembles, sweat matting bangs to forehead.

You called the police? Stevven says. Fuck. Fuck you, Barbara—Stevven squats down—Mary, get up.

I can't walk. My legs, Mary cries.

You're scaring me—Eli shakes Maryarm.

Mary hugs Eli, cries.

Get up!—Stevven hoists Mary up.

Maybe the police can help us, she says in tears.

No, no they won't. Fuck, move those legs.

Drone swoops in from South. Stevven freezes.

It's okay, you're safe now, Barbara says to Mary.

Don't listen to her, Stevven says.

All persons, stop, remain where you are, police bot says, hovers two arm lengths overhead. Stevven Pane and Mary Saito, step away from each other and unidentified person 49238.

I'm not hurting them, Stevven says.

Yes, she is, Barbara says, retreats.

Release them, police bot says, or I will have to use force.

They tried to stab me, Barbara says, streams tears, points at Stevven.

Why would you say that? Mary says, clings to Stevven.

Mary, let go of me now. Eli, step back. Stand up on your own.

Eli cries, squeezes tighter.

This is your final warning, police bot says, lowers to Stevven.

This isn't right! Mary cries.

Mary, if you don't let go, this robot is going to zap me. Barbara, tell this thing to stand down.

You've terrorized everyone long enough, she says. The game is over.

Stevven shakes Mary off. Electric prongs discharge, bite down on Mary. She shudders and drops. Eli screams, runs, reclings to her.

More police are on their way, police bot says. Stevven Pane, put your hands above your head.

Stevven grabs stunner lines and yanks down on drone before recalibration, hitches drone to lamppost, quick, messy knots.

Do not attempt to flee. More police are on their way.

Adrenaline peaks. Let's go, Stevven says, shoulders pack, grabs Eliarm.

No!

Stevven pulls on Eli. Winky drops from pack, rolls against Mary.

Ow! Eli cries.

Stevven Pane, release unidentified person 49238.

Mary, Eli cries. Mary!

Gino, help me, Stevven says.

Gino moves out from shadow, scoops Eli in long clay hands. Together they move fast, lichen and moss sloughing off Ginobeard by fistfuls. Eli rises to full wail, tears slopping.

Stevven looks over shoulder. Barbaradigieye glints blue. Mary still, sleeps like dying.

THEY RUN, SHEDDING, SWEATING, HEAVING. Eli chokes on tears.

I can't carry— Gino coughs.

They can run, Stevven says, loosens Eli from Ginoarms.

No! Eli cries, ropes feet into ground. Ow! You're hurting my wrist.

See that fence over there? Stevven says, tugs Eli into jog. That's where we need to go. Pretend you're a bunny rabbit. Hop—Stevven chokes air—Hop to it.

Stevven loses balance on slime, scrapes knees, recovers. Ginobreath flickers, face dripping. Mouse leaps from Ginoforest, scurries into gutter.

Following? Gino asks.

Stevven looks back. No, they say. Turn here.

They walk to fence, harsh parking lights from opposite side sharpening double chainlink. Shrubs and short trees stubble perimeter.

I hear nothing, Gino says, gravel breath. We can rest.

Let's get across the fence just in case, Stevven says.

Stevvenhand reads dogwood tree polish from footwear. They unshoulder pack, find footing, climb, tight squeeze through thicket. Barbed wire splits and rolls away at top, open. Stevven leans against tree, looks over employee bus facility. Airport lights tsunami into sky, trouble slim moonlight. Giant moth slaps LED light closest to dogwood.

Okay send BluBerry and the pack up, Stevven says.

Pack rises through leaves. Stevven takes strap. They straddle fence, look again across dark vans scattering long parking lot. One van rolls out lot road, merges onto high traffic employee road.

Stevven takes BluBerrybottle strap between teeth, tumbles pack over. Flump, bag hits ground and rolls. They step leg over, climb down, chink, chink, chink, crunch down onto crumbling cement.

Through fence, shrub, Eli and Gino hold together like root, rhizome.

I'm sorry, child. Gino strokes Elihair.

Stevven wipes salvia string from mouth, cradles BluBerry in hands.

It's an easy climb, Stevven says, words catching on chainlink like plastic bags.

Eli and Gino sit down together against dogwood base. Gino whispers to Eli.

Eli? Stevven says, hooks hand on fence. Come over here and we can talk? I don't want to talk to you like this. Just hop on over. We'll figure something out together.

Eli does not want to keep moving, Gino says. We will rest here tonight.

Stevven squats against fence, watches Gino nest Eli in great lapspan.

The police can find you over there, Stevven says. You will have better chances on this side.

Stillness torques. Scratchy grasses jab Stevvenankles. They turn once about, nerves transforming, locking.

I can't get back over, they say.

Ginoeyes chip red, steady on Stevven, knowing, straining, shaming, certainly. Stevven throws back against fence, sits down on tough grass, sets BluBerry in sweaty lap.

Would you like some water? Gino asks Eli.

Stevven eavesdrops tenderness, water bladder changing hands. Stevven trembles, bites down fevering emotions, weathers changing fast. They focus on parking lot, movement inside windows, yellow vest figure retrieving snack from vending machine, disappearing behind walls.

FLUTTERING, FEATHER, BIRD. ROBIN SWEEPS down from lamppost to parking lot, beaks into grass tuft pushing up through asphalt. They glide into darkness above Stevvenhead, dance to seat on barest branch.

Robin sings. Song echoes, carries on breeze, like brushstrokes on tangling silence. Gino prays.

Stevven battles breath in shallow throat.

Electric roar overtakes prayers. Lighttrain passes, ghosts sprinting in wake. Robin dives and bounces lightly away.

Stevven wiggles out semisoft seat. Small pebbles make tiny indentions on calves. They take one shoe off, other. Wet bandage drops off foot. They fold up and pocket bandage, worry chip in pocket. They watch trains run places into nonplaces. Dogwoodleaves pedal darkness. Heavy.

They sneak look through fence, at Eli hiding inside Earther embrace. Mary, Eli speaks. Mary. Mary, Gino replies, sentences quiet, too grievous for Stevven to hear properly.

Stevven ruminates emptily, fabricating unspoken justifications, explanations from wide words. Words without weather, without names. Every passing light train washes Stevvenmind blank. They ache. Bones.

Knuckly sleep finds them, lays them to earth.

LITTLE PARTICLES SWIRL, GREEN HUES, predawn.

Ignition sputters. Van rolls out lot end, headlights yellow. Stevvenneck shudders. They roll onto back, rub out tendons. They gaze through cold fence. Gino sleeps. Elihead rides Ginobreath, walnut eyes cracking with half sleep.

Stevven sits up, gathers BluBerry. Leaves swell, stick to container walls. Stevven holds BluBerry up to fence, tentative smile.

Eli gently climbs from Ginolap.

Can I hold? they ask.

I can't get them through the fence, but you can touch them, Stevven says, opens bottle.

Elifingers reach through, brush top BluBerry leaf.

Are you hungry? Stevven asks.

Eli shrugs.

Stevven retrieves unripe tomatoes, wiggles them through fence. Eli eats tomato, brings them to Gino.

Stevven rubs face, pasty, unfeeling, poor sleep crusting eyes. They move slow, put BluBerry into pack, breath stiff with morning allergies. They stand with pack, scan path down to bus service center, orange sunlight catching on silver rims. Parking lot lights blink off in sets as sun climbs.

Stevven faces Gino and Eli, all standing now, gathering strengths. Gino hands empty tomato wrapper through fence. Stevven fidgets with it.

I don't know how to get you on a train, Stevven says.

There's a service road along the fence, Gino says. We will take that, go West.

And then?

Perhaps you will see us in Tennessee.

You know I have to get on the train, for BluBerry. This was always the plan if GreenRoof™ caught up with us.

Gino looks down at Eli, strokes hair. Elieyes hang, unfocus on space before fence. Stevven watches train launch, pass.

Can I give you anything? Stevven asks.

The forest will provide, Gino says.

Refill on water? I don't think I can take this on the train.

Stevven unhooks bladder, opens spout. Gino pulls bladder from chest. Dull trickles. Stevven spills water all over Ginohands. They return bladder onto pack, shaking. Gino slides Elipack onto shoulder.

The police would have caught up by now if they wanted to, Stevven says. I don't know why they haven't. Something to do with Barbara. Her elaborate plans.

These are not the words for now, Gino says.

He puts hand on Eliback. They take first steps along fence together.

Hey, Eli, wait. Stevven walks along fence beside them.

Eli ignores Stevven, tear stinging.

I will introduce you to the trees, the birds—Gino smiles down at Eli—The ones that I know. And the ones we don't know we will discover together.

Gino stops to cough, continues. Private plane shakes air, dissonance.

Eli, Stevven says.

Eli keeps walking. Small bugs rise up, float around bare skin. Young forest waits for them Northside. Stevven follows along fence for minutes until they meet corner, set hands onto chains, dam. Gino and Eli pause before semi forest expanse, Stevven thinks, to turn and say something to them.

But Gino points. Stevven cranes to see.

Bat, he says. Another one. They're eating the insects.

Eli looks up, wonder piercing through grieving eyes.

I'M COMING OVER, STEVVEN SAYS, heart jogging. I'll go with you.

Eli and Gino look to Stevven for first time since they began walking.

Maybe there is a better place to cross ahead, Stevven says.

Gino nods. They walk together on both fence sides pinching towards security gate. Sweat slickens Stevvenpalms as they near security entrance for cars and maintenance vehicles, slide gate doubly thick.

I'm coming over, Stevven says again. One way or another.

We will wait for you under the cover of the trees, Gino says.

Gino and Eli flake from view. Stevven tucks thumbs under shoulder straps, eases toward security checkpoint, avoids eyes with small steely square room, outpost on boundary. Grasses teethe crumbly road edges leading under slide gate, gap large enough for Stevvenbody. They hurry.

Bluejean legs step out security box.

Where do you think you're going? muscly voice says.

Stevven runs.

Stop!

Security intercepts Stevven at gate.

Both breathe adrenaline.

How'd you get in here?

Decided not to get on a plane after all, Stevven says. Just going to step out. Is that right?

Stevven steps once more closer to slide gate.

No, you don't, security moves, reaches.

Stevven slides onto asphalt, fire on legs, shoves BluBerry and pack through gate gap. BluBerry rolls off asphalt into Bermuda grass, drainage ditch.

Great big hands haul Stevven to feet, rattle them.

That was stupid, security says, grins green teeth.

I can give you my ticket, fake ID, all of it, Stevven says. I don't want trouble.

Should of thought about that before trespassing.

Stevven throws knee up. Heavy oily hand catches. Smells wrap them, malty, excretion, sour sweat.

Let go!

Stevven elbows, kicks, hits. Security throws them up against hot metal outpost wall, shoves slick arm against chest.

I'll bite your fucking dick off, oilboy, Stevven says.

Security moves hand to Stevventhroat, forces bruising silence. They press in, stench cementing. Securityhand tugs at shorts buckle.

Bang! Eli shoots imaginary gun.

Security loosens Stevven from wall, turns to Eli. What the hell? Where'd you come from?

Stevven dives at securityknees. They go down. Stevven crushes crotch underknee, beartrapping themselves in squeezing, screaming thighs.

I got BluBerry, Eli says, holds them high.

Stevven steps up from security curling into fetal position. They follow Eli under gate, drag pack in after. They run into trees.

Gino catches Stevven from falling forward. Stevven vomits. They watch acid, hot and green sink into grasses. Ants scurry away from stinking pool.

How's BluBerry? Stevven says, trading breath.

BluBerry is okay, Gino says, hands them water bladder. Breathe.

Stevven looks back at Eli clearing dirt from BluBerrybottle, gentle touch, like older sibling. Stevven rinses, drinks from water bladder, stands. Beet color still cries through cheeks, hormones at boiling point.

Rest, Gino says.

Stevven inhales, stretches upright. They turn golden light in hands, look up to sudden pines, broad needles stirring, thin trunks leaning over squat hardwoods. Leaves ocean, fall onto lichens, moss. Yellow wasp circles around Stevven clumsily, flies away.

Feebe, feebe, bird calls.

Sparking tanager, bellydrum woodpecker. Stevven hears them, remembers. Creatures rest songs as airplane passes, resume. Old wood, sulfuric water, scat overtone. Stevven smells them, remembers.

STEVVEN STEPS FALL INTO PLACE.

Gino smiles. Lead the way, he says.

Stevven wades up to ankles in green, stirs mosquitoes, noseeums. Hundred steps, they climb out onto service road, security gate going, gone.

Stevven stirs bugs away. They float back.

Anyone want some marigold? Stevven asks.

They unshoulder pack, fish out oil. They pool oil in palm, coat face, shoulders, shine. They offer marigold to Eli.

Eli shakes head.

They're not biting you? Stevven asks.

No.

Stevven packs oil away. They walk.

American beech rustles, fronts small wind from South. New growth pours into road, boils in summer heat. Virginia rails sing in marshes downslope. Box television, gutless, only rusty metal frame and plastic, sits mutely next to road, audience and host to green brier. Moth lands on bend in frame.

How are your knees? Gino asks Stevven as they step through purple nettles onto paving road.

The blood has dried now, Stevven says.

The day demands tithes, Gino says, sheds reptilian skin from arm.

Eli walks slow next to Gino, holds Ginohand. Silence marinates, molding moods. Behind them, green overtakes airport fence.

Sun steals in, out clouds, sky gathering storm.

WHITE PINE NEEDLE LOAM FROTHS fading yellow road lines, spongy underfoot. Wood rib sounds, croak, croak, croak.

STEVVEN GATHERS MEATY MILKY CAP mushrooms, stores them in pack.

HERON STARTS FROM TREE BRANCH, glides across street, becomes forest again.

SMALL STRIP MALL AND GAS station mark town outskirts. Two cars pass intersection under lightless traffic lights, through branches and garbage narrowing road to one lane. Stevven collects sumac berries from under Exxon sign, eat as they walk.

Eli does not eat berries.

Thunder. Sky.

Bramble shakes just one blind reach away. Stevven stops, searches for beast. Only birdsong, godspeech.

SMALL WIND RIPS OPEN CLOUD bellies, soaks, floods Earth. Water slaps trees, sparks ground. Lightning claps.

They bow before storm, steer under store awning, *Tuesday Morning*. Gino squats down, beardforest heavy, dragging water. Eli hugs bare arms, sits legs outstretched to Stevven. Mud darkens shoe soles. Stevven unvelcroes shoes.

I didn't even know you had these shoes, Stevven says.

Eli blinks hazardously.

Stevven peels off Elisocks. They set BluBerry next to Eli against storefront post, open lid for airflow.

They look out into big falling wetness. Across street, kinky gas station roof streamlines water into topless car, orange rust, green kudzu. Gutters froth, foam three feet high.

I'll find some things for the fire, Stevven says. Gino, still got the starter?

Stevven walks along strip, turns through plastic chair shards, cans, old home decor with cursive lettering, *#blessed*. Stevven picks sign up.

Might burn, they say.

They gather arms full, cheap combustible plywood knickknacks. Gino teepees dry sticks inside fire ring.

Nice work, Stevven says. Where'd you find all that dry stuff?

Gino points to dead oak at strip mall end. Witch hazel flashes berries beside oak. Stevven sets combustibles beside Gino, crosses to witch hazel, gathers moist sprigs with pocket knife. Gino sparks fire starter, snap, snap, snap. Flame takes bait. Stevven lays witch hazel on pack, moves broken lawn chair closer to fire ring, flame yellowing, oranging. They place Elishoes and socks on chair.

Eli cuddles into Gino. Gino blinks slowly, strokes Elihead, eyes dead ending in fire, far. Stevven spits pit into fire. Crackle.

I'm going to see what I can find inside, Stevven says, rises, hooks headlamp on head. Just keep this fire going best you can.

Wasp runs around Stevven head, lands on shoes drying by fire. Long copper wings fold, yellow legs articulate into strong supports. They eat up salts. Stevven looks up to awning, wasp nest hanging from plywood.

Gino, when you get a chance, pull down some of this ceiling for the fire, Stevven says. Not this panel right above us. The wasps live there.

Gino nods.

Stevven steps to store entrance. Redyellow signs peel from toothy glass: *STORE CLOSING! EVERYTHING MUST GO!*

They enter.


PITTER PATTER, RAINWATER DROPS INTO unseen isle.

Stevven walks penumbra around register, disturbs plastic piles, startles sparrow from nest in nearest shelf. They rise on tiptoes, peek into nest. Empty.

Stevven climbs over rainbow pillow bog into picture frame isle. They toss few pulpy frames back towards entrance, move deeper, slower, reading into dark.

Water slaps closer. Stevven clicks headlamp on. Light chases small creatures into hiding. Rodenteyes twinkle back at Stevven. Small dark pond, critters plopping. Light tacks onto silver cookware handles. Stevven stops before large soup pot on side, lid askew. Inside, oblong white eggs sit on damp leaves.

Stevven looks all around feet, head, meets rateyes, shimmering thick healthy coat.

Seen mama snake in a while? Stevven asks.

Whiskers twitch.

Stevven selects small pan from shelf, gently shakes out fisher spider, eight eyes bright. They pick up egg, cool, rubbery. Stevven beams light through soft membrane, lighting pink corkscrew body, dark gray eye. One egg into pan, two, three. Stevven stops at six, leaves six eggs in nest.

They carry eggs back to storefront, to decorative tin pails *Made in China.* Stevven takes pink pail, shoulders picture frames, leaves store.


STEVVEN DROPS FRAMES IN BURN pile, sets eggs between Gino and Eli. Gino blesses them.

Stevven sits, rips off one grimy shoe, next. Skin tears on both heels. Cut on foot aches, aflame. They wash foot in rain, dress cut in oregano, fresh bandage. They roll out legs, dig into hamstrings, point and scrunch.

Sky lulls to slow rain. Late afternoon, yellow climbs water pools. Pineneedles and deciduous leaves ornament everything, drop off in clumps.

Fly takes to Stevven sock in frenzy. Front legs rear up, wings sputter, fall one way then other, nerves collapsing over one last meal. They peddle air, die, wings splaying like rocking horse blades.

Choo! Rifle shots roll like rockslides through Western valley.

Mosquitos. Stevven adds more wood to fire.

SNAKE EGGS AND MUSHROOM SCRAMBLE tic and simmer on scalding pan. Gino finishes dressing wounds in witch hazel, spoons scramble into cup for Eli. Eli smells, eats with hands, sucks bleeding embryo from fingers.

Sky deepens, bends into clouds, smears yellow, crescendos.

Where is Mary? Eli asks, stares into Stevven.

Likely with the police. Maybe somewhere better.

I want to go back to Apartment, Eli says. With Mary. With you and Gino and BluBerry.

Stevven rotates clothes on drying chair. We can't, they say.

Gino? Eli says, face orange in fire light.

Yes, little one?

Do you know where is Mary?

No, I'm sorry, child.

Is she okay?

I've been praying for her all day.

Do you want to go back to Apartment?

Hmm, Gino closes eyes. Apartment was good. But it was never for always.

But I want it always, Eli says.

This is hard, I know the feeling, Gino says. You will carry Apartment with you always. Like a bird carries seeds in his stomach when he goes North for the winter. Borders are always changing. Never solid, sometimes forgotten, more often burned or stolen.

Stevven unfolds bedding, throws wood into fire. Sparks float up, Stevven floats down, head to pillow.

Have I told you the story of Man and the Medicine bag? Gino says quietly. Eli shakes head.

Gino flows gaze into old rain, violet sky, recrosses legs. Hair, feather, and forest roll down Ginoshoulders.

It was in the age of Earth, when places had names, he says. One of these places the people called Eugene. The buildings were made of good material and the mountains were snowed every winter. There was once a man who lived on the outskirts of town alone so he could spend all his time crafting. He took frequent trips to the mountain to enjoy good wine alone on the vista, and went into the city only to buy what he needed. No one knew what he was crafting but the people felt that it must be great, for the man traded all his money for the finest beads, leathers, gems, and metals. What are you making? The cashier would ask. How long until it is ready? The barista would ask. What is it for? The carpenter would ask. The man shook his head politely, smiled, and thanked each one of them for their business. He worked for many months.

Just as many of the people were forgetting their curiosities, the spring season ahead, the man was spotted walking though town with the most beautiful bag slung over his shoulder. Its beads of blue, purple, white, sunset, and conifer spiraled elaborately. Buckles sterling and sturdy, buck leather fitting to his body, tassels fine as horsehair. It was the most beautiful bag made of all the good things of Eugene.

The questions continued. What do you keep inside? For a vessel so beautiful must contain something of high value. The man smiled and answered: The whole world, he said. And the cashier rolled his eyes, gave the man with the fine bag his groceries. The barista, overtaken by the beauty of the bag also asked, what do you keep inside? Seed, he said. Salt, he said. The valley, he said. Bone, he said. Medicine, he said. The whole world. Show us, the carpenter replied, like the others. The man would smile knowingly and then laugh and not show them. The man would pull out his money and tobaccos not from the beautiful bag but from a fanny pack dragging about the other side of his waist. Was the bag in fact empty? Just for show, fashion and no function?

Then one day a child found him resting on the side of the mountain trail, full on wine and sunshine. They took up the bag resting on the log beside him, unbuckled the flap and peered in. And in there, the child saw the whole world.

Gino closes eyes. Poplarleaves pedal like gold coins, drip water.

I don't get it, Stevven says, eyes street sign flashing assault rifle bullet holes.

Where would we be without our vessels? Gino says. Meals without bowls, our water without cups?

Where would we be without our gun holsters to carry our guns? Stevven says.

Gino smiles sadly, adjusts seat against store wall. It is a story without violence, he says.

But you said the whole world was in that bag. Guns must be in there, too.

I do not like talking about guns, Gino says, turns down for sleep.

Was Mary in the bag? Eli asks.

Yes, Gino says.

And BluBerry? And me?

Yes, Gino says.

Eli crawls over to Gino, lays head in Ginolap. They blink wet eyes, fiery sheen.

Stevven? Eli asks.

What?

Are you sad about Mary?

Yes.

Why aren't you crying?

I don't feel like it.

But you said you—

Crying takes too much energy. Happy with that explanation?

But Mary—

Just go to sleep.

Stevven turns away, uglygreen in belly, moves BluBerry into eyeline.

Charcoal wings splash in from South, falcon riding bronze breeze. Whoosh, great oversize truck drums on distant highway. Dogs bark, less than mile away.

Stevven shrinks into sleep, wet flame, leather, gunsmoke. Sleep like circuits frying underwater.

WHEELS, GRAVEL POPPING.

Stevven wrings fog from eyes.

Fire low strength. Big dark night.

Headlights climb into road. Horse silhouettes swell. Hooves and synth. Electronic music. Double truck, two scouts on horses leading. People dance on truck roof, dangle legs from odd perches. Truck climbs slowly, then revs up on straightaway.

Excavator slugs behind truck, ten foot long water mill melding to excavator claw, generators gripping yellow body. Monstrous wheels kick mud.

Stevven slowly grapples shoes and BluBerry, reaches to rouse Eli.

Horses, trucks, excavator pass. Rumblings, wheels and bass subsides.

Stevven looks between fingers hovering over Elibody. Eli blinks, watches Stevven, sleepless, fearful.

Stevven recovers hand, sits back onto sleeping mat. They meet Ginoeyes, soft with deep breathing, ritual. He reaches fist over ashes as if to conjure more flame. He holds something to Stevven.

For your nightmares, he says.

Gino slips rock into Stevvenhand. Rough in one direction, white, calcite. Stevven lies back down, rubs thumb up and down rockface.

Drip, drop, moisture slides off awning, plit, plop. Crescent moon siphons clouds, light and moisture mess. Little stars pimple gas station pump, little fateful stars.

GRAYAAAWL. YIP!

Dogs snap for dead rodent, breaking dawn. Limpear dog with more ribs pushing through skin trots off with fuzzy carcass. Other licks paw, pauses and stares after, trembles.

Stevven turns, aches. Sticky skin pulls cheap Tuesday Morning blanket with.

Gino squats, stokes small flame.

BluBerryleaves, fleshy, plump, balloon out waterbottle, number doubling overnight. Stevven rubs eyes. Looks over BluBerry again.

We're going to need some food, Stevven says. Big day ahead.

They stand, stretch hips, hams, then step off concrete strip into grass. They cross to high point in parking lot, gather dandelion. They return to camp with salad, clover, dandelion, borage. Gino sprinkles nuts onto salad.

I want McDonalds, Eli says, groggy.

You like dandelion.

Eli rubs eyes. I don't feel good, they say.

Eat it. I know you're hungry. You're always hungry in the morning. Tell them, Gino.

Stevven places salad pan before Eli, takes handful for themselves, munches. Bitter, feathery, green. Stevven slips on shorts, shirt, still chewing.

Gino tries to get Eli to eat. Eli does not eat. Gino finishes salad, collapses fire.

THEY WALK WEST.

Two white clouds loaf above, day hot and lolling. Backs slicken in clothes.

Paved road becomes country dirt road, mud road, then elevation, sandstone. Raindrop impresses orange clay. Foliage, purple undertones, decomposition. Deer bone, human bone. Puddles teem, small insects, gray matter.

Do I look like Mary?

You're her kid, so yeah.

We have brown eyes. But my hair is longer.

Careful here, Stevven says.

Brittle limestone sinks crumble like termite homes, water breaking earth.

What's in there? Eli asks.

You want to see?

Eli nods.

I'm going to hold your arms as you lean over. I don't want the ground to collapse under you.

Stevven grips Eliarms. Weight shifts over chasm.

Keep your feet back, Stevven says.

Clink, clock, crystal water.

How deep is it? Stevven asks.

I don't know, Eli says.

I'm going to pull you away now.

Okay.

THEY VEER LEFT AT T intersection, merge from dirt road onto sore gravel, SR 1124 West. Heartsize moss clump drops from Gino calf, exposes rancid pink skin.

I miss Snake, Eli says.

Apartment Snake? Stevven asks.

Yeah.

Why are you thinking about Snake?

I saw a snake in the leaves.

Why didn't you point them out?

I thought you would be angry.

Why would I be angry?

Eli shrugs.

No, tell me.

But you're angry right now.

I'm not. I think it's cool that you found a snake.

Gino assists Eli over century old oak falling across road. They stop together. Gino points out foliose lichen. Here they break, drink water.

Eli whispers inside Ginoear.

Stevven drags branch through mud, expresses sloppy shapes, avoids listening until they cannot.

But when do I start? Eli asks, Stevven overhearing.

You mean, when were you born? Gino asks.

No, Eli says, moves hand in, out from body, plays with space.

You mean where you, your youness begins?

Eli nods.

I believe you are your breath, Gino says. Your soul. Your breath and your soul dance your name. The earth is marked Eli.

Birds light upon trees, voicing like crystals. Gravel and dirt intersect asphalt. They take pave road North toward rumbling cars. Sounds broaden into four way intersection, lively gas station. American flags underscore bold red letters: *Tommy's Market*. Trucks and horses hitch to gas pumps, convenience store, pub. Barbecue grills smoke behind building.

Gino stops first. Stevven traces gaze.

Oilman insignia hangs from convenience store windows: red banners, gold etching, busting oil derricks, oil barrels, black rivers flowing from valleys.

This is where the demons spawn from, Gino says. We should go around.

They're human, and fanatics like anyone else, Stevven says. We just got to adapt. Besides, there's no going around. They are the roads now.

Ginoface pinches in great yellowing sunshine, beard deserting fast. They're not fanatics, he says. They are an organized army of soullessness and disease. You are too young to understand how horrific these signs are.

Maybe, but I bet we can hitch a ride from someone. Let's see who we can talk to.

Gino moans, closes hands into prayer.

Stevven threads arm through Ginoarm, breathes loamy, green air intimate to Gino. We'll sit you down next to a nice cool fan, they say, takes up Eliarm. Lions and tigers and bears, oh my!

Stevven leads companions down yellow stripe road towards bearding men with beer bottles and broad fingers gathering around market entrance. Men spot them emerging from forest, talk in smirks and low, looping growls.

The horses are so big! Eli says. Can we say hi?

Let's start with the person sitting at the bus stop, Stevven says.

I know his clan, Gino says. He is not with the oilmen.

Good! Stevven says, zephyrs towards figure shadowing in bus stop. Open the conversation with that.

Slowly, Gino says, begins earthing approach.

Stevvenlegs shake moving so slow, morph into tactile feelers more than wheels. Feet count rock pieces turning between shoe and pavement.

Figure steps from bus bench wearing sleek harem pants and long black trench coat, red sash swimming loosely around neck and head. Dark eyes stare out from dark complexion.

Gino bows, hands to third eye. Arms linking, Stevven and Eli join bow.

I am Gino, Earther, former Red Valley Compostist.

I am Addan, son of Addan Nahid-Maruduk, he replies, young, wild eyes, blood medallion swinging. You're a Compostist?

Before, Gino says. Now I am earthing without a people—Gino risks eyes at oilmen corralling outside building, now moseying into store—When I was a child, while I was training as a priest, I saw you young men come through our camps, on a mission to kill the oilmen. I wanted to go with you.

Addan smiles coolly, canines white, tips gold. That was during my father's time, he says. He remembers your generosity well. But he also remembers the fourteenth cycle. My father, he was one of the last to enjoy the Compostist's help.

I am not afraid. I am not a Compostist, Gino says, hangs head, closes eyes. I remember the very cycle, the meeting where it was decided to stop homing your clan. I was sad at first. Now I know it was best—Gino deeps eyes into Addan—We were aiding your mission to kill in vengeance, which is neither righteous nor brave.

So, you are friends with the oilmen now? Addan scoffs. You know, we could have protected you when the government came and scattered you like frightened rats.

Gino recrosses hands peacefully over beard, chest. Addan, where are you going? he asks.

I have a mission to kill two more American oil men, he says, smiles.

Addan unsheathes blade, steps into light, points to deathmarks near blade guard. Two more, then I return to the desert across the sea for exaltation.

Killing, Gino says. It does nothing good.

You are dumb in your old age.

Gino breaths in shakily. Words crumble into coughs. Stevven and Addan bring Gino to bench. They settle into shade, steady breaths. Eli sits on ground beside bench, watches horses.

Addan smiles across Gino to Stevven. And what is your name, desert flower?

Where does this bus go? Stevven asks.

Addan smirks. If this is your father, you have not been taking good care of him—Addan turns to Eli—What about you. Do you have a name?

What's the fare? Stevven asks, intercepts gaze.

Addansmile gives. You will have no trouble if you have gold, he says.

We don't have gold, Stevven says.

What do you have?

Tobacco, Gino says, reaches inside coat, lungs puttering.

I can tell you if it is enough, Addan says, takes gallon ziplock bag in hand, rings on pointer fingers. This should be enough passage for you alone—he slides gray eyes to Stevven—What else do you have?

Eli taps Stevven. We can share BluBerry, Eli says.

What? No, they're not ready for that. They just got their leaves.

BluBerry wants to, look!

Quiet down. Their leaves are falling off because they're stressed, not because they want to multiply.

They're reaching. I know.

That's just how woody plants are. They're not reaching for anything besides sunlight. We're not making another cutting.

Why?

Because.

That's not fair! Eli stands and stomps.

I don't have to explain.

You act like you know BluBerry but you don't.

We'll figure out another way onto the bus, Stevven says. Let's just sit down out here for a second, see what we got to share.

I want to say hi to the horses.

Not right now, Stevven says, unzips pack.

Gino taps tobacco pipe and stuffs new leaf inside. Addan strikes match, lights. They pass pipe between them.

I don't like the smoke, Eli says.

Then lets go sit with a tree, Stevven says, lugs pack to curb.

Eli drops into teeming grasses in lone elmshade, frowns at Stevven. Eligaze drives down road, interest hovering somewhere between manufacture homes bloating walls into streets, mattresses lipping out ravine, orange berries shriveling on gooseberry branches, clouds.

Here, Stevven says. You can hold BluBerry.

Eli sets BluBerry in lap, scratches arm where spittlebug tracks linger. They unscrew bottlelid, stick nose inside, inhale.

You'll suffocate BluBerry breathing on them like that.

Eli pulls nose away.

You have to be gentle, Stevven says, holds honey jar in light. They're three days old.

Eli sets BluBerry down, breaks sticks, snap, snap, snap. They pick up thick stick, unsnappable, poke, poke, poke. They scoot to silty bald spot on soil, draw.

Stevven sorts through clothes, medicine. What are you drawing? Stevven asks.

Chow chow.

From the city?

Eli nods, lazy.

Did you like that dog?

They licked my hand, Eli says. I love them. I miss them.

Eli draws tail and ears, big floppy tongue. Ants march across, texture fur.

RUMBLING, HEAVY MACHINE, HISS, REV, rev. Tree branches crack under buffalospan wheels. Gray sulfuric fumes shiver over giant red, white, blue bus ballooning over bend, impenetrable windows swabbing pollens and particulates from air. Grate plow steers straight towards Stevven, Eli, BluBerry.

Breaks squeal. Blood jumps inside Stevven, pattat, pattat, pattat. Horses snort and pull reins. Bus engine cuts.

Attention passengers, Conductorvoice rattles from inside. Gonna fill up here at Tommy's before we get on the highway and the eleven hour stretch to Chatt, stopping at Greenville and Murphy. I encourage you to use the bathroom and shop. We will be here twenty minutes, no more no less. I *will* leave without you.

Tall, scratchy glass doors shake open. Old white couple with round bellies and necks exit, shade eyes, cross into store. Limber city hippie wearing early twenty-first century sweats, sports jersey #4, jingly watches and gold rings swings out bus, guitar first.

Hello, they say passing, white pomhair and pombeard bobbing. I've got to piss!

Conductor walks down steps as if brick foot, squints and smiles black teeth inside wiry orange beard. What a crowd, he says, eyes widening and reddening. What a crowd!

He leans arm onto metal, soily orange trench coat rolling up to elbow, buckles and poles bracing atrophying limb.

Headin towards Memphis? We're stopping at and only at Greenville, Murphy, and Chatt. If you give a fuss, we'll throw you off a movin bus. You can recharge food and water at the stops. Extra cost for lag. Digidollar shit don't work here—Conductor narrows eyes—And neither do hippie liberal snowflakes.

Gino offers tobacco bag to Conductor.

Right to it, he says. I do appreciate a businessman.

Conductorfingers, flat and mechanic, tear bag open. He leans in, whiffs. Eyes pop.

Hell, where you get this? he asks. This ain't no bigtown tobacco.

We grew it, Gino says.

Got any more?

No.

How bout papers?

Just my pipe.

Lemme see. Hell, that's beautiful. Make it yourself?

It was my mother's.

Aw, I can't take your mama's pipe. But I'll take what goes in it! Hehe. Welcome board. Whatta I call you?

I am Gino. Does this cover the fare for my friends?

A little bag of tabacky is only gonna cover one seat. What else you got?

Stevven offers binoculars, solar light, Zeebee honey.

Got any metals? Good American dollars?

Stevven glances at Eli. We have seventy dollars, Stevven says.

Shit that don't hardly cover gas to Chatt, Conductor says, steps onto grassy patch next to elm, unzips, pees.

I will pay for their passage, Addan says, counts glowing pieces from hip pouch. Halflife coins.

Conductor looks over shoulder, zips up. Fine pieces you got there, he says. Throw in that drink and we'll call it a deal.

I should have bought a smaller bottle, Addan says, pulls whiskey from pouch.

They used to say no drinking and driving, now they say no driving without the drink, Conductor laughs, takes bottle from Addan. Twenty minutes.

He enters store, hollars hellos and howareyous.

Gino steps into bus.

Eli looks up to Stevven. Can we see the horses now?

Let's not bother them, Stevven says. I'd feel better if we just got on the bus. Addan, thank you for doing this.

I won't bother them, Eli says.

Just get on the bus.

You're being mean, Eli says.

It is no problem, Addan says. I can guard you from the oilmen if you need to go to the bathroom.

We don't need anymore help, thanks, Stevven says.

They might have toys for him inside, Addan says.

Elieyes swell.

Now you're doing the opposite of helping, Stevven says.

Toys! Eli says, bobs. Can I please please go in?

Eli stops squirming, steadies eyes on Stevven. I'm done holding BluBerry for now, they say.

Stevven stares back at Eli, figures. Okay, they say, take BluBerry in hands, gentle.

Eli runs.

Eli!

Eli breaks through men exiting convenience store.

Stevven drops pack at Addanfeet, breezes past laughing men inside, charges jumbo inflatable Bud Light mascot sitting on cooler.

Shit, sorry, Stevven says, raises hand to cashiers, uprights inflatable.

Eli runs down middle aisle. Stevven hits hip on cornershelf, knocks down plastic jug, ga glup.

Ouch! Eli!

Stevven picks up jug, pen scratching out soap brand letters, and in all caps: *MOTOR OIL*.

Eli turns aisle corner, rocks *Sweet Side* pastry tower. Cheap orange treats tumble out.

Eli, cut it out, Stevven says. I don't want to be running with BluBerry like this.

Eli watches Stevven from slushie machines, red and blue churning around head. They stick tongue out.

Where the fuck did you learn that move?

Eli turns and runs past register where cashier and customer watch with expiring amusement. Eli bursts out back door.

Stevven apologizes to cashier growling behind shiplap bar, wall behind them stringing cigarettes and pornos. Bull skulls in oil man colors stare down from crossbeams overhead.

Stevven shoves orange pastries into baskets, jogs out back door after Eli.

FULL WHITE LIGHT, HISSING, GRILLING sounds.

Barechest men joke around grill, picnic tables. Women in ball caps, open crown hats and long ponytails wag ruby toenails in sandals. Electric fans whiz. In sheetmetal shelter, butcher saws off leg from deer, prepares cuts and jerkies.

Butchereyes meet Stevven. They point bloody bonesaw to path breaking into trees behind parking lot.

Thanks, Stevven says, leaves bone crunching sounds for thin forest.

They climb concrete slabs, stairway into second reforesting parking lot. Something brushes head. Rib bone dangles from string.

Stevven stops before vertebrae, antler, toe bone, femurs, radials, rodent mandibles.

Eli?

Stevven ducks under bone chandelier, stumbles out into small clearing.

Four children and Eli gather around limpleg cardtable weighty with drying bone. Behind them, ten foot tall bone flesh creature expresses hundred faces and inorganic appendages, titanic. Deer femurs stick out topmost head structure like tusks, pubic bones make pointing noses, and cattle ribs claw hands. Two big caverns in face resolve into dark eye portals, hatch strange airs and movement. They wear giant crown made with antler, feather, and colorful twines. Strings tie into trees, tie into dangling bones. They all breathe together, tree and bone.

Welcome to the Bone Witch Lair! Pale child in Adidas shoes says, raises arms ritualistically above head.

Stevven catches Elishoulder, spins them.

What the hell was that? Stevven asks.

I don't want to go on the bus, Eli says, huffs.

You have to or we'll leave you here, Stevven says.

I don't care!

Small sunburning kid tugs on Stevvenshirt, hands them finger bone. Giant tumor glistens on kidneck.

What do you want me to do with this? Stevven asks.

I can't reach, Sunburn says, points to Bone Witch.

Stevven sets BluBerry on table and looks at Eli.

BluBerry needs you, Stevven says. That's why you need to get on the bus.

Stevven heeds Sunburn pulling on shirt.

It goes right here—Sunburn points to pinky knuckle on hand, then points to Bone Witch hand.

Okay. Have something sticky?

Sunburn fetches broken plastic bowl, disturbs drying pine sap with fat stick. They dribble sap onto fingerbone, smear Stevvenfinger also.

We're trying to stick this to the Bone Witch, not me, right?

Yeah, Sunburn says, hands black with stick and dirt.

Okay, I'll put it here.

Coolness comes over Stevven as they touch Bone Witch, attach bone.

How's that? Stevven asks.

Sunburn nods. Again, they say.

I got to get back to the bus, Stevven says. But this was fun.

Whistle crackles through trees into Bone Witch Lair.

Kids, fatherly voice says, you're gonna wanna come take a look at this fish.

Kids scurry out lair, bones rattling after them.

Eli blinks at Stevven.

Sorry for being mean, Stevven says. This is a neat place.

Eli nods.

Stevven sighs—You can go look at the fish. But then we go back to the bus. Deal?

Eli nods.

Take BluBerry for me. My hands are sticky.

Eli escorts BluBerry from Bone Witch Lair.

Stevven turns again to look at Bone Witch, knobby fangs, thousand fish bone alveoli, curling toes.

Bone Witch winks.

Stevven falls back as hummingbird flies from Witcheye socket, streaming green and purple. Bird hums, becomes trees.

Pattat, pattat pattat. Stevven recovers some heart, face smearing grass. They stand and regard Bone Witch once more. They walk away sticking and unsticking sap fingers.

KIDS FLOCK AROUND MAN WITH heavy styrofoam cooler. Kids squeeze in, layer tight, Eli tiptoeing behind them, beaming. Fisherman sets cooler on butcher table, lifts out giant grayfin critter, dangles them in light, hand inside maw.

Woah! kids squeal and punch each other.

Fishhead bulky, smooth, porpoisine, fist size growth eclipsing small blue eye. Pale bright intestine droops out lips, two crustacean legs curl into belly. Cartilaginous tail fin knobby as Garden carrot drags through ice.

Dale, butcher says, I figure we kin make loads of fish tacos wit him but pops might wanna stuff this one. See, it got a full set of legs.

Pops won't want issun because he didn't catch it. And I don't wan it. Cook him up and give the kids them bones, will ya?

Yay! Sunburnt screams. Can we give the tail to Smarty?

Big black dog responds to name, cocks head, swings big tail, sweats tongue.

Doggy! Eli says.

You saw the fish, Stevven says to Eli. Now let's go.

Stevven raises hand. Sorry to bother y'all.

No trouble, butcher says, waves saw. Y'all have a good one.

They walk around building. Stevven looks back towards fish. Fisheye stares back.

LONG TAILS FLICK FLIES. HORSE heads bend for feed slop. Convenience store awning extends over them, metal posts kneeing in. Rod iron and car parts pile and rust nearby. One horse reaches for hubcap with water, stirs mosquitos.

Eli squeaks and hurries to horse. Giant nostrils sniff all over, turn Eli into giggle fit.

Stevven smiles, grabs hose hooking onto nails, turns spigot on, fills barrel with water. Black and white horse nuzzles Stevven then drinks straight from hose stream.

Stevven laughs and watches Eli.

Horselips close on BluBerry leaf protruding from open bottle, yank up, break leaf from stem.

Stevven drops hose.

Hey! Stevven leaps and snatches BluBerry from Eli, shoves chewing horsehead away.

Horse rolls eyes, nudges back for second bite. Stevven leaves stable, crosses to bus shade. They squat down, aid BluBerry.

I'm sorry! Eli says, crashes down next to them.

Stevven bristles. This horse could have pulled all of BluBerry out of the bottle, they say. Ate them all.

I'm sorry. Are they okay?

The leaf came clean off the stem. We're lucky.

I'll be careful. I'm sorry.

Just go take a pee break and get on the damn bus.

Eli climbs onto bus.

Stevven screws lid onto BluBerrybottle, hugs them in.

Cigarette smoke. Stevven opens eyes to Conductor sucking cigarette.

Tough traveling with children, he says.

Stevven stands. No doubt. How long did you say the journey to Chattanooga was?

Eleven hours, give or take.

I'd like lag.

You're gonna get your boyfriend to pay for that too? It's worth at least a whole fare.

Stevven digs out temp chip from pocket.

I have a one-way ticket for a train, attached to a fake eID.

Legit?—Conductor brings chip to face—Model looks right. But why the hell you ain't use this to get to Nashville?

Because I was stupid.

Hm. Conductor looks at Stevven, looks at chip, looks at Stevven, flicks cigarette away.

Let's get you set up then, he says.

Conductor waves bye to trucker, swings leg onto bus. He flips open compartment door on dash, throws chip in piling paper maps, trinkets, pistol. Driverseat frays, radio chatters, grease and grime slide in paperbag litter.

Go ahead, take your seat, Conductor says. I'll get the stuff.

Four rows outfit unique seats. Eli curls up against window next to Gino on blue moquette bench. Addan sits behind them, smiles at Stevven. Stevvenpack hangs in overhead nets.

Across aisle, young, fickleeye Metakid glances up at Stevven, spaceships beaming and orbiting white hoodie. Holographic interface like hamster ball revolves around Metakidhead. In neighboring armchair, someone sleeps, IV dangling from arm, golden liquid, honey, lag.

Stevven stops before Gino. I am going to sleep the rest of the way, they say.

Ginoeyes shift to tubing slung over Conductorarm.

You're going to use? Gino asks.

I need to go over some warnings with ya, Conductor says. Go on, pick your seat.

Stevven slides into chair behind Eli and Gino next to Addan, seat foam sticking to calves. They secure BluBerry in waterbottle holder on seatback pocket.

Hello, I'm glad you made it, Addan says, secreting sweet cloves, sweat.

Conductor kneels metal knee in aisle. Have you used before? he asks.

No.

So you know lag's a nullifier. I say it's like staring out from a cooldark hiding place in the shallow part of your head.

I'll be mobile? When I wake up?

Sure sure, you'll just be a machine going without a brain, without emotions. No one's had trouble getting where they need to go. But the hangover can be something fierce, when all your nerves start waking up. The hangover being the inverse of a hangover, a giant rush of emotions and nerves.

Conductor attaches tubing to ceiling, fishes out needle in medical plastic— Which stop are we waking you?

Chatt.

Roger that, he says. I'll be feeding you the stuff from the compartment behind my seat, a safe, standard amount. Secure with two locks, so no one can fiddle with it. Watch me here, new needle, new tube, new everything. No risk of infection. Once everyone gets settled I'll stick ya.

Okay, Stevven says.

Conductor crosses to bus front, leans out door.

All aboard!

Old couple washes in, settles in back seats.

City hippie smiles swinging in, greets every person. Jen tie, gajaj katoj, they say to Stevven.

Salunton, Stevven replies.

Sterling white eyebrows jump out goldrim shades. Vi parolas la bonajn vortojn! Cityhippie says.

Iuj.

Mia nomo estas Cullo.

I'm Stevven.

Conductor shoos Cullo to seat, breaks wipe from sterile packaging.

Cullo shakes head sadly. Ĝi estas malbona drogo. Ambaŭ miaj fratoj perdis la vivon pro ĝi.

It's not always bad, Stevven says. It's a tool, to help me get along.

Temposalti, malbona.

I don't understand, Stevven says.

To timeskip, Cullo says, tunes guitar. To feelskip, it's never good.

Conductor sanitizes Stevven wrist with wipe, tears plastic from IV and needle.

Stevven catches Elieye surge, watch them through seat gap.

I'm going to velcro your arm to the seat so it don't swing around, Conductor says. Easy to undo. See?

He demonstrates, grabs needle. Stevven looks up to ceiling, to soft luggage bulging in nets. Small pinch into forearm. Tape, velcro.

And we're in, Conductor says, groans to stand.

They double check tubes, return to front, release lag. Gold slugs down tube, merges with Stevven.

Stevven turns to Addan.

Why did you pay for us?

I recognize the fire in you, Addan says.

Bus doors clack shut. Engine turns.

No really, Stevven says.

It's true, Addan says, jolts forward with bus.

Stevven looks past Addan to crosshatching cars, approaching highway.

Conductor cranks wheel, merges onto merger, gathers speed, faster than Eli running, faster than Donnaboat, faster than anything. Stevven begins to forget movement, settle into placeless limbo.

You don't think you're coming back from your mission, Stevven says.

Addan continues to look out window. Bus grumbles and shakes over rough lanes, passes smaller vehicles.

What's that? Eli says.

I don't know, Gino says.

Can we go see?

Unfortunately no.

Why?

The bus has to keep moving.

Why?

Because we were just stopped, and most transportation in today's world is a business of efficiency. People pay to get from one place to another very fast.

We're moving too fast, Eli says.

Yes, Gino says. I prefer less, also.

Because you're earthing?

Yes.

Birds like to move fast. But not turtles. You're like a turtle, Gino. Do you have turtle in you?

No, but my arm here is prairie skink.

It's flaky.

Yes, infected. Too much friction, stress.

Gino?

Yes?

What's Stevven doing?

They are using lag, a form of anesthetic.

Like Ms. Jones?

Yes.

Why?

Fear. Always fear.

Is Stevven still mad at me?

They just need their space, like at Apartment.

Conductor blasts horn, shoves through traffic.

Gino, when was before buses? Eli asks.

Long before me, two hundred years ago, maybe. Does it sound like a long time to you?

Yes, but also no.

Why do you say it like that?

Because, because rocks live millions of millions of years. But I've also been alive a long time.

Gino makes affirming noise, points out window. How about that rock? he says. It has a nice pink color.

Cullo plays soft Spanish ballad on guitar. World runs outside, runs, runs.

Tear on Stevvenface hardens, drops like punctuation. Blood cools and stalls further tears.

WHAT'S THE ISLAND? ELI ASKS.

Stevven eyes tap tap open, ebbing. Reds, oranges, violets. Addan reads from pocketbook, Arabic.

Oh, the grass? Gino says. I don't know if there is a name for it.

Median, Stevven whispers, voice hollow.

Addan sets poetry book down, offers Stevven water.

They drink, sun setting inside plastic.

That's where deer go to see their reflection, Gino says. It is an old tale I heard as I child. I will try to remember.

Elifingerperson runs along grass median.

Sounds melt. Rattlings, chattings, strummings, clickings, hummings all slide into flat puddle under Stevvenchin.

This land used to be so forested that even the wildfires couldn't break through the canopy, Gino says. It was becoming jungle. There was clean water everywhere, where deer and their forest friends would drink. The water was always moving, rippling with activity from within and without. It was beautiful.

Then came roads, the first clearings, where horses came through. Then this was finished with black tars, which became hot in the sun. Cars rolled over the roads like thunders, making toxic storm clouds. Deer could still cross without too much trouble, but then one day a car hit one, going so fast. The deer were frightened, but continued their migrations across the land for food, water, and shelter.

Soon the roads grew, and whole fields of trees were cleared. Their favorite watering holes became dark, murky, muddy, from all the erosion. More cars killed more deer, and it became impossible to cross the road. Many brave unwise creatures tried and tried, but died. Until one succeeded in reaching grass.

The littledeer thought he had made it across the road, only to find the road directly in front of him, and behind him, but grass extending endlessly on both sides of him. He walked this grass hoping for a break, but instead he walked further and further from his family, feeling lonely. And he was getting tired and hungry, the cars swarming down the roads on each side of him, forbidding passage.

Stevvenlegs slide away from body. Eyes sore gathering cars. Metal rubber plastic crisscrosses, cascades, rust shine tumbling together, forward, over again, looping loops looping, battling air, sliding under, four wheels spinning into noplace.

Eventually he came to the lowest point in the small valley, Gino says. Where the drain had clogged and the water pooled. The sun was high, baking the deer's back. He was thirsty. When he leaned down to drink, another deer looked right back at him.

Was it his reflection? Eli asks.

Stevven wipes drool from chin. Hordes shovel by, shapes going shapeless. Darkness crosshatches vision, coffining, Bone Witch, fisheye morphing into Barbaradigieye. Light boils, then pales down, down, silt death, mud mind. Small, teeming, none.

CLAP. CLAP.

Hands clap air, dull, far away.

Stevven blinks eyes open.

Wake up, Conductor says. There you go.

Haze like drum symbols. Edges harden, shape. Conductorface wrestles panic, turns away. He crosses to control board next to frontmost bus seat, flicks big switch up, down, updownupdown. He curses and grips overhead strap, squeezes fist white.

Stevvenhead rolls, cheeks headrest. Callous greeneyes watch them from opposite seat. Two lag IVs hang, untethering between them, drip gold in bus aisle. Red blood bubble dries on Stevvenarm.

Eli peeks over seat at Stevven.

Stay in your seats, Conductor says. Stop moving. Stay!

Eli plops back down.

Greeneyes rolls out hands and ankles, takes out pocket case from steely jacket, shakes out glasses, lenses square and black like beard, assumes executive look.

Metakid trembles, eyes Greeneyes nervously. Interface planets revolve blue, orbit Metakidhead.

Stevven looks windowside. Stillness, dusty heat, no Addan.

Conductor wipes stubble face. Now, he says, it's been some time since one of my passengers ripped into the wires. I don't very well like it. I ask whoever is messing with things speak their terms—he puts hands to hip pistol—so we can get back on schedule.

Sandshifting silence. Heads revolve. No one speaks.

Conductor points to Metakid. You, gamer boy, he says. Stand up.

I didn't—

What's your job? Conductor asks. You employed?

I'm a grocery store clerk. E-Grocery.

You sure you ain't just a hacker and trouble maker? Think this is fun?

No—Metakid trembles—Not at all.

Turn of your computer.

It's stalled, if I turn it off without—

Conductor crosses to seat, imprisons Greeneyes and Metakid in shadow. Sweat slops as he moves, drops onto Stevvenarm. Stevven watches bead roll numbly down. Body prickles, half asleep, unsensational.

I said turn off your damn city tech! Conductor yells, reaches for Metakid headpiece.

Blue light bites Conductorgut. Taser.

Greeneyes pushes Conductor, limp and moaning, into aisle. They steal pistol and stand. They refix glasses to face, step over Conductor, press button on control board.

Idle bus revs, gadgets twinkle and beep. Metakid turns toes in, cries into seatback. Greeneyes faces passengers.

Small detour, Greeneyes speaks in multitone. I must notify you that you are now hostages detained by the Warthogs, special ground forces of the People's Liberation Army of China.

Cullo opens hands. Please, I have a child, they say.

Let's hope your government gives a shit, Greeneyes says.

But they do not. They do not!

Cullo knocks guitar onto floor, feverish. They recover instrument, cling as if to life buoy.

Please relax, Greeneyes says. I have control of the situation.

Greeneyes climbs into driverseat, fiddles with gears and levers, familiarizing.

Stevven reaches over seat, grabs Ginoshoulder, whispers through seat gap: Hide them inside you.

Gino shifts, stows BluBerry inside tunic.

Cullo scoots closer to Stevven, leans over isle. Ĉu li diris kien ni iras? they ask.

Ne, Stevven says. Ne zorgu.

Ne zorgu?!? Jen via drogo, kiu parolas.

Jes kaj ne.

Bus rocks forward. Greeneyes maneuvers bus onto highway.

Ĉu ni ataku?

Ne.

Shhh! Metakid says, tear staining. You'll get us in trouble.

They don't care that we're talking or they would have shut us up already, Stevven says, searches Greeneyes face in bus mirror. No, this isn't about us. They just want the bus, to provoke the oil fascists.

We are useless, then? Cullo says. Kial li ne forĵetis nin?

I'm not ready to die, Metakid says, trembles lip.

Saying shit like that gets us nowhere, Stevven says.

You are more cold than before, Cullo says.

Bus climbs over fallen pine. Branches rake underside, crshh crshh. Bus merges left onto circular ramp. Fading yield sign smiles happyface stickers and bullet holes.

Why is everyone scared? Eli asks Gino.

We're in the hands of military people now, Gino says. We are scared because we don't know what is going to happen.

But we always don't know.

We don't know, but we have an idea.

Eli looks through seat crack at Stevven.

Stevven does not feel but turns to watch one hundred foot pines texture spiral road with shadow. Secondgrowth climbs over highway, steals back sun day by day. Stevven floats, world numb, all pinpoints soft.

BUS MERGES ONTO OLD HIGHWAY North. Air grows sulfur. Truck fitting three soldiers roars past, honks. Greeneyes waves.

Terraform vehicles in large dugout collect yellow dust from atmosphere. Soldiers camouflage green and flaxen yellow, take measurements from meters. Multiterrain AI carrying crates zips over road shoulders, enters short underground tunnels with doors that reseal and blink red lights.

Camouflage nets dapple small tech station that sends drones into sky. One drone escorts bus down exit towards roadside inn.

Liberation army units flow like termites through rooms and industrial mounds. Giant sign signals to highway in sky blue letters: *Ducktown Copper Inn*, duck mascot smiling with spraypaint canine teeth, swastika eyes. *High-Speed Internet*.

Bus crunches to stop in lot.

Doors open. Two soldiers step through dragging early morning heat after them. Metal alloy calves glisten. They salute Greeneyes.

Greeneyes commands them in Mandarin. Soldiers hoist and haul halfconsious Conductor out bus.

Bus windows rattle as Chinese battle tank careens out brick carwash station, body wide as road. Great wheels kick up kudzu, grasses, soils. Main gun barrel steers North. Foot soldiers march after, metal body parts and guns winking sun.

Boom, hiss. Light flashes in East. Bus rocks.

What was that? Eli asks.

It came from deep underground, Stevven says. Detonations in the mines. And setting fire to the yellow dust. There is a reason the only trees here are pine.

Few other popup structures operate in parking lot and inn. Paths to mines and bunker doors signal larger operation respiring underground.

Out, Greeneyes says. Line up. We'll proceed to screenings. Leave your things.

Stevven leads line into air tensing electricity, combustion, white light. Soldier stops line in full sun clearing. Stevven, numb, stands least sensitive to heat barreling around them, marks cardinal positions, traffic flows.

Two foot soldiers claw toothy feet through red soils, drag bloody, American armyman from mine. Cuffs bind armymanhands. They push armyman onto knees before old brick wall, former foundations for ore bins.

Shlunk!

They shoot armyman. Blood hits brick, head slops to ground, wet clopping sound.

Cullo screams.

Gino bows head, prays.

Eli chest pumps fast. They look up to Stevven.

Stevven does not react.

Greeneyes stops before line, looks Cullo up and down.

Follow me, Greeneyes says.

Please, Cullo mutters, breaking. Please.

Soldiers shove Cullo forward into interrogation tent posting outside inn, small distance from dead armyman. Sobbing continues inside tent.

Clank, clonk, weight shifts on bus. Soldiers carry out packs, batteries, Culloguitar, everything. Stevvenpack disappears inside Ducktown Copper Inn.

Soldier turns to Stevven, red eyes flashing.

Who are you with? soldier asks.

Stevven looks at feet.

Who are you with?

We're together, Gino says, nearly touchless hand on Stevven. With the child.

Stevven regards him, emotions bustling deep, unknowable inside, only pinpricks.

You three, soldier says. Follow me.

Soldiers escort Cullo outside tent. Cullo trails salt to old mine entrance, loud, terrible.

They're taking him underground, Stevven whispers. Where that armyman came from.

Gino prays as soldier leads them all into interrogation tent.


SMALL FAN PUMPS USELESSLY OVER small steel table, chairs.

Sit, Greeneyes says.

Soldier unfolds third chair for Eli, steps back, motor flicking quietly, awaits orders.

Hold still while I identify you, Greeneyes says.

Greeneyeglasses gloss Gino.

You have too much hair, they say. They command soldier in Mandarin. Soldier leaves tent.

My name is Gino. I am earthing. This is no disguise.

We will see, Greeneyes says, glosses Stevven.

Stevven Pane—Greeneyes smiles, reads moving pictures in lenses—Ha, you're trending.

What?

Many people want to know where you are. For entertainment news.

I'm on the news?

Bright images carousel, vanish from lenses. Greeneyes refocuses on realtime Stevven. We are very lucky to have scooped you up, they say. It's really hard to lose people in today's world. What will your people think when they know we have you?—Greeneyes clears throat—Stevven, why did you get on the bus?

I'm going West.

Why?

I don't know.

Greeneyes claps hands impatiently. Try again, they say.

It's the safest place I can think of.

For you? Or for the little one? Greeneyes says, smiles at Eli, glosses quick as wink.

Greeneyes turns to Stevven. This child is a nonperson, they say. Huge capital. There is no safe place for this one. I could take them from you now and do anything I want, they say. No laws protect them. Not that your country's laws can be enforced at this point.

Soldier returns to tent bearing scissors and buzzer.

No! Gino shouts as two more soldiers enter and hold him, Gino no match for alloy arms.

Eli cries and hugs Stevven. Small skip inside Stevven chest, small unravel.

Buzzzz. Cut, snip. Buzzzzz. Life clods drop and die on dirt floor. Forest goes, bit by bit, dead buzz. Gino protests louder than falling sequoia.

Eli stares, grips into Stevven, miserable.

Buzzer presses into chinskin, cheek. Clicks off.

Only thick black whiskers shake, dark and wet below Ginonose. Ginojowl long, nude, cold. Square teeth sweat. Ginohands fly to face.

Grieving begins.

Soldiers yank Ginohands down. Greeneyes glosses him.

Eugine Foster, Greeneyes says, smirks. Domestic terrorism. Same charges as all the other Earthers. Do you hate the government as much as they hate you?

Ginoeyes close tight inside clay hands, skins flaking, failing.

Overhead fan clicks, pushes air like walls, choking.

Greeneyes smiles at Eli, stands, fixes shirt collar. You will stay in the mines for now, they say.

Stevven and Eli stand, thread. Soldiers force Gino to stand, escort them outside.


BRIGHTNESS SQUINTS THROUGH SENSES. STEVVEN winces, throat pinches.

Outside, Gino drops onto knees. BluBerry tumbles out tunic.

Stevven dives, hugs BluBerry to chest.

Click click click, gun barrels spin like rattlesnake. Semiaquatic soldierfeet grip earth inches from Stevvennose.

Get up, soldier says.

Stevven climbs up, massages mud from BluBerrybottle. Soldiers yank Gino up. Mud stuccoes trembling knees.

They walk onto roadshoulder, muddy feet collecting old leaves. Plastic cars sink in smooth green dust, windows cracking like eggshells. Kudzu, kudzu, kudzu.

Are you scared? Eli asks as they march over road.

I'm prepared, Stevven says, swallows. Not scared. Just keep walking.

Gino drags behind, frown like deepest dark fault on Earth.

Me too, Eli says, sniffles. Is BluBerry okay? Can I hold them?

No, Stevven says.

Mine entrance grumbles like some gummy snoring maw, boulders frothing at edges.

Stevven, why did they attack Gino? Eli asks. Is he going to be okay? I'm scared.

Metal and railroad tie stacks swallow them into slimy, hungry, sunless foyer.

SHORTSIGHT LIGHTS STUD WALLS, GREEN, yellow, blue, like oil on water. Drip trickle, drip drop. Water circulates, eats rock inside all direction. Air blues, darkens.

Digisign floats at first cave intersection, English and Mandarin: *Boyd Drift, Cherokee Drift, Calloway Drift, Central Shaft.* Legs kick unseen pebbles walking into Calloway Drift. Stalactites dribble water in Stevveneye. They rub out calciums and trip over railway, swollen spokes reflecting red light, red rust.

Wooden ladder leans against North wall, rots. Soldier with more flesh than metal glances up from personal screen, face blue and wet like copper basin.

Clink clonk, bang. Metal falls some distance down opposite tunnel. Shouts, viscous laughter. Wet echoes leap through ore cart hollows, compound all around.

Old iron gates lock away one side at acute angle from cave floor to wall, prison room like giant sewer grate peeling from earth.

Stevven catches eyewhites staring out from prison. Cullo.

Soldier turns lock on prison door.

Enter, they say, lift door on aching hinges.

Gino drops, sinks to ground against prison bars. Eli nestles into Gino, strokes arm, consoling.

Stevven steps in, turns and watches door screech, clank, close, lock. Rust flakes rain down. Soldier leaves, cold lights blinking down tunnel. Calloway Drift continues across chamber, sweating deeper darkness. Stevven blinks eyes slowly, coaxes sight that will not come yet.

Breath sneaks up to neck.

Monstro, Cullo says, tobacco breath sour. We are not alone.

Cullo faces Stevven to darkest prison corner, hides behind them.
See? See?

Eli rises, awes. It's a flower! they say.

Monstro! Cullo moans. No no no no.

Someone low, wet, growling. Hunching back grows in purple umbra. Growler squats, one hand gripping slick wall, itchy dark nails, gray stringy hair, boisterous eyes. Growler crawls forward, naked below ribs, knobby feet caking black like coal, shiny. Black fingers roil next to bioluminescent purple flower.

Hello, hello, hello, hello, voice says like wet mortar stones.

Gray teeth smile. Fingers trip over rock, brush flower petal. Growler turns nose into flower, breathes in, shudders, purrs.

Florence and I welcome you, they say, red tongue lapping.

Behind Growler, cave floor slopes down, widens into crevasse. Water rushes below, sounds refolding themselves on craggy cave walls, dispersing everywhere.

How do we get out of here? Stevven asks.

Not a sand falls! Growler cries. Oh, I thought we were going to be easy friends.

This looks like it's been trying to fall apart for centuries, Stevven says, examines prison bars.

They grip bars, shake them, hang on them, full body weighing, drop.

Op! Growler dances and laughs. I haven't seen that one before! they say.

Growler runs back to Florence, inhales fragrance, rebounds off cave wall to crevasse edge, swings down. Ten boulderous fingers cling to cliff, then slip away like water drops.

Stevven sets BluBerry by Gino and steps towards crevasse.

Wait, Stevven says.

No! Cullo cries, yanks Stevven back. Monstro, monstro!

I want to watch them for a way out, Stevven says, shakes Cullo off.

Stevven crawls hands and knees to crevasse.

Pale white figure drops into darkness, zigzags walls, marsupial. Growler scurries upstream, ascends again on far darkness, climbs into hole. White thighs and calves, then infinite dank dark.

Shit, I can barely see anything, Stevven says.

Soft thunder, storm generating outside cave.

We're still not far from the surface, Stevven says.

Dudek metroj da roko aŭ du milionoj da metroj, Cullo says. Ni estas kaptitaj! Gino rocks and cries, dwarfs.

We could climb into the crevasse, Stevven says. But the rock is slick. Maybe there is a way out, or maybe we can hide down there until the soldiers think we we're missing.

Eli walks towards purple hues, illusory, ebbing. Florencetendrils texture dark wall like veins or tendons. Eli stares into Florencepetals.

Get away from that, Stevven says.

Eli wiggles from Stevvengrip, sits under Florence, crosses arms around BluBerry.

Keep BluBerry out of it, Stevven says.

Eli hugs BluBerry down tighter.

Florence could be poisonous, Stevven says. Back off!

Ouch! Eli says, slides out grip.

Stevven closes fists over eyes.

Quiet down, Cullo, silenti! Stevven says, spins rage each direction. And Eli, I swear to Good Harvest, keep pushing me and see what happens.

Something inside rocks Stevvenhead, yellow, fearsome. They sit down next to Gino, rest calling, then force themselves back up.

No, Stevven says. We can't get comfortable. Gino, what do you think? Help me out. I can't be the only one thinking here.

Stevvenvoice ripples, going nowhere, echoes ugly.

I didn't think you would give up this easy, they say.

Gino does not stir.

New weeping approaches, fills cave.

Metakid trips across rail lines into chamber. They struggle to feet, fresh blood dotting palms, miserable tears, glasses kinky, foggy, impenetrable. Soldier pushes them ahead towards prison.

Where are we? Metakid says. Please, I can't see! I don't wanna go!

Stevven squats next to cage door, picks up rock.

Soldier unlocks door, shoves Metakid in. Stevven slips rock in open frame as soldier drops door, catching rock and Stevvenfingers. They bite down yelp as door latch turns outside keeper, locks onto nothing.

Yes! Stevven says smallbreath as soldier turns away.

Metakid wails into Cullo, clammy blood hands electrifying, seizing. Please, please, help me! Metakid cries into Culloface. Cullo wrestles them away. Metakid trips, pinwheels arms, sightless.

Haltu! Stop! Cullo reaches out, catches air.

Metakid takes heavy seat into crevasse. Head smacks on back wall, spins them quarterways. Crag strikes jaw. Bloody, silent crumpling, then heavysack sounds, shallow splash.

Cullolegs give, fold and fasten him small like Gino.

Moments suspend, corroborate violence. Eli approaches ledge.

Stevven finds breath. Get away from there, Stevven says, cracking.

Eli looks back at Stevven, looks into crevasse.

Stevven crosses to Eli, pulls them back by shoulder.

Don't touch me!

It's not for your eyes, Stevven says, pain waking.

I want to see, Eli says.

Let me look first.

I can do it better.

What do you mean? Stevven says, massages fingers.

You will get sick, Eli says. You always get sick when people die.

I don't always, and anyways, that is just part of it. I don't want you to see. Mary wouldn't want to you see.

Water changes below.

Stevven and Eli look over crevasse.

Metakid somewhere, camouflaging in dark hoodie.

Pale body emerges from hole in dark, climbs down onto Metakid lump. Growler. Dragging, sloshing, thudding. Cracking, squelching. Growler writhes over Metakid, looks up, sinewy velvet strings dangling from maw. They wave hand, glistening dark wet blood.

Stevven sits, rolls onto back, turns ear to wet rock. Knees drop wide, rubbering.

Flesh tears, sounds painting air entire, violence echoing. Stevven focuses on constellations, cave cricket eyes, draws lines between them, swallows down bile.

You look sick, Eli says.

Lag is wearing off, Stevven says. Things feel again.

Do you want to hold BluBerry? Eli asks.

That would be nice. Thanks.

Stevven reels BluBerry into chest, body itching for Eliembrace.

Tell me what you're feeling, Stevven says, concentrates on Eliface.

I don't know.

Squish, squash. Growler guts Metakid. Feasts.

Stevven hugs BluBerry in tighter, closes eyes. Explain to me what you think is happening down there, they say. What you think they're doing down there.

Eating, Eli says.

Do you understand why I'm sick?

No.

I'm sick because that usually doesn't happen.

But life eats life.

Not itself. Not like this.

BluBerry eats their dead parts. I saw them.

That's different.

Why?

Stevven blinks, tears well. I don't know how to explain.

Eli slumps. I want to go to Apartment, they say.

Bloody appendage erects, grabs ledge rock. Growler leaps from crevasse.

Stevven sits up, rolls tailbone on rock, lungs empty, nerves sparking. BluBerry jumps across uneven surface between Gino and Eli, buries themselves in soil

Don't you touch my Florence! Growler says, slinks towards Eli.

Left, right, Stevven feels for rocks, sharp, bludgeoning things, none.

I like Florence, Eli says, catches tears. I like them.

Don't touch!

I'm sorry!

Eli drops, scoots back to BluBerry.

What's that? Let me see, Growler demands.

Elihand magnetizes to BluBerry, picks them up, presents.

This is BluBerry, Eli says. They don't have flowers.

Growler sheathes teeth inside bloody lips, takes BluBerry in bloody hands. Oh, a new friend! they say.

You can smell, Eli says.

Growler carefully unscrews BluBerrybottle.

Ah! Growler inhales, smiles messy smile.

They set BluBerry on ground next to Florence, clap hands together. Easy friends! they say.

Eli laughs relief. Cries once, wipes face.

BluBerry's not like Florence, Stevven says, winces to upright seat. They need sun.

Growler frowns at Stevven.

How do we get them outside? Stevven asks, trembling like centuries.

BluBerry is sick, Growler says. They're stuck in a cage, like you. See?—Growler crosses floor, inches from Stevvenface, reeks iron.

That's right, Stevven says, shakes, emotions elaborating, sweat. I got the door open. Which way is out?

Hahahaha! Growler grins, teeth coppery. So clever clever clever! But so impatient!

Shut up!—Stevven runs hands through hair, squats before Gino. Get up. It's time to go. I got the door open. We will figure it out as we go. Get up!

Gino slumps like dying.

Fuck! Gino, please.

Nausea kicks, tears come like splinters, sting. Breaths harden, brittle, break. Stevven squats down, laps sulfuric air.

Growler squats down, level to Stevven, pouts. Oh, so sad. UUuahh!

Stevven hands smear face, headache complicating.

UUUUAAAAHH! Growler wails, bloodspit unraveling from bottom lip. What will we do?

Stevven screams and covers face.

Growlerhands rip Stevvenhands away, force eyes. UUUUUUAAAAHH! Dark, enormous eyes reel, terror, two voices, three.

Jittery sounds upwell, adrenaline breaking to fingertips.

Stevven laughs into twisting face, twisting bloody face contorting more, forever. Spittle webs shake, mouth widening and widening, swallowing space, place. Dark glow grows deep within, eclipsing, blinding, bleeding, incomprehensible. Overwhelming swirling weight, unknown boundaries. Stevvenhands grip ceiling floor walls, great directionless skyless earth. Blood rhythm filling inventing weather and beasts, mind growing everywhere all at once, blazing.

WET CHEEKS, SLIME, CAVE FLOOR. Stevven breathes cave soots, trickling water, salts.

Stevveneyes suckle, focus.

Blinking through wetness, Cullo. Cullo rocks Stevven awake.

Tempo por iri, ĉu?

Hands off, Stevven says, rolls onto rocks, sponges more gray, wet grit.

Stevven breathes. Trickle, drop, trickle. Stevven adapts.

Little Elihands cup together before Stevveneyes, part. Cave cricket sits on fingers, fine antennae fishing wide, tasting Elihand. Long, horned femora, hooks, compound eyes, color and color.

It's so much, Stevven says.

They have red dots on their legs, see? Eli says.

Yes, beautiful.

You fell asleep for a minute. Do you feel better now?

I definitely feel more, Stevven says, winces to seat. But Cullo is right. It's time to leave before that cave sicko comes back.

Eli returns cricket to pooling florescent light. Florenceflower swells.

Have they always moved like that? Stevven asks.

Eli looks between Stevven and Florence, nods. Your eyes have adjusted, they say.

We've been here too long. Gino?

Ginohead sinks in thick arms. Sleeves suck away from wrists, exposing wet inflammations.

I didn't mean what I said. I know you haven't given up on anything—Stevven looks between everyone—Where's BluBerry?

Babadadummm! Growler climbs crevasse, one hand wriggling around BluBerry bottle.

Hey! Give—

Growler sets BluBerry in Stevvenhands, capless.

Go right, follow the tracks, climb, Growler says.

What did you do with the lid? Stevven asks.

Hahaha! BluBerry be free! Growler cheers, runs back to Florence.

I feel we were unfairly taxed, Stevven says, examines bloody BluBerrybottle, gnarly bottlecap strap. They sigh.

Cullo, help Gino, Stevven says.

Cullo wraps Gino arm around shoulders, tacks eyes onto Growler.

Stevven edges prison door open, creeaak, wide.

Sentry soldier light blinks, illuminates tunnel, unchanging.

Stupid robots, Stevven says.

One foot up, second, prison break. Stevven wipes dripping eyebrows, watches Soldierlight blink steady.

Right tunnel, right tunnel! Growler sings, dances in Florencelight.

Cullo goes left.

Ni iras dekstren, Stevven says.

Ne. Tiuj estas la direktoj de la diablo, Cullo says looking back. I don't know what is that way.

But you know what is waiting in the one we came from.

Cullo shakes head, relinquishes Gino to air. Parduno, he says.

Stevven waits for Gino to collapse to one side. He does not.

Parduno, Cullo says again, leaves them for light tunnel certain with soldiers.

If he doesn't get past them they'll be after us, Stevven says, turns toward right tunnel, darkness sloshing at *no entry* sawhorse barrier legs. Come on.

Growler smiles gray teeth through bars.

Thanks for your help, Stevven says. And thank you for your light, Florence.

They move into dark dark where garnet sparkles go to sleep.

HOLD ONTO ME, ELI SAYS to Gino.

Stevven reads wall with one hand, places foot after foot on uneven rock, trips. They stand up, wrangle breath. Crickets feather antennae, jump away from searching fingers.

Breath, sniffle, breath.

Gradual curve through rock begins to write Growler, Florence, Cullo, and soldiers away. Water gathers on gentle downslope, swamps shoes.

Snap snap snap! Bullets, snakestrikes whistle off crags, skip water.

Cullo screams. Echoes zip by them and land somewhere in deeper dark, or light.

Stevven nerves sputter, make sloppy steps. Sensation like tripping over intestines. They drop, yelp. One foot dangles into dissolved joint, strange frightful depth.

Both Eli and Gino drag them back.

Blood dots Stevven thigh, streams down into subterranean lakes.

A chimney, Stevven says. Keep your feet to the walls.

Eli and Gino follow, careful slowness keeping up with Stevven easily.

Shouts begin to chase.

Stevven touches rockpile sliding from above. Soft glow sugars limestone ledge some ten meters above, sky.

Looks like we have to climb, Stevven whispers.

I'll go first, Eli says.

Careful.

Eli steps up. Small rock dislodges, splashes.

Careful! Stevven says, raises hands to Eliwaist. Okay. You got this. You're good at this. Just like at Apartment, like the Blind Ghost game.

Eli rises, gray, amorphous along rock, now outside handreach. They disappear from view. Light plays with faint Elishadow. Then shadow takes all.

Scrape, shufflings.

Eli? You out?

I see the sky, Eli says.

Yes, good. Gino, you go. Now!

Soldiers sweep down tunnel, short minutes away.

Gino climbs, slow, feels out solid holds.

Shouts carry closer.

He keeps pace. Stevven pinches rock next to Gino, climbs alongside, wiggles feet down to snug, blistering grip. Gino matches feet, reaches, slug.

Go! Stevven hisses.

Gino rises.

Battering and splashing elaborate, near. Flashlight feeds on rock edges, swells.

Stevven throws arm around sharp sloper. Belly protests against rock. Feet find higher hold.

Hand me BluBerry—Ginovoice startles Stevven to slip down harsh step, bruise knees.

I can't, they say.

You can't climb up with one hand, he says.

Stevvenfoot slides and calf skin tears. Wrists pump fire, fingers swell. Stevven sends wall, matches feet, teaspoon daylight sparkling blood, mud rivering arms.

Toss BluBerry to me, Gino says.

What if you drop them? They'll be lost.

You'll need both hands for the next part.

I can barely see you. They're coming. I see their light.

See me. See these hands. Gino waves, penumbras, blur, buzz.

Stevven kisses BluBerry, breathes in one, two, three.

BluBerry takes off into big dark, maybe hands.

Teeth grind into long silence.

Got them, Gino says.

Stevvenbreath fledges and pushes body up. Rock surface slides like beastbelly under feet. They lean across chasm, rope arms around rock. Two big hands under Stevvenarms hoist them up.

They stand up into cave, light like turmeric, twenty meters across and sloping like funnel up flowstones, portal to outside. Eli crouches on boulder, swaddles BluBerry, wet black hair heavy to toes, eyes dark, large.

Gino crosses to ledge fanatic with flashlight. He lays two big shaking hands onto boulders, sends them down.

Shouts and lights sputter below. Crack, crack, rocks go tumbling. Gino hands ripe, dripping, tip every unsteady rock over edge.

Clonk, scratch, clank.

Shkshkshkshk! Bullets skip and spark, few escaping into top cavern.

Gino heaves, steps back.

You're shot? Stevven asks.

No, Gino says.

Stevven leads bear crawl from cave.


QUIET ROCKS, DEAFENING TREES. SUN like flash bulb, blinding, hollow. Patchwork gray rain clouds, green canopy. Stevvenskin shudders, rejoices.

Gino trudges forward, ahead.

Caw caw caw, tactile crow launches from pine.

Stevveneyes slide off silken feathers to Gino, pulpy, cutting open, wandering away.

If I stop moving now, I won't be able to start again, Gino explains, voice grog.

Okay, Stevven says, wipes hands on grass. Keep North with this rock face. And watch for soldiers. Eli, can you walk?

Eli sniffles, nods, follows Ginosteps.

Ook-up ook-up ook-up! Vireos chatter, dip, distance in West.


IT WAS A SQUIRREL, ELI says.

What? Stevven asks.

Now it's the wind.

Where?

In the tree.

Stevven looks to tree, perception slipping.

I'll hold BluBerry now, they say.


THEY MEET HORSE TRAIL ZIGZAGGING steadily up mountain, slow. Insects carve cities from shit stacks. Trail intersects gravel road, syncline rock wall. They keep to shade side, pass offroad picnic table. Pond. Wet skin splits inside Stevvenshoes.

I'm tired, Eli says.

We can rest at the top, Stevven says. Less mosquitos.

THEY WADE ONTO OVERGROWN OUTLOOK, sit on mossing sandstone boulders. Maple tree clan, twelve generations, cling to bluff. Wisest trees bow, slip roots through limestone, overhanging overhang. Eli slumps down on rock, groans loud, kicks off shoes. Dark brown moist leaf litter respires, rests bare feet.

Stevven kneels at cavity in rock holding water. They scrub hands, arms, sensitive open wounds. They wash until blood stops, submerges BluBerry up to bottle lip. They gather two maple branches with immature leaf swirls, swab soils from bottle walls.

Gino shivers in sun, flutters eyes.

I'm tired, Eli says.

Stevven crosses to young sumac, digs into soil, takes root. They open festering Ginohand, thin fingers, place sumac inside. Gino holds loosely.

Eat this when you can, Stevven says.

They cross to Eli, offer root.

Eli shakes head.

It will help with whatever you're feeling, Stevven says.

I want Mary, Eli says.

Stevven sets root next to Eli. Blackwing, bluedot butterfly touches Stevvenarm, opens, closes wings. Earth magic swirls around them, turning rocks into soldiers, soldiers back into rocks. Stevven dizzies.

I miss being barefoot in Apartment, Eli says.

That was something special, Stevven says, forces wet socks back onto Eli feet. A real luxury.

I don't want to walk, Eli says, kicks Stevvenhands away weakly. Hey, this looks like the tree the Wanderer climbed in the secret night.

Which one?

This one with the golden eye lichen, Eli says, points. Maybe Mama Spider is here, too.

Stevven gazes into alluring bark. They resist sinking into moss, giving up all perceiving body to earth, oak.

Do trees have ears? Eli asks, sniffles.

They sure have something that knows, Stevven says, aches to stand.

Can you tell the Wanderer story?

Only if you keep walking, Stevven says. Help me get Gino moving.

Eli pouts, body complaining, indecisive.

Pee-o-wee, pee-o-wee, wrens say, float overhead. Stevvenhips ache, jealous.

Eli crosses to Gino, takes hand. We have to go now, Eli says, rubs eyes with free hand.

Gino rocks forward, first step like forgetting.


THE WANDERER WAS THIRSTY, STEVVEN says, walks. She followed the river upstream.

What river? Eli asks.

Give them a name.

Michael.

Okay. The Wanderer followed the Michael river until she found a dam. She began to climb the embankment. Rhyzome raced her to the top, and wagged and barked.

What color is Rhyzome?

You already chose Rhyzome's color. They're blue. Do you want to change their color?

Green!

Okay, Rhyzome is a camouflage green. The watchman in an office at the top of the dam leaned out of his window as the Wanderer climbed. He told her that she was trespassing on government property. What do you think she did next?

Um, she invites him to a tea party!

Deer spring across road, white tails exclaiming. Stevven inhales, gathers second wind. Legs assume gangly grace, like limber saplings.

Hello fellow human, do you have hot water for some tea? The Wanderer asked. He was stunned, and a little afraid. He'd never seen someone climb the dam without so much as a wink, much less ask him for tea.

A wink?

A figure of speech. Like how she didn't think too hard about it. She just felt it and did it like the human animal she was. Anyways, he was affected by her. He said he had a coffee machine they could use to make hot water. In the tower there was a simple desk, two chairs. One chair he used to stack his feet on as he watched the cars go by the top of the dam and the water stop on the other side.

Stevven slows, points at pile, rich purple bear scat respiring on yellow road line, full with rain. Beetles roll.

Why do you sit up here? The Wanderer asked the man, taking a chair. Rhyzome sat on the floor at her feet. To keep things moving along, he said. People aren't allowed to stop here and walk the shoulders. This road is too narrow for people and cars.

She could tell he was lonely. Sometimes she shared her animal body with the ones estranged from the earth. She could be falcon, lynx, frog, horse, and many others. They drank tea together, the spirit of the river aching under their feet. If only he was a woman, she thought, the force of our lovemaking could break this dam.

Stevven falls silent, feeling June.


SUGARS STRIKE STEVVENNOSE. THEY KEEP gait, road curving like smile underfeet. They outpace Eli and Gino.

Oh—sound escapes Stevven.

Blackberry bushes swelter, call out over road, vapors begging in yellow sun. Stevven walks into bramble, sharp green poles, takes juices into hands.

Oh, this is good stuff, right here.

They pick out one blackberry and eat. Puckery soapy sweet blast, small skins tearing, flesh giving to bitter seed. Stevven closes eyes, drops to seat, brambles nicking clothes, devours handful, dives in for more.

Above head, painted signs read on pine: *Welcome, willkommen, bienvenido,* אבה דורב, *karibu, ulihelisdi.* Dirt road veers through great blackberry patch into deep forest.

This looks like an old campground, Stevven says. Come over here and eat these with me.

Gino still, silent as dry stone.

Eli squats on haunches in shade, back to berries. Red cheeks, neck. They drop to knees.

Blackberries fly from Stevvenhands. They catch Eli under arms as they sink down.

I don't feel good, Eli says.

I see now.

Can you carry me?

Yes, Stevven says.

Great loud cicada, blackberry juices staining.

G INO, TAKE BLUBERRY, STEVVEN SAYS. Eli, put your arms around my neck.
Stevven gathers Elilegs around waist, stands up. They trudge forward onto camp road, no hands left for blackberries.

There might be someone here who can help us, Stevven says. You think, Gino?

Gino clasps BluBerry to chest, eyes soft, dying.

I hate being the optimist, Stevven says.

Eli slides like wet plaster down back. Stevven hikes them. Legs thrum like sewing machines down gravel roadway. They pass welcome signs into young afternoon shadow.

Chicki tuki tuck, red tanager rustles inside oak.

Steps crunch, crunch. Wind creeps up slope carrying hums, shuffling earthbound beasts, human. Grilling onion aromas spiral into nostrils, stirring focus.

They stop at shelf in road, overlook camp. Dozen patchwork vehicles and vendors populate clearing. Honey bees fly into houses fitting to high suspension vehicle. Crosslegging beekeeper talks to buyer on carpets. Plants fuzz on mobile gardens. People number more than thirty, less than fifty. Third gen solar panels edge clearing, face South, channel light into metal charge station. Electric hum.

Large pavilion backbones market, kitchenette steaming. Tall, white male walks down pavilion steps into light, waving arms. He jogs through market and long picnic tables waving arms, beard curly, head hair wiry, nude except sandals. Arms open as if to embrace, he stops feet away.

Hellooo!—he says, blue eyes jittery—Welcome to Kewee Water Retreat! I'm Jordan, he/him.

Hi Jordan, can we rest here? Stevven asks.

Of course you are welcome, Jordan says. All are welcome always. Is the little one okay?

Fever, I think. Just need a place to rest for the night. I don't have much to give in exchange.

Oh no no no no no. We ask for nothing. Your presence is a gift.

We?

Us! The Retreat! It's always busy during May Eve celebration, but we *always* have room for more. Let's get you settled. What are your names?

I'm Stevven. This is Gino, and Eli, Stevven says, glances at BluBerry secreting inside Ginohands.

He smiles big at Stevven. Nice to meet you all, he says. Did you happen to try the blackberries on the way in?

They were wonderful, Stevven says.

Jordanthroat twitches. Please, come, welcome, he says, smiles, turns to camp. I want to ask the girls if you may use their teepee.

Stevven hoists Eli up, struggles down decline. I don't want to push anyone out of their space, they say.

No worries, they'll be anywhere but their own bed tonight, I know! Jordan says, smiles again, waves to person harvesting basils on green trailer.

Jordan birdcalls to pavilion. Three women giggle to attention at entrance.

Girls, we have some new guests. I'd like to offer them your tent for tonight, if that is alright with you.

Of course, says woman wearing constellations, silver blue hair spinning off into tantalizing crescents.

She winks.

Stevven shudders, looks away to Jordan.

Okay, this way, he says, eyebrows Stevven. I can imagine you might like a wash. Your tent is right next to the creek.

Trail wraps behind pavilion to coniferous slope. Five hexagonal tents anchor to dirt platforms spreading across two foresting acres. Jordan steers towards one on steepest bluff, lush creek one fatal leap below.

Beautiful, Stevven says.

My personal favorite, Jordan says, unzips tent, parts flaps wide.

Stevven and Eli slip inside. Stevven kneels, sets Eli onto cool furs, undoes Elishoes, sets them outside tent.

Gelatinous fairy string lights bisect tent. Drying flower parts bur furs. Stevven picks some stems and petals out, sets them on small wooden stool shoring dozen oils and balms.

Jordan points over Stevvenshoulder to opposite corner, steps one foot inside tent. There's a fan, he says. Some water and a towel. But I'll send someone to bring you a fresh one. We also have a doctor on site if you would like to meet them.

Stevven puts hand to Eliforehead. A doctor would be good, they say.

Stevven twists Elihair away from reddening face. Small chest pumps. Eyes open, see Stevven, close.

I'm going to leave BluBerry in here with you, Stevven says, sets them on stool next to rosemary lotion. I'll be right back.

Stevven brushes Elihair again, realizes tenderness, slips out under Jordanarm. Mesh flaps close. Stevven rezips tent.

I will take you to meet our doctor—Jordan turns to Gino—Some friends have set up a kettle station under the blue tarp. Feel free to brew teas there. We will be eating an hour before sundown, marked by three bells.

Gino sits down on stump facing bluff.

Jordan raises eyebrows at Stevven. Shall we go?

Stevvenhand touches Ginoshoulder. I'll bring you and Eli some things, Stevven says. I won't be gone long.

Gino does not respond.

Jordan leads hike up trail to main camp, long wiry strides.

Gino is normally very friendly, Stevven says, follows. He's an Earther, but an officer at Ducktown cut down his forest. He hasn't been the same.

That is horrible. Horrible what people do to each other—Jordan flicks eyes to Stevven—I think that there are a couple practicing Earthers here with us today. Perhaps we should introduce Gino.

Really?

I believe so.

That's exactly what Gino needs. This is great.

Jordanface suddenly heavy, eyes further.

We appreciate you so much, Stevven says, fetches smile. For the easy welcome, for the place to stay. I would like to help where I can, repay your kindness.

Stevven wrings hands together, reads.

We have many helpers for our May Eve celebration, Jordan says. The best thing you can do for us is rest and keep up the good cheer. We could all use a higher morale these days.

Excuse us, says person crawling out from under pavilion. They drag out lights, parachute cord. Pole meets ground, becomes pentagram. Greenpurple lights flick on, small in daytime. Cushions mountain and sun nearby.

Stevven peers into crawlspace under pavilion. Tools, buckets, rope. Chicken nests in basket.

Jordanface pinches. Oh yes, I forgot, he says. The doctor is organ sharing right now. Unless this was a real emergency, I would hesitate pulling them out.

They're organ sharing?

Jordan points to purple tent in elm shade, zipped tight, private. They will be done by feasttime, he says. You can get their help then.

Jordan!

Someone like stouter, older Jordan calls, swivels through shops towards them. They hip hands, squint frosty eyes, nose hilly, beard square and white.

It's my dad, Jordan explains. Dave. Not doing his job.

We got trouble up on the hill, Dave says, breath short.

And it's following you down here, Jordan says, massages temple.

They want to speak to who is in charge.

Three people in western hats and leather boots stir up topsoil, cut through switchback trail, huff and hustle like canyon river.

Stevven steps into pavilion, shadows.

I told you to wait up there, Dave says to cowboys. I'm bringing him up to talk to you.

But Sweetbuns, the 'nado don't stop just cause you want it to, leader says, polishes grin, long dragon blue hair bouncing. You must be the one with the breeches around here, uh, save for the breeches. Folks call me Cash, zey/zem.

Cash takes Jordanhand. Brisk shake.

Stevven remembers zem.

Welcome, Cash, Jordan says, finds smile. You're here with the jerky exchange?

That's right, zey say. Haven't been here a minute before I'm asked to hide my guns. Your old man here wasn't gonna let us sell til we got our pieces squandered away in that fancy shack o yours.

Yes, this is a gun-free zone, Jordan says. We ask all weapons be shelved at the cabin.

Gun-free? Cash says, laughs. You've seen the kind of vermin crawling around these parts? I'm not just talking about the Chinamen. You've got a bad case of trappers. And a couple of them drones whose got their wires melted in this heat. One detonated next to our wagon on the last hill up here. Lucky we had a spare tire.

Doesn't sound like your gun stopped the drone, with all due respect, Jordan says.

Now, sir, Cash says, steps closer. My team's been trucking our jerky through here since your ass was still bare as a bell, since the Assembly Crash of 2059, and not once have I put my piece away for nobody.

If you would like to sell here, you must check your weapons on the hill—Jordan swallows—You will get them back when you decide to leave.

Cash steps forward to speak, then stops, closes mouth, fire dimming.

Stevven sneaks glance at moongaze from pavilion lounge. Silver hair woman wide eyes Cash like cat.

Alright, then, Cash says. Let's put them away.

She winks at Stevven, spreads arms on couch firs, sparkles toes.

Thank you, Jordan says, breathes.

Yeah, yeah, Cash says, shoos posse back up hill after Dave.

Thank you, and welcome to Kewee Water Retreat! Jordan calls after safe distance, claps hands, whoops relief. Stevven, can I get you a drink?

I'm okay for now, thanks, Stevven says, peels away.

They glance again at mooneyes. They catch up with Cash at top switchback.

CASH.

Zey turn, blue eyes happy fire.

You may not remember—

Hell, if it ain't Stevven! Zey reel Stevven in, hit them with heavy hand. I never expected to see your face again. You look worse for wear, been crawling in the mines?

Yes.

Cash laughs, hits Stevvenback again. You're still the damned funniest, when'd you get here?

Just fifteen minutes ago, Stevven says, walks up hill together.

They take your gun, too? Hey now Stevven, this is Brownie, and this little bitty one is Bingo. We deputized him crossin Arkansas. Fellas, Stevven's a friend from some years ago.

Brownie dips black gambler hat, Bingo howdys.

Nice to meet you, Stevven says. How's the jerky business?

Fine, fine. We're trying to set up a permanent operation in this side of the country since it's so popular, but we're having a little trouble with the madcows. I thought the badlands were lawless til we tried things out here. It's just another kind of something in the jungle. Can't get all ten toes on the ground before somethin jumps you like a fire ant, or a coked up ape. Had any trouble out here?

Yeah, we got a shakedown from the Liberation Army. Escaped today.

Cash blinks at Stevven. How do you keep such a straight face all the time?

Zey pinch Stevven cheek, fish out smile.

Dave hurries ahead to gun cabin, unfastens lock on door.

Look at this total nugget of a man, Cash says, surveying. I can crack that thing easier than a biscuit.

The man or the lock?

That lock's nothin but a hog egg. This little go-away-gun operation is gonna fail within the week. You know why? Cause here kids fly little attack drones with bombs strapped to their little robot coochies and turn squirrels to dust. I've seen it.

Cash draws pistol: Chinese Liberation Army. 40 cal.

Check this out, zey say. I lifted a whole rack of these from an unstationed camp at the mines. No offense, but you reek of the very place.

Why would they leave all these?

I'll raise you ten pounds of maw's pumpkin pie it was them same kids who shoot eyes out of squirrels. They're wilder than Apache.

Isn't your mom Apache?

And my paw Chinese, Cash says. Turned out by their own people and then by their new people. One of them oilmen shot my paw a couple weeks back because they thought he was with the Chinamen. Like they didn't even see the oil sash. He was comin in as representative of the Midwestern clan. And they shot him.

I'm sorry.

He's alright now, just out one leg. I'm tellin you, things are twisted swampside.

Cash collects guns from Brownie and Bingo.

Hell, Stevven, what are you doing in these parts? I thought you were living it up in the South Carolinas with uh, what's her name?

June.

Right. Junebug! Yow!

She's dead.

Dave takes guns from Cash and friends, hangs them on rack inside cabin door.

My condolences, Cash says. How'd she die?

Corporate interest. It's a twisted place, like you said.

You still workin with—

No. I'm just working to stay alive now.

Ain't we all, Cash says, turns to friends. Let's go on and get the shop set up, give her tired wheels a break. Down this same trail I reckon.

I can help, Stevven says.

Alright then. We got a funny wheel on this side so why don't you stand right along here and make sure she don't tip. This road's a battle zone.

Cash removes hat, douses face in water.

You okay? Stevven asks.

I've just hit a sort of spell. Not feelin my right self.

Yeah, Cash, what was that back there? Brownie says returning from pee break, dusts dustless cap.

What you mean?

You just let them take our pieces.

I told you to leave it, Cash says, unhitches jerky trailer from truck. I ain't got to explain everything to y'all.

Cash salutes to Dave rocking on cabin porch chair, leads wagon down trail.

Brownie, you know Stevven was running the food exchange over at the old school up in Sewanee since they were itty bitty, Cash says. That's where we met. Let's see, you couldn't have been more'n twelve years old when you were directing the whole operation. Natural leader. How old are you now?

Twenty two.

Time flies, Cash says.

I'm trying to get back to Sewanee, Stevven says, helps trailer around first bend.

You know it ain't a school no more, Cash says.

I suspected that much. Have you been recently?

Oh some time since. Heard from a friend they went private.

Private?

Not like corporate, just—Cash sweeps hand through air—skimmed like cream off the public radar. Last I checked, full of no-bull-shitting young firecrackers like you.

What are they doing?

I reckon they're doing what they can, with the facilities they got now. Sciencing.

Got any water? Stevven asks.

They jog up to front, take water skin from Cash.

You come in with anyone? zey ask.

Just Gino and Eli, Stevven says between drinks. Wouldn't have stopped over here if Eli wasn't sick.

They family?

I don't know.

They payin you to escort them? I always said you'd be a good guide through these parts.

Stevven shakes head.

Just the folks you get roped up with, then.

Yeah, they were living at the same place, working the garden, helping out. I don't think I've spent many days without them, actually. In the last two years I've been at Apartment.

These are the folks you've been chowin with every night for the past two years, and you don't call them family?

Stevven shrugs.

Don't surprise me none. You've always been scared of intimacy. Til Junebug came along.

How about we set the wagon over here? Stevven says, points to nearest open gravel in market.

Fine spot, zey say. We'll ease her right next to the cute honeybee.

I should go check on Eli, Stevven says.

Say, what time is supper?

Hour before sundown, I think. They said they'd strike the bells three times.

Damn hippies dropped all their pocket watches? Cash says, turns to first customer, renews charm. Your fine highness fancy a jerky?

Mobile vendor catches Stevvengaze. Sign hangs around neck: *Save the sun for plants, ditch Solar!* Three plastic jugs full with coiled tubes jostle around in free hand.

Howdy-do! they say, hairy, sweaty. I would like to be the first to introduce you to the mosquito generator, the nomad's first choice for energy. Bait the trap with some yeast and sugar mix. And behold! The trapped mosquito flies down the tube lined with the energy-collecting membrane. And bam! Charges all your small electronics.

Stevven looks from jugs to vendor. Electricity from mosquitos? they ask.

Ah, you want to know how it works! But of course! First layer of the membrane is composed of tiny drum-like cells that vibrate to the mosquito's buzz.

The second layer is a piezoelectric material that generates a current from the first. Less than ten mosquitos are needed to charge your small devices.

I don't have any small devices.

We can fix that! My sister store has all the gadgets you could need.

This is really cool. But I'm okay for now.

Tell your friends!

Stevven circles to purple tent. Small glow inside. They finger joint in fabric walls, widening small crack, peep in.

Low light room, candles. Two people hold hands across wicker table, eyes closing. Jar between pulses, full, red, veiny. IVs string from jar organ to arms, one blood, one heart, two people. Stevven feels private membrane breaking and escaping. They back away just as monitor rises from stool in corner, shoos them out.

Face hot, Stevven stumbles into constellation woman, spills drinks.

I'm sorry—Stevven watches dark juice seep into ground—I was just looking for the doctor.

I can see that, she says, crescent smile. I have your drink, most of it, anyways.

Oh, I, uh, thanks—Stevven takes small pottery in hand.

How is the little one?

Oh, Eli, yeah, they'll be okay I think. I better get back—

That's good to hear, she says, looks across courtyard. Have you ever seen anything like it?

Stevven follows gaze. Things, and people things make, people, and things people make stacking on rugs, changing hands. Hands change hands. Company, bargains. Samples and innovations. Humidity sticks like life to them all.

Love, beauty, fertility, she says, voice molasses. See the band getting set up down there?

Stevven searches downslope through trees. At creek, they recognize big excavator, water wheel turning with falling water.

I can't remember the last time I heard live music, Stevven says.

Where could you have possibly come from, then?

She chuckles and sips from drink.

Off the coast of Charleston, Stevven says. One of those tidepool places people wash up to. It's not really on any map you can find today.

What do you call it?

Apartment. The roof we called Garden.

Stevven reaches for BluBerry in pack. No pack. No BluBerry.

You okay? she asks.

Yeah, it's just been a long day. I should probably go check on Eli.

Let me send one of the girls to check up on them. It sounds like you've been traveling with them a long time. You deserve a break.

How do you know?

Signs of wear written all over you, she says, smiles. That's not to say you're not attractive.

Stevven crinkles dirty cave shirt.

I guess I really haven't had an afternoon away from Eli since... Since we met.

Take a walk with me? I want to show you my favorite place.

Is it far?

The best places are never far.

Stevven sniffs drink, rich and dark.

Blackberry wine, she says. Though I can tell by the edges of your lips you already had a taste of the blackberries.

Stevven wipes lips. I'm a mess, they say.

The spot is this way, she says, laughs.

Stevven sips wine. Eyelids flutter, ecstasy.

Stevven follows blue constellations swirling on skin, body like photo negative, phantasmic.

What is your name? Stevven asks.

Teles, she speaks over shoulder.

Tikettle tikettle tikettle, thrush song. Green leaves turn, play with wind, sunlight, laughter.

What is this place? Stevven asks.

Teles scales schist stairs on trail upslope. She turns, looks out, rests chin atop wide foresting world.

It's my home.


DAPPLING TRAIL ROUNDS ROCK LIKE tightening bow, creek slipping further down. Trees shift from scaly bark to lenticel, coniferous to deciduous, fruiting, blossoming. Cherry, glossy citrus leaves, orchard. Perfumes turn through body like deep water currents.

Teles slips off sandals, sets them on top aging stump beside three other pairs.

Stevven peels off muddy shoes from heel to toe, drops them, sighs, massages feet into cool, soft foot trail.

Pomegranate pollens sparkle, fairy dust. Green and green.

Teles smiles at Stevven. Lemons, she says, touches green orbs clinging to twigs. Stevven runs finger over reptilian skin.

Hybrid? They ask.

I don't know what kind specifically, she says, but they're not GMO.

You say it like GMO is evil.

They are, disrupting the natural rhythms of lover Earth.

In the way they've been commercialized?

GMO's are toxic in every way.

We have always touched the genes of foods as they have touched us. We make each other.

Not in an unnatural lab with white suits, Teles says. You see fruit doing that to us?

Stevven smiles quiet, traces BluBerry inside waxy leafface. They look at Teles.

Is this the spot you wanted to show me? they ask.

Teles smiles, tethers Stevven deeper. She slips down path between apple trees.

So, does Jordan run this place? Stevven asks.

What an interesting question, she says, parts branches in path. In a way. He bought this land when the park service died out. It's over 200 acres. He made a vow to protect this land, use it in a more natural way, restore it.

Restore it to what?

To how it was before colonists ruined it, she says. We're almost there.

Path crests to great beech tree shade and fescue grasses. Two nude humans lounge on platform, rag rugs, fading quilts, weave each other floral hoops and hair garlands. They wave, Teles waves back.

Teles stoops under low twisty elm branch, walks narrowing path to old cabin, purple wisteria rewilding doors and windows. Sun stretches out sinking doorframe, illuminates fine white sands at foundation, casts ceremonious circle around cabin.

Is this where you sacrifice me to the Great Harvest? Stevven asks.

Teles laughs, disappears into doorless cabin.

Trip, trop, trip. Water creeps somewhere nearby.

Are you coming in? Teles asks.

Stevven peeks in head first.

Two collapsing walls open to vista, sun and bluff. Festival prepares at creekbank below. Spiderling trails shine. Fox darts into foliage.

Teles pats seat on couch facing overlook.

Stevven sighs onto cushion, soft, rosewood, relinquishes power from flesh legs to wood legs. They bring wine to nose, sip.

You look tense, Teles says. You're safe to relax.

Stevven arms disobey mind, sink like silts. Jaw slackens. They laugh.

I could fall asleep right now, Stevven says.

You're welcome to, Teles says. I'll guard you as you sleep.

What kinds of things do you have to guard me from out here?

Oh, nothing really, just saying you can rest easy.

Those men with the guns? Stevven asks, sips, slips further into cushion.

Where? On the hill? Oh, they're just there to make sure no one brings guns into the camp.

Right, Stevven laughs. Keep your secrets then.

Stevven drinks.

Teleshair swings to one side, grey eyes strong soft. I'm glad you're here, Stevven, she says. You're a special one, I can tell.

Cup stops at Stevvenlip. They upright comfortable seat.

I'm curious what you mean, Stevven says, swirls wine in cup, blackberry grains kicking up and settling.

This camp, Teles says, it's not normally so full of people. We can't support this many mouths with this amount of land. We are forced to be very selective about who can stay beyond the festival days each month.

I should be getting back to Eli.

Maybe you need a break from Eli. Stevven, trust me, I know how hard it is raising a child. We all love kids, but it's too much to raise them by yourself. Humans are finally starting to remember what polyparenting is.

I'm not Eli's parent. Things are just different right now. Their mom was taken by the police. I've never had to take responsibility for anyone like this.

But that's what I'm saying. Who's telling you to take responsibility? The patriarchy. You're doing a brave thing, but this isn't the only way.

Why are you so concerned? Stevven says, sits up straight, prepares sore feet to walk again.

Teles meets them, puts hand on Stevvenshoulder. We know they're nonperson, she whispers. They're in danger.

Stevven backs outside Telesreach. So you want to protect Eli by inducting them into your little commune family? they ask.

You and Eli both, Teles says, smiles. I can feel that this is right. The moment you came down the hill.

You don't know us, and we don't know you. And we're just staying for the night, besides.

Dong, dong, dong.

Dinner, Teles says, looks out and long over land.

STEVVEN STANDS FIRST, LEADS OUT cabin, orchard. They wrestle soggy shoes onto feet, descend into center camp, silence simmering, pushing Stevven inward. They search for break.

Fire, garlic, and splitting fruit press through understory, melt nose and mouth. Stevven barely hears feeding woodpecker two heads above them, thwak, thwak, thwak. They hurry towards dinner.

Market gives way to two long tables, people finding seats. Colorful table cloths float local dishes, green lettuces in seven salad bowls, steam sailing from pottery.

Stevven joins washbowl line, soaps up. Teles picks up conversation with young teenager blinking same misty violet eyes.

Stevven shakes hands dry, headache on horizon. They cross and squeeze into seat diagonal from Cash, listeners shoring zem like ocean.

Cash wheels hands around head, ropes people into story.

So my paw saw to it that nobody messed with Thibaut the friendly bull. Thibaut would spend the rest of his days rolling around in that tall grass, security cameras always watching over him like angels. Whatever came knocking, the only bullshit my paw paid mind to was, in fact, some very special bull shit.

Cash winks at Stevven. Laughter tumbles all around. Stevven smiles.

Tink, tink tink, Jordan clinks glass, stands. Hello, thank you everyone. Thank you!

Pain rocks behind Stevveneyes, ricochets down spine. Stevven blinks through swelling eyes, searches for Gino and Eli through wetness.

We are so happy you are here to celebrate May Fest with good food and fun from our lover, Earth, Jordan says. This year we have received many gifts from her. Though, we have also had continued trouble with the forces fighting against her. The drones, the armies, and the lost ones. Thank you for your perseverance so that we can take pleasure together again.

Stevven turns in seat, browses faces on other tables. Teles winks, shivering Stevven fierce.

You have all brought something to contribute to our celebrations, Jordan says. Look what we can create when we all work together, and when we make love, not war, to Earth, when we worship her sun and caress her sweet waters and give ourselves abundantly!

Whoops and whistles.

Cash rolls eyes, raps fork and knife, stirs giggles from enamoring neighbor.

I know I am between you and the food, Jordan says, ticks eyes to Cash. So I just want to say thank you. This space has been a dream of mine for as long as I can remember. And Teles, we all know we wouldn't still be here without you. Enjoy! Thank you everyone. Thank you blackberries. Thank you!

Jordan falls into seat like he can take no more steps. Teles squeezes Jordanarm, whispers affirmation. He dabs sweat from forehead, nods.

Blackberry canes bloom in colorful glass vase sitting high at table head, bones and talismans surrounding. Lover Earth.

Stevven, Cash says, dollops generous potato salad onto clamshell plate. If I didn't know better, I think water makes these folks really wet. Ha!

Stevven accepts turkey from neighbor. Do you know if there are extra plates?

No, there should be enough plates set out for everyone, neighbor says. I made sure.

My friends are not here, Stevven says. I want to take them some food.

Oh, you are the one with the sick child. I think the girls have been checking up with them.

What? Which girls? Is Gino still with them?

Gino? I haven't heard that name.

He's probably isolating himself, grieving, Stevven says, piles plate with double servings. I'm taking this to him now.

Weakness bends eyes. Stevven shakes head, drops plate on table, slops jello tower onto paisley flower table cloth.

Are you okay? neighbor asks.

Stevven meets neighboreyes, violet moons. You have the same eyes, Stevven says.

You should eat, they say. It will make you feel better.

Stevvenhands move, shovel potatoes onto fork, fork into mouth. They eat fresh vegetables, cut into savory eggplant flesh. Stomach fills, something swims inside.

WE ARE HUNGRY, SO WE eat.

Stevven reels back, fights us. They look out beyond feast.

Gino. Gino up, walking. Gino walks, passes pavilion, dinner tables, eyes far, far. He walks to Western hill, wounding, soul bleeding out each step. He stops, faces sunset.

Stevven strains to see Ginoface, edges blurring, Gino like gravestone.

Gino, Stevven chokes.

Hands slap Stevvenback, launch food from windpipe. Stevven stands for breath, life, and Gino.

Sit, sit, rest, people say.

Hands guide Stevven into seat, impossible gentle tide.

Gino lingers before thick trees, sunning nakedness.

What are you doing? Stevven asks, no sound coming. What is happening?

Stevven looks at hands, unstirrable.

We take Stevven together, together again. We eat.

You alright there? Cash says.

I can't move, we say, eat garlic butter cream corn chicken, beans, squash tomato. I can't—our chest swells, moves like lead worms.

What you want me to do for you? zey say, set meat knife to plate.

Gino's over there. Can you tell him to turn around?

Cash turns, looks behind zem to western trees. Searches, finds Gino shrinking away.

Oh, that your fella?

Get him, please, we say, sink deeper.

Cash furrows, stares at plate.

I can't, we say.

You won't?

I can't, we say.

You feel it, too?

Gino walks into forest. Going. Gone!

Dark wine, reflections, eyes, visions compounding.

We are thirsty. We drink.

You should slow down or you won't be able to dance, we say.

We wipe lips. Burp, laugh.

Why do I feel like I'm still eating?

Because some of us are still eating.

I can taste vinegar still.

Yes, me too.

Your eyes are purple.

Yours are too.

I feel light. Should we dance?

Yes.

I hear the drum.

Yeah doggy.

We step away from table human by human and walk downslope, form lines down lanternlight path. Sun oranges and pinks and grays. We reach embankment, box drum, strings, synth.

Artificial lights and colors break dusk. We sit on log and sand. We sweat, dance, sweat, strip. Copper, amps spark, strings gather, bloods blend.

We spin round and round, light.

Tents ebb on high slope. Gino. Eli. BluBerry.

Brow sweats, skin, changing inside and out, woody smoke flavors rising. Stevven pulls away from us. We reach for them.

Beech tree branches brush stars, dancing, singing. Water cascades blue and red, violets, gold from stage lights. We cheer.

They're cheering for us, Teles says.

Stevven sways with her.

Tawny and fawn skin melt into each other, hair turns in air. Damp silver wisps cling to Telesback as she spins, eyes Stevven, enchants, with but apart, above.

Stevven gapes, bare chest heaving.

Teles pulls us into dance, drum and tambourine striking like thousand matches. Sandy soils kick up, kiss ankles. Locking fingers, breath full. Frolicking round and round, clapping. Twirling animal bodies.

Thieves take one from us. Terror skips like stone through dance, ripples, becomes.

Supercharge spin ricochets Stevven from dance. They hit tree, tumble, rock with laughter in mud, slowly siphoning breath for voice. They laugh, half with us, half without, laugh at dark gaping mouth holes, joysound, lusting, reveling faces. Light runs down throats like Ducktown mines, teeth blackberry, blood, Growler.

Stevven watches dancers carousel, glitter losing gold. Owl hoots and breaks world like dark flower.

Gino. Eli. BluBerry.

Stevven crawls backwards, breaks through leaves, faster, runs with trees, up.

Trees lead Stevven into clear, light pentagrams and wet, writhing flesh. Red bodies blaze, moan, orgasm. Our arching, swelling, panting pulls Stevven.

Stevven resists. Hand brushes Stevvenankle as they crumble into tears inside dark again, trail past pavilion to tent. Stevven bristles against colossal roaring creek, night mist, pores open wide.

Sobbing, trembling, they find tent, fumble for zipper. Stevven falls inside, lands hard, rezips tent behind them.

Eli? Eli, I'm sorry. Stevven cups Eli, huddles, makes constellations.

They fear. They pull at fur, soft, studding dirt, soft, old sweet musk.

Perspiration runs Eliforehead, mats hair. Stevven gently rakes strands away from eyes.

Eli?

Small moan.

Hey there, Stevven says, tucks Elihand close to body.

Elilashes quiver but do not open.

I'm so scared, Eli. I don't know what was happening. Something in the wine. Blackberry gods. They made me eat. They made me dance. I got away. I was going to bring you some food, I promise. But they kept making me do things.

Elilashes quiver. Stevven?

Yeah?

Where's Mary?

I don't know where she is but she's thinking of you.

Do we have to keep walking?

Stevven ties fingers into Elifingers, holds them under snotty chin, cries.

Just focus on resting tonight, okay? I won't leave you, again. I won't.

Stevven quiets, massages Elipalms with thumbs.

Are you drinking water? Stevven asks, feels for glass on nightstand, knocks over mason jar, wets furs. Shit. It's like I'm learning to walk again. Shit.

Small water swishes inside glass.

Drink this for me please, Stevven says, supports Eli head with shaky hand. Then I'll let you sleep.

Eli drinks.

That's good. Good job. Nothing for more now. No more.

Stevven sets glass on table, cocoons Eli, fetal, finds Elihands, strokes them.

DARK.

Light.

Black hair. Clammy, dirty feet.

Cicada.

Amp fire.

STARS.

River hushes. Juniper shushes.

What are you doing here?

You're gonna be okay, baby, June says.

Wait. June. Wait.

Elms crackle.

Moisture dews.

Moth, greening. Worms, swimming, tug inside skin. Veins. God lives in blood, rhizomes, leaves and tongues.

WATER PEBBLE GELS MESH WALL, rainbow swirling inside.

Easy, easy up.

Thighs alight, calves reel. Paddle one foot, other.

Hand to Eliforehead. Warm, not hot, fever breaking into pieces.

Stevven panics atop next inhale. BluBerry?

Hands read every inch around nightstand, frantic, feeling for bottle, dirt. Stevven searches around Eli, under blankets.

BluBerry going, gone.

Fingers rake tent zipper. They stand up outside tent, squint through noonday forest, rushing creek, thrushing birds.

Sitting stump swells dark soft wood, forests mosses and lichen. Hands read every inch around stump, frantic, feel for bottle, dirt, nothing. Stevven circles, then circumferences wider. They sweep slope towards creek, overturning leaves, hard rocks. Hands and knees and feet zigzag, thrash about wetly.

Fuck!

Stevvenbreath jogs. They drop shorts and pee, watch Western trees cast shadow over trail, think.

Long pink neck, black bill, bird. Flamingo condenses on foggy slope. Knobby legs ginger forward. One foot raises. They stop and look, sideeye hens working around web feet. They walk, evaporate into trees.

Stevven wrings eyes, searches for creature, absurd pink question mark without answer.

STEVVEN HIKES UP TRAIL TO pavilion, furious as bear mother.

Dink yo ti, Towhee calls from pentagram string lights above sloppy cushions. They flicker away as Stevven storms, walks up steps into pavilion. Two crocheters crochet on couches.

Where's Gino? BluBerry? Stevven asks. Where's the big guy who looks like he should have a beard? And the odd looking plant in a bottle? Know them?

Crocheters look at each other, shake heads.

Lit lanterns hang on each tall hardwood post. Hodgepodge candles drip, form rainbow stalagmites on floor. Stevven kicks, shatters one.

Where's Jordan? Teles?

Laughter. Girls giggle, river through sleepy market with water bowls, rags, herbs in string.

Stevven jumps from pavilion, intercepts them.

Oh, good morning, front girl says. We're going to check up on the little one. We made some balms and tea.

Where's Teles?

Are you okay?

Stevven hits water bowl from girlhands. She stumbles back, gapes. Other girls net arms around her.

Where's the plant? Stevven demands. Where's BluBerry?

Blackberry?

No, the one that was in the tent!

Oh, the one in the waterbottle? smallest girl says. They were looking a little cramped. So we repotted them.

You did what?

There, in the pavilion, she says, points timid finger.

I was just—Stevven runs back up steps, scans couches, concerning faces.

Stevven spins to kitchenette, to shrub and herb families in pots. BluBerry, sizing to two year old deciduous sapling, nestles inside green cousins.

I didn't recognize you, Stevven says, kneels before them, rests hand to chest.

Thick woody stems raise plump fruity leaves. Stevven touches nose to leaves.

You like it out here, Stevven says. June would be so happy.

Stevven tugs leaf to lips, teeth, tongue. Sweet, acidic, healthy.

Now how are we going to get you out of here? they ask.

Stevven lifts BluBerry by brown plastic pot. Leaves fill face.

Not like that, they say, set BluBerry back down.

Stevven looks out pavilion. Girls gone. Market lulls in noonday heat, unknown moods eclipsing. Stevven shivers.

First things first, Stevven says, pats BluBerry soil, hurries out pavilion. We're done being fucked with.

Stevven jogs trail to gun cabin, steep uphill. More flamingos preening feathers. They pay no mind to Stevven.

Dave rocks in cabin porch chair, rifle across lap.

You're the guy who guards the guns? Stevven asks.

I don't remember you checking one in, he says, puckery skin swallowing blue eyes.

It's a soldier pistol. Branded Chinese Liberation Army. 40 cal. Maybe.

You hardly look fit to handle a weapon.

Just give me my gun. You know which one it is. Cash checked it in yesterday.

I am not handing out guns to hot heads.

And if I take it from you? Stevven steps up to deck.

I'd rather not shoot a lady, Dave says.

I don't have any other choice. I'm leaving this place and I need a gun.

Dave flips gun in lap, finger soft on trigger. If you want to be stupid, go right ahead, he says.

Stevven presses hands to head.

We invite. We invite. Thoughts pass light between us. They grow heavy.

I hear your will. Hear our will.

I am under strict orders, Dave says.

Dave will not hurt us. He will not hurt us.

We turn door handle.

Dave eyes us, stonehard.

He will not hurt us.

We enter cabin. Overhead light buzzes, flies tripping all over. Stevven wriggles free from us.

They step to hooks on wall, large semiautomatic with red strap, war machetes. On floor, stolen Chinese Liberation Army pistols reek metals. Stevven collects one pistol, releases magazine under overhead light, checks chamber, mostly full. They replace magazine, step outside.

They stare at Dave. Dave stares at Stevven.

I disagree with the way Jordan has been treating the folks coming through here, he says. He's a good boy. It's the devil woman, learning the secrets of the blackberries, playing mind tricks with him and the lot of us who have complete rights to these parts.

So it's the blackberries doing this?

We didn't have a problem with the special berries til she showed up. She knows the secrets and teaches them to the other girls. Does what she wants with the rest of us.

What else do you know about Teles?

You aiming to shoot her?

It depends.

I ain't ever believe in Lucifer magic til I saw it juggled between her hands. Guns don't work on her.

What?

The guns. They don't work on her.

What do you mean they don't *work*?

Caw, caw! Crow drops from hickory. Lichen twigs sprinkle Stevvenhead.

What works, then?

You'd know better than me, witch.


STEVVEN SKIDS DOWN TRAIL, STIRS hens into feathers and clucks.

Hey, you, Stevven says, startling nearest human. Have you seen a tall Earther, but without a beard?

Naw man, I'm sorry. Good luck. Woah, that's a gun.

Stevven flags down doctor in long net shawl stooping next to pavilion. Doctor looks up from forage basket.

I'm looking for a giant man, long hair, no beard, Earther, Stevven says. Have you seen him?

Doctor opens mouth, maybe to speak.

Good morning, says cosmic voice behind Stevven.

Stevven turns, gunhand tightening.

Relax, Teles says.

Thank the Good Harvest my mom taught me how to use one of these, Stevven says. Where's Gino?

Teles steps closer. Who?

Stop, Stevven says, levels gun.

Teles moonbeams. Relax, she says.

We relax some.

This place is a great bend in the river, Teles says. Sometimes it carries sand here to build the embankment. Sometimes sediments pass by, destined for another part of the river, or the sea.

Where. Is. Gino?

Don't be afraid of the tide, Teles says, reaches, gestures in deep time. Let it wash over you freely.

Gun grows, weighs. Stevvenmuscles fight, sight gun on Teles. They want to melt, merge, become.

Teles smiles and cocks head, looks beyond Stevven.

Hi little one, she says. Feeling better?

Eli? Stevven says, spins around.

Hair moist black, eyes gaping, mouth tight, feet bare.

You said you weren't going to leave, Eli says.

I didn't. I, I was looking for BluBerry and Gino. I was coming back. I promise.

Eli blinks. Where's Gino?

I don't know—Stevven sores eye on Teles—I'm trying to find out.

Where's BluBerry? Eli asks.

Up there, on the pavilion.

Come, Eli says.

I'm in the middle of something.

Only the beginning, Teles says, dreamily.

Shut up. I have the gun.

You sound like a man. Don't be so silly. There is no real power there. Now go on, see BluBerry.

Teles palms push air like two moons, move Stevven.

Eli grabs Stevvenhand, carries momentum into pavilion. They stop all three together before BluBerry.

They're so happy! Eli says, runs hands up and down BluBerry.

Stop fighting for control, Teles says in Stevvenear.

Two giant waves smother heat into Stevvenarms. Gun drops into Teleshand.

I'm going to set this over here, she says, places gun on side table.

We drop tear.

Sit, she says.

We sit on couch across from crocheter, jaw slack. Crocheter bundles yarn and hooks, hurries away. Eli brings BluBerry leaves, sits on Stevvenlap.

So yummy! Eli says. They will make you feel better.

Eli sets leaf in Stevvenmouth. We chew, juices scintillating tongue. We close eyes.

I know you know, weasel! Cash yells.

Cash chases Jordan down to honeystand in market, grabs Jordanarm.

Cash! Stevven yells.

Relax, Teles whispers.

Cash looks around, sights Stevven in dark pavilion. Oh, hey there pup, zey call. Wild night, huh? Find your friend? I bet we can crack this one open and find out.

Cash jostles Jordan, drags him to pavilion. Jordanface streaks red, tears wet. He mumbles, shivers, grieving not unlike Gino.

Cash frowns at Teles. Pretty lady, you know how to crack this crazy? Or are you a toad-swallower too?

Let go of him, Teles says.

Cash furrows eyebrows, loosens hand on Jordan. Hell, I might just, zey say. Hey, that ain't my gun you got there?

Shhh—Teles sweeps into Cash, sits zem on couch like sleeping spell.

Cashhead drops on Stevvenshoulder. Oh, hell, zey mumble.

Teles peels Jordan aside, speaks harshly into ear. Jordaneyes puff red, sleepless. He groans.

I almost had him talking, Cash says.

I want to whisper, too, Eli says, lies across Stevven and Cash.

I've been hammering him all morning about Brownie, Cash says.

What happened to Brownie? Stevven asks.

Do you want to eat BluBerry? Eli whispers to Cash.

What happened to Brownie?

Someone took him. Stole him. If Jordan didn't, I know he knows who. Fuck, how come we can't move? And how come this little bit here weigh two tons?

She's the one doing this to us, Stevven says. Teles.

Teles pinches Jordanmouth, sits him in armchair. She dusts hands, closes eyes, gathers breath.

There, settled, my little sand mites. You three have caused quite the ruckus.

Excuse me, Eli says, crosses to Jordan. Have you seen Gino?

Jordanmouth pulls down, head rolls up, groans.

Speak, Stevven says. Speak, we say.

Silence.

Speak!

It wasn't always like this, Jordan says. It wasn't so many.

Teles flames at Stevven. You don't get to tell him what to do, she says.

We listen, pry chains. We release Jordan.

The trappers, Jordan says, moans. They wanted Eli. I couldn't give them another child, once you saw what they do—Jordanface pinches, trembles. So they took many others. Too many to hide. Everyone knows. The festival, it is ruined.

The festival is not ruined, Teles says. Just you, pig.

The trappers took Gino? Stevven asks.

I don't know, Jordan says, crumbles. Probably. Yes!

Eli crashes into Stevven.

Where's Gino, they ask, worry eyes.

We search answers in Teles.

You already know, Teles minds to Stevven. You just can't admit it to yourself.

We ache, we know.

The trappers took him like they took Brownie! Cash says, teeth gritty.

This is where all your hypnotism comes in, to prime the victims? Stevven asks. Were you planning to hand me over to them too?

Teles blinks. Yes, she says. But you returned to your tent. I didn't want to lead them to the child.

Stevven cups Eli face, tears brinking. Help me up, they ask.

Eli pulls Stevven to standing.

Sit, Teles says.

Stevven stands.

What is happening to our heads? Stevven asks.

Funny, you don't even know. You don't deserve the power of your body. You hide it and hate it yet you abuse its power.

Stevven shoves Teles aside, takes gun from table.

The blackberries have a parasite, Teles says, swallows, steps back. It makes you more suggestible.

To you?

Yes, especially to females. It subjects you to what everyone else around you is compelled to think or feel. You and Cash will never be in your same mind again. And if you fight it, it will eventually kill you.

Jordan rolls and moans, delirious, blind in armchair.

We're leaving, Stevven says.

Teles nods.

Tell us where the trappers are, Cash says, pin on couch.

Yeah, Stevven says.

South, to the palm factories, then west, for cow biz, Teles says. They could hardly make up their minds, though.

Now release zem, Stevven says.

Teles crosses arms over chest, closes eyes.

Cash rockets up, shedding chains, dizzy. I ought to—

She's telling the truth, Stevven tells Cash. This is all she knows.

Cash licks long lips, seals them into straight line, crosses to Stevven. I'll take my gun now, zey say.

Stevven hesitates.

What, are you buddy buddy with her now?

I want the gun, Stevven says.

Come on, now, pup. You ain't studying to be a half-wit, I know. Give me the gun, and let's go get our men!

Teleseyes twinkle at Stevven, sits hands gracefully, resolutely over stomach. Yeah, better go get them, she says.

Stevven hands gun to Cash.

Cash exhales, checks chamber, readjusts hat. Gonna go pick up the rest and start the truck, zey say.

Cash jogs into sun, cuts through switchbacks uphill.

Gino wouldn't just leave, Stevven says, turns to Teles. The trappers must have taken him. I know him better than you.

You know him better than you think, Teles says.

What are you going to do to Jordan?

I'm so tired of all this talking—Teles touches fingers to head, closes eyes—Feel the tide, the one voice washing between us, washing over all our intonations. Making all unsecret, except what we womankind can bury in the womb. Do you hear it?

Waters rise, filling chalice. Frogs croak underskin, driftwood bones budding. We ripple, spread.

ELI TUGS ON STEVVEN. STEVVEN shudders, returns.

Are we going to get Gino? Eli asks.

Yes, Stevven says, looks for Teles.

Teles going, gone. Jordan gone. Light prisms dangle beside entry, tilting after some presence, going, gone.

Someone cries on stool in market, hands contorting over face. Southwestern turquoise beads chatter against long nipples, stir mud from soil and tears at feet. Peace sign paintings and stickers on vendor homes bleach in chiggery sun.

And then we can go home to Apartment, Eli says.

Eli, Stevven says, kneels. I have a very important question to ask you.

Okay.

Did you eat or drink any blackberry since you've been here?

No, Eli says.

Stevven swallows Eli in arms, holds embrace. Good, Stevven says. Eat some BluBerry, okay? I'm just going to pull some rope from below. We won't be out of each other's sight.

Ever? Eli says.

Never ever again—Stevven squeezes tighter, slots fingers between Eliribs—Eat, Stevven says, unravels.

They exit pavilion, stoop and wiggle into crawl space.

I see your feet through the boards, Stevven says, squints up.

Elishadow shifts above. Dark Elieye peers down into crawlspace, winks in dimness.

Stevven grabs rope. Broody hen growls from inside rusty pail. Cobwebs and ruby black spiders stir quietly. Dust lunges into throat. Coughing.

Stevven returns to BluBerry in pavilion, measures rope by arm lengths as they walk, rip dust into air. They form rope net around BluBerry, handles sagging on two sides.

Let's get to the truck, Stevven says.

Eli takes one handle, Stevven takes other.

Want to walk ahead or behind? Stevven asks.

We can walk next to each other, Eli says.

BluBerry rises into air, gentle swing upwards. Breeze runs out pavilion with them, touches Stevvenneck, rushes down spine like dragonflies.

STEVVEN, ELI, AND BLUBERRY HIKE up hill to vehicles parking on dirt shoulder. Cash throws rifle in passenger seat, helps lift BluBerry into truck bed.

In ya go, our big leafy friend, zey say.

Stevven lifts Eli in. They sit against back windows, sandwich BluBerry between them.

You can wrap yourselves up in that tarp there if there's too much sun, Cash says. Don't let it blow away. Always hold onto something.

Stevven, Eli, and BluBerry hold each other tight. Rusty tailgate latches. Cash crosses to driverside. Truck starts up, guzzles, lurches forward.

Gravel turns to asphalt. Cash spits out onto road, steers down mountain. Branches kick up, kick as truck steals around next bend. Power lines cross overhead. Blackberry canes dip far into road, whack fruit against truck.

Don't eat those, Stevven says, wipes juices from Eli skin.

Look, Eli says.

Life rustles under tarp nest in truckbed corner. Black snout, white tuff, watery eyes. Skunkhead sniffs, risks one paw outside, two. They sideeye Stevven, Eli, and BluBerry, incisors twinkling white. Skunk eats blackberry, smack, smack, swallow.

W HITE PAINT PATCHES BLINK THROUGH trees. Mobile homes tic by.
Cash turns truck onto *US-75*. Billboard: *Ocoee Ziplines. Adventure Park.*

Tools roll from left to right, chase skunks from hiding, mama skunk, baby skunks. Squeak, squeak, skunks rush over shaking tarp, wind pulling fine hairs like lightning. They cover each other next to door latch, huddle down in hard wind.

They're beautiful, Stevven says.

Mama skunk stares at Stevven, tail high, then softer. Black eyes blink blackberry irises.

We feel each other, like palms grazing, then hold, same body. We open.

Look, they're coming to us, Eli says.

Little baby scurries out from Mama skunk, runs over Stevvenankle, nests against crotch. Full family follows, little paws pressing into Stevvenlegs, marking them with dirt. Mama curls up over babies in Stevvenlap, swirls black eye upward, feeling.

We breathe, heart rates small and quick like acorns.

Do they want touch? Eli asks.

Yes, Stevven says.

Eli scratches Mama skunkhead. Stevvenhead. We share sensation, daring to trust, ferociously.

Are you scared? Eli says. About Gino?

We watch skunkhair swirl in windtide, fish for words. None bite.

I feel like these skunks, we say. They just want a home where they won't be bothered.

INDUSTRY THRONGS, SMOKESTACKS STACKING METAL in air. Chattanooga. Traffic slows, Cash slows to stop behind semis.

We should get out, we say. We don't want to ride anymore. We should find a log. A nice smelly log, and a hole.

What about Gino? Eli asks.

Stevven chases breath, moving too fast, panic. They rap on window.

Cash slides back window open. What? zey say without eyes.

We need to get off, Stevven says.

Come again?

We got to get off! How close can you get us to Sewanee?

Cash scrunches hands on wheels, flicks look in rearview mirror.

I can get you close to Sewanee, Cash says, but what about your friend?

He was dying, Stevven says. He was looking for a place to die.

He's what?

Dead.

How do you figure? Cash keeps ear to Stevven.

Feel me.

Cash meets Stevveneyes. We merge, crest, exchange, break apart.

Salt brims Stevveneyes. They turn and sit back against window.

Traffic resumes, some honking, hating. Skunks squirm in Stevvenlap, troubling.

Stevven? Eli asks.

Yeah?

Someone's been watching me.

Eli points to greasy yellow car tailing close. Stevven squints through windshield at old sweat and smirk. One hand on wheel, one hand in lap.

What are they doing? Eli asks.

They're masturbating, Stevven says. Fucking perv. I'm going to make them stop. Can you hold our friends?

Eli nods.

Stevven invites skunks into Elilap. Clear, they scoot to tools pinning under ratchet strap, yank out tire bar. They raise weapon over head.

Pervsmirk swivels. They look for escape into next lane.

Stevven hurls tire bar into windshield. Crack! Windshield spiderwebs. Tire bar spins off highway bridge to disaster below.

Honk! Honk!

Cash hollers from drivers seat, accelerates getaway truck.

What the fuck you doin back there!—Cash makes hard exit at *152A*—We're getting off at Jasper.

Stevven stumbles down next to Eli. You okay? they ask.

Eli nods, stares wide at Stevven. Is Cash mad at you? Eli asks.

Yeah.

For throwing their stuff?

Yeah.

Truck stops at intersection. Only two other vehicles mill about shop station, flying American flags high. Cash parks beside express carwash islanding swamp, snakes.

Skunks tear away from Stevven like arms and legs, leap into foliage, free from foul belching machine. They dig claws into dirt, run home.

Tear drops. Eli hugs Stevven as Cash storms around, opens tailgate.

The driver was a perv, Stevven says.

We're all fuckin pervs but we can't afford to smash everyone's face with tire jacks!

They were looking at Eli.

Yeah, well, shit—zey pinch nosebridge.

Truck engine idles, coughs. Stevven helps Eli off truck.

Listen—Cash crosses to front, returns with pistol—Take Battle Creek Road, zey say, wrap gun in motoroil tea towel. It goes right up along 64 but without the cars. If you meet anyone, they'll be on foot, too.

Cash lays gun in Stevven hands. Stevven stares into dark fibers pulling around trigger guard, soft thing and hard thing.

And take you some water, Cash says.

Stevven draws water skin straps over shoulder. Cash lifts BluBerry off truck.

Fine rope, zey say.

Thanks.

Cash plays with hat, dragon blue hair dangling over eyes. You understand I can't keep you in the truck with this mind business goin on. We got too much head between the two of us.

I understand, Stevven says.

I was havin crazy visions of varmints.

You weren't imagining it, Stevven says. There were skunks.

Get you some rest, Stevven, Cash says, quarter smile.

Zey kneel down to Eli.

Little boss, make sure they get plenty of hugs, zey say, flick Eli nose.

Cash closes tailgate, steps into driverseat, shuts door. Zey wave hand, rev up to highway West, join great vibrations, vehicles sucking to and fro.

Eli, Stevven, and BluBerry stand in wake, adapt to metamorphosis, air.

Chow chow? Eli says, points.

Black hill rummages in wreckage below highway exit ramp, black bear.

No, that's a bear, Stevven says.

They watch Bear sniff, sift garbage. Cicadas in tall wet grasses shout.

Do you still want to find a hole? Eli asks.

What, to lay in?

You said you wanted to find a hole.

Maybe if it has food, Stevven says, stomach squeezing.

We could eat some BluBerry, Eli says.

I don't want to stress them, Stevven says, swigs water. We'll find something else along the way, I'm sure.

Stevven tucks tea towel around gun, sets gun on BluBerrysoil. Eli and Stevven pick up BluBerry by rope handles, walk Battle Creek road West.

Bye bye, Bear, Eli says.

Bear sniffs air, continues shopping.

Smoke strings from house half hiding in old growth. Kitchen pots clang, voices tang.

Why did Snake bite Jayme? Eli asks.

Because Jayme didn't know there was a snake, Stevven says.

Do you remember Jayme's eye? Eli says. It was grey.

Only after he died.

Because Snake killed him?

Yes.

Stevven chews on sumac.

Is BluBerry Jayme? Eli asks.

A little bit, Stevven says. I guess.

Is BluBerry me?

We didn't compost you, did we?

Yes, hair.

Oh, right.

DEPARTMENT STORES SHED BRAND LETTERS from crowns, cracking windows shining like spiderwebs, spiderwebs shining like cracking windows. White clouds thumb shadows on expiring sidewalks.

Rope swings and plastic playground equipment sink like barges in wet lawn.

Hairy person works on truck in driveway. Toddler muddies dolls inside embracing wildflowers. They stare out at Stevven and Eli, unflinching.

I'm hungry, Eli says.

Can you smell that barbecue?

It smells so yummy.

They break, munch on dandelion and kudzu. Then they walk.

I want barbecue, Eli says. We can smell it and find it.

You're right, but I just don't want to deal with anyone out here.

It smells like the one at the market but not as sweet as the song house.

The song house?

You were asleep when we stopped and it was night. We went inside for food and soda.

Who's we? When was this?

Gino, Addan, the old people, the driver, and the poofy hair person.

Cullo.

Yeah.

Cullo played music with the band on the stage. It was really creaky and white because there were so many feet on it. I ate a pulled pork sandwich.

How did you like the sandwich?

I think Mary will be mad at me.

Nevermind that. How'd you like it?

It was really yummy. I wish I had it right now.

Luckily no one came into the bus while you were in the song house, killed me or took BluBerry. Oh, are you crying? I'm sorry. I shouldn't say things like that. It sounds like you had a good time.

It's not that, Eli says, wipes eyes. I just really want a sandwich.

Stevven stops Eli, hugs them.

Eli, I promise we'll get you some good food before tonight. I promise, okay? Let's just take it easy now, drink some water. I'll pull up some of this cabbage. Rest here for a second. It's going to be okay.

Eli squats under elm, runs fingers along trunk.

Stevven pulls on young swamp cabbage, strains. They break and breathe.

I'm not strong enough, Stevven says.

Ferns shake. Stevven matches eyes to green, searches.

Did you hear that?

Eli nods.

Sounded kind of large.

Maybe a bear, or a chow chow?

Bears don't come as close as this, Stevven says, dries hands. Let's keep going. We have a gun, at least.

Helllooo! Eli yells into thick forest.

Don't do that.

Why?

We gotta be less than twenty miles from Sewanee, now. We can wait to make new friends there.

Is Gino at Sewanee?

I'm not ready to talk about Gino.

Why?

We're very close to Sewanee.

I'm tired.

You have to trust me, Stevven says, lifts BluBerry.


ELI HEARS THEM FIRST, STOPS.

Hymnal singing.

It's the most beautiful—

Shh, Stevven says. Keep walking.

They walk parallel to Jasper Highlands Christian Center. Hymns pour through brick walls. Church greeter waves hello from shade under eaves, stands.

Stevven pulls Eli and BluBerry on, clenches gun in freehand.

Hey neighbor, greeter calls.

Stevven picks up pace, rounds limestone boulders and Penske truck.

Greeter takes no more than two steps from shade, retreats back like vampire.


GRASSES ENTANGLE *JESSE'S GRILL* DINING furniture. They move from warm asphalt onto weeds and twigs. Stevven uprights dining chair set and table, sits, waves grasshopper off BluBerry.

They might eat BluBerry, Stevven says. Shoo them off when you see them.

Stevven oozes and stinks like persimmon. Toes soften, squishy in shoes, painful mush. They remove shoes, pick bandaid off.

Eli, can you pick some lichen from that conifer? A good handful.

Eli collects lichen, saves piece to play with.

Stevven packs lichen down into shoe. They rip fabric strip from shirt and tie lichen to foot.

No infection, Stevven says, slides foot into shoe.

What does 'ferocious' mean? Eli asks.

Stevven chortles. What do you think it means?

Hmm. Being a good friend.

Okay. Cheers to that.

Stevven hands Eli water skin. They drink.

I'm glad to see you're feeling better, Stevven says.

You look bad, Eli says. Maybe a pulled pork sandwich will help you.

Indeed.

CHEVROLET, BUICK GMC, SALES LOT.

*JESUS CHRIST*

*IS COMING*

*BE READY*

Worn letters speak from iron palisade fencing. Church ducks down below street like timid animal, local sandstones framing eye. Wheelchair ramp capsizes. Earthen sludge seals door.

Crack, shudder, deep movement. Colluvium under church slides down, chases valley to creek. Great roaring change. They watch foundations, worlds go with water, ruining.

Water is secure with knowing.

Landslide, Stevven says.

Woah.

EARLY EVENING COAXES HEAT INTO balminess favorite to needlenose insects. Mosquito swarms broaden, darken horizon, near and far, scratch around sign: *Creek Meadow Estates*.

I wish we had face nets, Eli says, rubs small beasts from eyes. Or Barbara's bug spray.

Barbaraname jolts Stevven.

If we stop moving we will get even more overwhelmed, they say.

Red brick church sinks into mountain swamp, white steeple molding. Large varicose creek veins dive underground, upsurge into ponds. Mosses suckle on church pews. Trees young, sky open to foresting hills. Cloud reflects sticky orange, static air. Revelation brews.

Boom! Mechanical rushing, air, plane diving.

Stevven drops cold, awaits trumpets.

Nighthawk swoops back up to sky, slender, tapering body, inconspicuous beak. White flash, wings raising and lowering. Nighthawk carries chipmunk in talons, dive still sizzling, cracking air.

Wow, Eli says, smiles, watches hawk make distance.

I haven't seen one of those in years, Stevven says, stands shivering. I thought I was dead.

Childlaughter whistles through reeds, hundred yards off. Play.

Stevven scans yellowlight homes in Creek Meadow Estates, squeezes Elishoulder.

Let's find some real food.


THEY WALK DROWNING GRAVEL DRIVEWAY around chainlink fence. Red truck browns and deflates in water, setting sun skipping off paint. Dull green vines climb through mud, reach from chainlink and trees.

Child play resounds.

Stevven smiles, hoists BluBerry higher. That's the sound we need to hear, they say.

Kids are good, Eli says.

Kids are good. I should have known that no kids at Kewee Water Retreat meant that something was wrong.

Soft smokiness snakes through slugging air, gunpowder, cherry bomb country. Stevven and Eli rest BluBerry and squat under late blossoming magnolia tree homing curious sparrow.

Down road, two human kids play game, toss pebbles into cable dish on roof. Smaller one mostly fetches rocks for bigger one to throw.

Settle down now, old voice crackles from inside house.

Kids stop throwing rocks, giggle, hurry from yard.

Smaller one spies Stevven and Eli, points.

Stevven raises hand, greets.

Kids scamper off. Small spotty dog leaps from reeds and runs with them, barks as they holler and play.

Stevven and Eli consider cable dish house leaning with mosses, old clapboard swamp wood. Shutters wilt on window edges. Old bench sleeps under clothes, dollar store junk.

*Come on in and sit awhile*, reads wooden placard hanging on string.

Wait here, Stevven says. I'll go knock.

They take gun in tea towel from BluBerry. They cross through swampy yard on stepping stones. Bottlegreen dragonflies dive for gnats. Violet stripe dragonflies. Bloodroot red dragonflies. Stevven creaks one porch stair, stops, looks back at Eli, waves.

Eli waves back, BluBerry patient at side. BluBerryEli, EliBluBerry.

Stevven steps up to door, poises, sweating, knocks.

Hello? Stevven calls into home.

TV blabbers inside, blue light flickering on blistery windows.

Sorry to bother you, Stevven says over TV, but we're hoping for a place to rest and drink. Can you help us?

Soft sweeping sounds from inside. Door unlatches, croaks open. Dirty screen veils old face, dark and crinkly as shriveling fern. Glass eyes crank from Eli to Stevven, lips in long thin line disappear into jowl folds.

You kids hungry? rocksalt voice says.

Yes, thank you.

Come on in and we'll fix you some poptarts. You can call me Nana.

Nana turns back into house.

I like old people, Eli says, steps to porch, heavy with BluBerry.

Stevven helps lift BluBerry. Yes, Stevven says, But never let your guard down.

What's my guard?

It's a phrase. Your guard is your eyes, your senses.

Eli opens eyes wide as bird bellies.

Stevven, Eli, and BluBerry enter house, smile.


TELEVISION TALKS GAMESHOW. BLUE LIGHT spins, catches onto mountaining clutter. Well worn leather recliner boasts corner room, long green couch sags center room facing television. Insects kick white ceiling light in kitchen, low flickering noises untucking everywhere. Floral wallpapers peel, century old. Decorative lace and cobwebs darn blind windows.

Stevven and Eli sit BluBerry in little clearing between laundry pile and door, then walk through narrow path towards kitchen table busy with mail, coloring books, memorabilia. Nana pulls out dining chairs. Eli takes seat.

Nana crosses to fridge, door full with family photos, road sign magnets, crochet kitchen utensils. Inside door stocks catsups, jams, sauces, pickles on pickles.

Eli folds hands politely on table, dangles legs, swinging, delighting. My butt is so tired, they say.

Stevven rubs in last mosquitoes like lotion beads, sits in chair, looks again around dense, mothballing room.

So, lived here long? Stevven asks.

All my life, Nana says, takes two glasses from pantry.

Something twitches inside washing machine. Stevven picks at tea towel pills, gun slippery inside.

Nana twists ice tray. Little frost pieces spring into air, melt onto soft paperweb hands. She drops ice toes into glasses. Ding. Ding. She refills tray at sink.

Stevven hides gun behind back, opens freezer door.

Thank you, Nana says, sets tray inside freezer.

Nanagown smells like butterscotch, mildew, talc and corn. Nana goes for full lemonade pitcher, lifts with both hands.

I can help, Stevven says.

I ain't helpless, Nana says, breathes softly through parted lips, caramel incisors glimmering.

Nana pours lemonade into glasses. She shuffles around table, places one glass for Eli, one for Stevven. She grabs poptarts from open pantry, sets box on table.

Holler if you need anything else, Nana says, flows through narrow path into living room, sinks into recliner.

Puzzle letters flash on TV: R. Yes. S. Yes. V. No.

Insect song pulses through open front door, screen.

You won't join us for a drink? Stevven asks, places hand on Eliwrist.

No, Nana says. Lemonade's for the kids.

Children laugh in distant swamp.

Stevven lifts hand from Eli wrist. Eli goes for cup, swallows three big gulps, exhales monstrously.

Stevven takes glass in hands—succulent cool shock. Water beads drop as Stevven raises glass to lips. Tart cold skips down, puckering, cough. Sugar zigzags behind eyes.

Eliface draws up into lemonsqueezy smile. They drink more. Stevven sucks icecube, puts icecube to neck.

It's so good, Eli says, pants.

Stevvengun slips out lap, clatters on floor.

Shit. Stevven dives under table, bangs head, recovers gun.

Um, Nana, thanks for the drink, Stevven says, hides weapon behind back. We were wondering if you would be kind enough to host us for the night. It's been a long day for us.

You can have the couch there, Nana says, ziptying to TV.

Stevven exhales, smiles at Eli. Eli smiles back, jazzy for good rest. Stevven lays gun on BluBerry—Wetness flops into underwear. Stevven checks with fingers, cherry stain.

What's wrong? Eli asks.

I'm bleeding.

Is it menstation?

Close, Stevven says. Menstruation. All my hormones are out of whack. Shit. Just what I need.

Does it hurt? Mary says it hurts.

Not too bad. I need a rag. Hey, Nana?

Yuh?

Do you have a towel or a—a cloth I can use—maybe—

Don't you go cleaning anything, now. Leave them dishes for me.

No I, I'm on my period.

Your period? Why didn't you say so? Top cabinet. The granddaughter started a couple weeks ago—Nana turns away from TV to look at Stevven, turns back—Thought you were a boy, to be honest. But I don't know what surgeries the LGBT are doing on each other nowadays. And I don't care to hear about it.

Stevven takes one pad, pockets two more, hesitates hands at dishware landfill in sink.

Where can I wash up? Stevven asks.

Bathroom sink works now, Nana says. You got panties?

Our stuff got stolen.

Take one of mine in the dresser in the back room, Nana says, throws gesturing hand over shoulder.

Stevven leans down, whispers to Eli: I'll be right back. Tear into those poptarts in the meantime.

Do you not like talking about menstruation? Eli asks, takes poptart box.

Why?

You're talking really quiet.

I guess I'm a little uncomfortable.

Is it okay to talk about it?

Yeah. Of course. I'm just always a little bit surprised when it happens.

Is it new? Eli says, yanks apart cellophane wrapper, scatters poptart chunks on table.

No, I just always forget. I have a hard time knowing my body. June got onto me about it, though she wasn't as socratic as you.

Eli vacuums Poptart.

I love my body, Eli says. And my body looovvees poptarts!

Stevven laughs, expels more blood. They step through indoor junkyard towards bedroom. Parts, pieces, pictures, and then panties in wooden dresser drawers, all dollarstore fabric pieces.

Thank the Good Harvest, Stevven says, scoops thin polyester panty, crazy neon colors.

They shed bloody garments, slip on large underwear with pad, wash hands in small pastel enamel bathroom, avoid mirror.

Stevven shuts off lights and steps into living room, Eli snacking sounds and mumbling TV. They exhale, bleed freely.

Want to watch some TV? Stevven asks Eli tearing into third poptartpackage.

Does it have Samurai Jack?

Probably not. It will be fun anyway. Moving pictures. Maybe some other old things you've never seen before.

Okay.

Eli plops onto couch next to Nanachair. Nana snores, mouth wide to heaven. Stevven grabs poptarts box and crosses to couch. They sit, finger stiff twentieth century blanket, adjust pillows, lean back. Stevven tears open poptart package, hands one to Eli.

Banana cream pie flavor, Stevven says.

They chow down on corn syrup, dextrose. Blue TV light swims in Elieye wetness, dances dreamily on BluBerry leaves.

American firework ad plays, skip option dusting screen corner. Early twenty-first century show resumes inside desert shootout between old cars. Bullets kick up dust, break glass. Pistols, shotgun. Bald man climbs out car, begs for life. Hard masculine squinty looks. Clack, pistol. Second police officer dies. Camera cuts to rock, southwest colors.

What's happening? Eli asks, wincing.

Something about drugs and revenge, Stevven whispers. Maybe we should watch something else.

Creak! Two children clatter into house through back screen door, one with overbite, two beaver teeth, other smaller, dark, shrinking inside themselves like turtle. They squeeze in next to Eli on couch. Children stare at each other until attention fades back to TV one by one. First, TwoTeeth, then Eli, then Turtle who sucks thumb.

TwoTeeth reaches remote on Nanachair. Screen turns blue, lime number switches from *Input 3* to *Input 4*.

Dreamworks movie begins. Little purple creature abducts fisherchild from crescent moon. Soon purple Boov people turn off gravity and relocate humans to Happy Human Town.

Stevven laughs.

Title letters float up to skyrise, *Home*, giant swirly O. Vortex fades.

Home, Stevven mouths.

I've seen this one a gazillion times, TwoTeeth says, swivels and speaks to Eli. Wanna catch some fireflies?

Fireflies? Elieyes match size.

Them light bugs out there.

Yes.

Aight, I'll get you a jar.

TwoTeeth scrambles over couch, toes grappling and releasing, frog sticky, opens cupboard. Mmm I don't got lids with holes and we need em with holes, TwoTeeth says, climbs off kitchen counter. We'll share.

Will you come? Eli asks Stevven, bounces on couch.

Okay.

Turtle tails TwoTeeth and Eli outside.

Stevven slides hands onto knees, stands. Muscles shake, fatigue. They eat last poptart and watch another movie minute, curious pill body characters with great round eyes.

Stevven crosses to door, brushes BluBerry, turquoise TV light writing stars into wax leaves.

Eli laughs, raises arms into firefly sky. They stand with TwoTeeth and Turtle on small swamp island. Stevven sits on back porch steps, slips off shoes, grime, wiggles out toes in soft air.

Junk piles soften into life, wild leaves and insects trellising into night world.

TwoTeeth unwinds metal lid from jar, soft airy click. Now watch this, they say. They jist float up in there like this. They're not too smart. It's easy.

TwoTeeth closes lid on firefly, hands jar to Eli.

You got to poke holes so they can breathe. Yeah sister n me used n old screwdriver we found n Tony's yard and poked them holes and that's how I got this.

Two Teeth holds hand out to Eli, dark circular wound.

You have to get a tetanus shot for that, Eli says.

I know I got it last year when the doctor came. He said I understand if you're afraid and I said I ain't afraid of no needles and he went WAM!—TwoTeeth pretends to stab arm straight down, shakes up firefly inside jar—It hurt like a bee nothin else.

Wow, Eli says, fixes on firefly.

Yuh. Here, you can let that little guy go n try n catch another.

Eli watches firefly climb out jar, slip away into dark.

Go get that one, TwoTeeth says. Watch it there, that waters deep.

Eli holds jar and lid apart above head, tiptoes. Golden bud hovers above opening, floats starward. Eli steps deeper into trees, tracks gentle as ghost. Firefly perches on jar, blinks, lifts off.

You done forgot to put the lid on em. You can look at em longer when they trapped n the jar. Hey you got hair like my sister. She's dark skinned n you're Asian but you got the same hair. Where'd you come from?

Garden, Apartment, East Coast, Earth.

What garden you come from?

Garden. It's really far that way—Eli points.

Oh, I ain't heard of it. I was born here. Pop says I got frog feet. He means I'm real good at this place.

Stevven says I have monkey feet.

You better not to climb n these trees. There are a lot of snakes here. That's how Mom got killt. Pop says if I climb a tree he'd kill me if the snake don't.

That's silly.

Yeah it's just a way of sayin things. Can I have that jar if you ain't gonna use it?

Eli hands jar pieces to TwoTeeth.

You play xbox? TwoTeeth asks.

Turtle tugs on TwoTeethshirt.

Hey can't you git it yurself?—TwoTeeth groans and looks at Eli—Hey my sis wants a sandwich. You like sandwiches?

Eli nods.

Ookay but you're gonna have to make your own. I got to make two already so its fair you make one.

Okay.

TwoTeeth jumps up onto porch steps, grazes Stevven, Turtle tumbling in after.

Eli, wait, Stevven says, holds out hand.

Eli falls into Stevvenarms, laughs.

Having fun? Stevven asks.

Yeah.

That's good. I just wanted to check in.

Eliface softens. They snuggle into Stevvenlap.

I want to check in too, they say.

I've been thinking a lot, Stevven says. Can I tell you what I've been thinking about?

Elihead rubs nod into Stevven. They inhale fragrant starlight. Fireflies open, close, all around. Eli silences, more bright and watchful than slim moon.

I've been thinking about Ms. Jones, Stevven says. I wonder how she's doing.

Are you worried about her?

Yes.

Why?

Because she's old.

But Nana's old and she's doing okay.

Yeah, Stevven says. But she's got these kids running around. I'm thinking we were like Ms. Jones' kids, in a way. And I feel guilty. I feel guilty about leaving her and leaving your mama. And leaving Gino—Stevven scratches head, searches for itch—I almost left you, Stevven says.

Eli rides Stevven breath, up and down.

What are you thinking about? Stevven asks.

Eli leans over, fingers something in dark, hair drooping over eyes, raggedy.

I like it here at Nana's, they say. Maybe we can stay longer.

We're almost where we need to be.

You're not listening.

Okay, sorry. I'm listening now.

I want to go back to Apartment. Apartment is perfect.

We can't go back to Apartment, Stevven says. But I think we can make any place perfect. If we just stick with it. There's a time for moving around and there's a time for sticking around and it's hard to sort out. Like this place feels perfect right now. It's hard to know. And all I know about Sewanee is that I hope for it. I think it will be good for you. And BluBerry.

Eli sits up, looks out into swamp, tenses.

Crows clap wings. Bearding trees become shadow.

You need more food, and some rest, Stevven says. Go help your friends with the sandwiches. I'm going to sit out here for a little longer.

Do you want a sandwich? Eli asks.

Yes please, but only after you've had enough to eat, Stevven says, combs through Elihair. You need a bath.

I'm okay, Eli says, stands. I'll get more lemonade.

Let's at least tie this up, so you don't get hair in your food.

Eli digs finger into pocket, pulls out elastic band. Stevven ties Elihair back.

You do it soft, Eli says.

Softer than Mary?

Yeah. It falls out, watch, Eli says, shakes head. Hair slips from tie.

I don't want it to hurt your head, Stevven says, ties band around hair three times.

It's not working, Eli says, takes hairband from Stevven.

Eli ties hair, trots off inside.

Stevven falls weight onto knees, watches dark. Light spores grow and sink, disperse. Monocot leaves glow green, insects silhouetting. Wings pitter, pirouette into shadow. Frog leaps, water sparks, reeds rustle.

Shapes squirm under eyelids. They force eyes exterior, deny bridging.

Kitchen clatters softly, soprano to swamp music. Snake slides down from rafters, flicks tongue. They pass through deck railing into tall grass. Slug slides around Stevvenshoe, trail glinting between kitchen light reliefs. Stevven peels bandage from foot, savors coolness.

Eli returns with two sandwiches. White bread, butter, mayo, ham, olives.

Thanks. Where are your new friends?

They said they're pooped.

Me three, Stevven says, bites into sandwich, soft, salty, creamy.

Me four, Eli says.

Five, Stevven says. BluBerry must be tired.

Eli bites, chews, wet sounds surround, within, without. Swamp critters compost, burp, breed.

Stevven saps butter fats from earthy fingers. Let's get a little water and some sleep, yeah? they say.

Eli swallows last bite, blinks eyes, drowsy. Stevven stacks plates, helps Eli up to stand. They hold hands, carefully step from porch to dim room, one lightbulb tinkering overhead. Bedroom door hangs open. Children puppy pile on bed.

Nana sleeps in chair before low volume movie. Stevven turns TV off.

Eli slumps over couch. Stevven shakes out old quilt, drapes Eli. Eli reaches out for Stevven.

I'm just going to turn off the light, Stevven says. I'll be right back.

Stevven brushes BluBerry, blue incandescence. They place gun on table, water BluBerry from skins.

Soreness creeps from hands to head, then fire. They spill water onto floor.

Shit.

Stevven caps skins, leans against junk, find breath. They scan room, ancient, slumbering. They flick lightswitch, plunge into dark.

Moment, adjusting. Feet gently probe one step, two, collect dirt, stick. Food wrappers tickle like tentacles, tangle. Feet feel, cling, relish sensorial world under soles. Stevven weaves into space, becoming place.

Stevvenhand slides over polyester coucharm. They climb onto couch, lie next to Eli. Eli pulls Stevvenarm over, cocoons. They latch in warmth, water, as if fungal, two living felt pieces, ecological, sympoietic, loving.

CEREAL HITS CERAMIC BOWL.

Elihair salts tickle nose.

Stevveneyes open.

I know you ain't gotta tell me to be quiet, TwoTeeth whispers. We're all out of chocolate milk. Mind me to bring some back over from pa's house later, nkay? I ain't gonna eat dry cereal never.

Eli shifts, face inches from Stevven, warm. They sync breath.

Whut? Course they ain't got milk. You saw them come in with a whole lot of nothing. Cept this here gun.

Stevven jolts up.

Guhmornin, TwoTeeth says, chews, spins gun on table. Hey my sister n me wonderin if you got any milk.

Stevven dizzies into kitchen, lays hand on spinning gun.

No, they say, wet, croaking.

They turn to BluBerry, leaves reaching one foot higher than night before. Stevven rewraps pistol, lays weapon in BluBerry soils.

But you can have some fruit, Stevven says, runs hand through BluBerry old growth.

That ain't fruit, TwoTeeth says.

I bet you it's sour like the freshest berries you've ever tasted, Stevven says, clears web in throat.

You're pullin, TwoTeeth says. You try it first.

Stevven gathers ripe BluBerry leaves. They turn to face children, yawn, smack lips, bite into one leaf. Tang bursts, minerals rush. They shudder.

Not as sweet as they could be, Stevven says, but they're working on it.

Stevven places BluBerry leaf in each childhand.

Turtle bites in first, chews slowly, stares at clean bite mark though leaf. They meet Stevveneyes, twinkle.

TwoTeeth digs in. Kind of like orange, they say.

Eli rises from sleep, yawns, peers over couch.

Back door clacks. Nana wears same nightgown, crosses to kids, Stevven.

Did they wake you up? Nana asks, intonations building.

No trouble at all, Stevven says, hoarse. Would you like to try some BluBerry?

What's this? Nana asks, takes leaf in palm.

BluBerry leaves. For eating.

I ain't ever heard of it.

Can I look at your gun? TwoTeeth asks.

Stevven turns and takes gun from TwoTeethhand.

No.

I know how to use it!

I don't care, Stevven says, coughs into arm, green, sticky cloud.

Small body leans against Stevven. Good morning, Eli says.

You wanna go to pa's for some more poptarts? TwoTeeth asks. She's not invited, TwoTeeth says, points at Stevven.

Sorry but we have to head out soon, Stevven says.

I ain't askin you!

Quiet now, Nana says.

Come on, sis, TwoTeeth runs out back door. Turtle follows, skips.

Nana smiles after them, shakes head, then touches BluBerry leaf in palm.

You can even juice them, Stevven says, drops leaves in Elihand.

Nana takes BluBerry to mouth, bites down soft.

Hmm, she says, closes eyes, nods.

Would you like us to leave some BluBerry with you? Stevven asks, clears throat. We'd be happy to share.

That'll go nice with my collection, Nana says.

Stevven looks to wilting flowers sitting on smoggy windowsill in kitchen.

They're more outdoorsy, Stevven suggests. I saw a big tire with an expired vegetable garden out front we could put them in. They'll grow to be a small tree, but I guess I can't say what they'll do out here in the swamp.

Nana smiles. Alright, that'll do nicely, she says.

Stevven brushes BluBerry, blood hot but two steps too slow. Stevven sits down, hangs head.

Eli, want to help make another propagation? they ask.

Yeah. Eli says, looks to Nana. Do you have more lemonade?

Course, Nana says. But first, what's your name, child?

I'm Eli.

And you?

I'm Stevven, they say.

Ain't right I know the plant's name before people's, Nana ruminates. Names. Don't hardly catch them no more.

I forget to introduce sometimes because everyone eIDs each other, Stevven says, rubs neck, grog from eyes. Everyone already knows everyone's name.

It's polite to say names, Nana says, draws drinking glass from pantry. Ain't about knowing, exactly. I say people are just more scared than they used to be n scared about each other.

It did feel weird, saying my name, Stevven says. Like a secret. Kind of.

Names are like seeds in places they're spoken, Nana says, pours lemonade.

That sounds like something Gino would say, Stevven says, sips hazy window view, sinks.

Eli, Eli, Eli! Eli broadcasts turning once about room.

STEVVEN AND ELI CARRY BLUBERRY to muggy porch.

Stevven sits, points finger on thick BluBerry branch. We cut here? they ask.

We can do more, Eli says.

If you think they can handle it, Stevven says, rubs barbing forehead. You know them best. Now what are the chances we will find a good, clean cutting tool around here?

Eli squats, hands in BluBerry, BluBerry in hands. Eli presses two thumb nails into BluBerrystem, slow. Small, white excretions bubble from broken veins, climb halfway up Eli thumbs, settle into amber sap.

They came apart for you, Stevven says.

They know when its wind and when its teeth, or hands, Eli says. Look how sticky.

Eli stretches BluBerry sugar between fingers.

Think that tire is a good spot? Stevven asks.

Eli nods, stands, croaks porch steps down to waterlogging yard. White feet glow, sink into dark marsh.

Heat rockets through Stevvenhead. They massage temples, chase heat down through ear canals, throat, upper back.

I'm gonna grab some water, Stevven says, plods into house.

Sizzle, sizzle. Salt and fats quiver kitchenair. Bacon skips in skillet. Nana opens squeaky styrofoam egg carton. Eggs bright white. She fishes out two, cracks them in grease among bacon.

I'll bring it out to you, she says.

Thank—Stevven coughs in arm, gathers phlegm in mouth, swallows down.

Better to spit that stuff out, Nana says.

Stevven crosses into bedroom, changes pad in privacy. They drop redbrown sludge napkin in kitchen bin, stare long at waste. Black plastic garbage bag blinks, horse fly.

There was once a better way to do this, they say aloud, look around. Shiver rolls down back. Body forgets every last moment for next one, rest hailing.

STEVVEN FORCES BODY OUTSIDE INTO white, searing sun.

Pee o wee. Pee o wee, flycatcher flurries.

Eli sits as lotus on porch edge. Next to them, BluBerry sweats in pot. Across from them, BluBerry roots in tire garden.

Stevven settles down next to Eli, matches crossing legs, joints chalky dry, head drippy.

Elieyes close. They breathe in, out.

I'm surprised you can meditate with the smell of bacon, Stevven says.

I'm not good at it.

Not with me interrupting. Just keep doing it and that's when you're good at it like Gino.

Is it okay to be thinking?

Always. As long as you are thinking about breath also.

Is it okay to be talking?

Then all you'd have left to do is open your eyes, Stevven says, chuckles.

Gino talks when he closes his eyes.

Stevven clears throat, nods. I see what you mean, they say. He prays.

Who does he pray to?

Nana places egg and bacon mountain between them.

Wow! Eli says, legs exploding out from meditation.

They shovel bacon into mouth before Nana can set forks down.

You poor kids, she says. Ain't you got anyone to feed you? My son fixes the meat from hogs out here. Can't keep our own chickens here no more cuz the hogs eat em. Can't shoot them all.

Stevven tastes egg, taste failing. It's delicious, Stevven says, rocks back into shade.

Eli chugs lemonade.

Eli, think you can finish off my bacon? Stevven says. I'm not too hungry, actually.

Stevven scoots eggs and bacon onto Eliplate, coughs into arm.

I see you're fixin to go, but you can rest up here longer, hun, Nana says.

I'm alright, Stevven says. We have to keep moving.

That's how you go on being sick, Nana says, takes Stevvenplate. Moving around from place to place.


STEVVEN SHUDDERS, EXITS NANAEMBRACE.

Eli lingers in Nanaarms.

You take care of your big sister, Nana says, trundles back towards television. Y'all come back anytime.

Eli and Stevven carry BluBerry off porch. They stop before BluBerry in tire. Eli sings to them.

They move on, both dragging some. They leave some BluBerry and names behind, seeding. Substantial.

They leave Creek Meadow Estates, merge onto asphalt road, move under corkscrewing powerline poles, kudzu.

Turkey vultures swirl rhythmically in blistering sky.

They rest while flying even, Stevven says.

Eli drags feet, drags BluBerry.

Keep them off the ground, Stevven says.

Eli jerks BluBerry up.

Hey, what's the matter with you? Be nice to BluBerry.

Eli frowns, drags BluBerry.

I'll carry them alone, then, Stevven says.

They bundle ropes into fist, loop straps over shoulders, raise BluBerry pot high against back. They trudge forward, plastic pot rim scraping flesh under shoulders through failing shirt.

Eli follows twenty paces behind, runs tree branch into ground like broken tail.

Colors blot behind Stevven eyes.


They meet creek crossing, sun boiling. Creek drifts kneehigh over asphalt.

Careful, the water can sweep you in, Stevven says.

I know, Eli says.

Let's put our shoes in BluBerry's pot.

Barefoot, they wade into water.

Careful, Stevven says again. There could be broken anything down here.

They pause in cool water rush. Trouble licks ankles, calls deep corporeal waters.


Stevven redresses shoes. Eli remains in water.

Come, Stevven says.

You never listen.

We're so close to being done with this, you don't even know.

You never listen!

Eli squats in water, current bending around body.

Stevven rests under elm tree. Stevven picks tic off leg.

I want to check you for tics, they say.

No! Eli splashes in water.

Stevven stretches hips, one leg over leg, bends, touches toes, rolls ankles. Blood swings inverse, abandons head. Stevven stumbles, knocks BluBerry onto side. Gun clatters to road.

Eli looks at them.

Rose up a little too fast, Stevven says, shovels soils back into BluBerrypot, vision hot and bubbling like petri dish.

Sweat slops off nose. They aim drip onto BluBerry, miss.

Eli steps from river, crosses to shade. Eli and Stevven share elm and silence while feet dry.

Eli cranks shoes on, gives up on sticking velcro shoe straps. Stevven picks burrs from velcro, fastens shoes tight.

We'll cross I-24 in a couple miles, Stevven says.

SHAPES AND LIFE AND GROWLS swim in periphery, high noon. Stevven blinks, all edges frosting.

Can we rest? Eli asks.

Further, Stevven says.

Rock walls, shadows, new beasts. Stevven wars drowsiness, paranoia breeding. They hold one eye to forest crown, flinch at bird and squirrel, ear keen to sudden rushes, clicks.

We are not alone.

We see each other, stop. We bristle, hail lightening.

Giant opossum, feather, claw, white eyes nothing and endless, space to leap through and out.

Eli?

Yes?

Am I hallucinating?

What is hallucinating?

Do you see them?

Yes.

What color are their eyes?

Lots of colors.

What are they?

I don't know. Maybe jaguar.

Devil, devil, we think each other.

Creature startles into trees, fast leafhush retreat. Going, gone, now anywhere. Tears drop from Stevvenface. They fumble for gun.

I need to see if this thing still shoots, Stevven says, watercolor slashing vision.

They fish for distracting words.

Did you know that the Charleston riot was the day the 2nd amendment was amended, the levees let loose? Stevven asks Eli, wipes sweat with tea towel. The government finally tried to take people's guns, and then that was it. China's second wave of cyber attacks started then.

Why?

Why what?

I don't know, Eli says, sits down on graywacke.

Just try and be more specific, Stevven says. Not talking? Fine. I'm just testing out this gun for whatever that thing was. For our own protection.

Do they have guns, too?

Who knows what they have nowadays.

Stevven slides fingers onto magazine release, chewy with dirt. They pick out dirt, pull release, catch magazine.

Hold this, they say. Don't mess with it too much.

Stevven sets magazine in Elihands, checks chamber.

I'll tell you how it works. Want to know how it works? We take the magazine, stick it to the chamber. Make sure that it clicks. Here's the rear sight, the safety. When this safety is flipped this way, it won't fire—they blink away fuzz—Stand back there. I'm going to aim for that tree.

Will it hurt the tree?

Like a bee sting. Maybe, not quite. They'll be okay. Cover your ears. You'll still hear if you cover your ears. Trust me.

Stevven stands, straddles BluBerry, gun tossing in finger sea. They steady center tooth between two poles, levels long sight.

Breath, sweat. In, out, in, halfout. Hold. Trigger, spring, hammer.

Bang!

Young elmleaves jerk two feet from tree. Head throbs, ears slug.

I missed the target, Stevven says. And now I can barely hear anything. Great.

Where's the fire? Eli asks, shivers.

It happened inside gun.

Where'd it go?

The bullet went right of the tree.

Should we get it and try again?

No, the charge is gone.

Stevven flips safety on, folds gun in towel, sets in BluBerry.

Let's not spend any more time here, Stevven says.

It was so loud, Eli says.

Want to help me with BluBerry, or are you going to make me suffer?

I don't want to make you suffer.

But you don't want to carry BluBerry.

Eli stares angry into Stevven.

Stevveneyes flock, fledging control too fast. They shoulder BluBerry like pack.

STEVVEN AIMS TO PASS BATTLE Creek Baptist church, but something grows.

Stevvenlegs stop, weakening fast. Sermons leap through walls, skull.

When you think about the future, Preacher says, how do you feel?

Stevven stops in road before faces, white pyramid awning over red church brick, crucifix. Preachervoice marbles in hollow head.

For most of us, thinking of the future brings all sorts of feelings. Worry, anxiety, hopelessness. We have lots of reasons to feel this way. The Chinese, not feeling safe in our own homes. Children going off to crooked cities, forgetting the good word. Sexual deviance and drug addiction. Abortions. Our bodies are hurting, aging. Sickness, death, and so on. Uncertain times are ahead.

Old rotting ceiling tiles drip light on congregation, aging hands and bowing heads.

Events and thoughts like this make us ask ourselves some scary questions. Questions like: Do we have any real security in this life? What does the future truly hold for us? Can we find freedom from fear, anxiety, and worry?

Stevven touches cheek to catch tear, but cheek is dry.

It's happening again, Stevven says. The sharing thing. I can see and feel inside the church.

We sit in pew, old hymn book square in seatback, comforting, consoling.

What if I told you the future is full of hope because Jesus Christ died on the cross?

Voices say Amen.

Let's read from Colossians 3:1-4. Since, then, you have been raised with Christ, set your hearts on things above, where Christ is, seated at the right hand of God.

Can you hear what they are saying? Eli asks.

Yes, we say, yank on hair, fighting ourselves. It's like I'm inside.

Set your minds on things above, not on earthly things. For you died, and your life is now hidden with Christ in God. When Christ, who is your life, appears, then you also will appear with him in glory. Our body will be made new. We'll experience a resurrection too. Now, what is Paul saying about resurrection? What does it mean?

I want to hear with you, Eli says.

I see the Preacher. His gray hair, shirt buttoned to neck.

I want to see! Eli yells.

Until the trumpets come and we ascend to heaven, let us not boast about what tomorrow will look like. Please turn your Bibles to James 4: 13-17.

Waxy thin paper tickles, verses flickering like moths all around. Pews and gravel. There is ceiling and there is sky. Thorn crowns become ravens.

Eli walks ahead, puts hands to church doors.

We rub black fur on tree, scratch into skin, sniff air. We mother cubs. Cubs climb over feet, legs, pew.

Now listen, you who say, Today or tomorrow we will go to this or that city, spend a year there, carry on business and make money. Why, you do not even know what will happen tomorrow. What is your life? You are a mist that appears for a little while and then vanishes. Instead, you ought to say, If it is the Lord's will, we will live and do this or that. As it is, you boast in your arrogant schemes. All such boasting is evil. If anyone, then, knows the good they ought to do and doesn't do it, it is sin for them.

Preacher leans from stand, manifests in searing stratocumulus.

We walk towards doors, white paint, already sitting in pews.

Folks, we cannot go about making plans as if we are in control, Preacher says. We submit our plans to God for the future is in his hands. What does this look like for us? Turn again to James 5: 7.

We stand between darkness, church doors, white and goldplate, plastic holly wreathes. Door creaks open. Stevven reflects in prism, eyes mirror eyes. We all look in on ourselves and we can see straight to blue blood pumping in, red pumping out, violet stream. Storm. Sacred body, join life on high.

Be patient, then, brothers and sisters, until the Lord's coming. See how the farmer waits for the land to yield its valuable crop, patiently waiting for the autumn and spring rains. You too, be patient and stand firm, because the Lord's coming is near. Don't grumble against one another, brothers and sisters, or you will be judged. The Judge is standing at the door!

White doors clack behind us. Urge to sit grows heavy, to bear words as Christ bears cross.

We watch ourselves, eyes incesting.

To verse 14 then, is anyone among you sick? Let them call the elders of the church to pray over them and anoint them with oil in the name of the Lord. And the prayer offered in faith will make the sick person well; the Lord will raise them up. If they have sinned, they will be forgiven. Therefore confess your sins to each other and pray for each other so that you may be healed. The prayer of a righteous person is powerful and effective.

Eli whispers: We have to pray to make you better.

It's just words. It's just words.

It's just a body. It's just a body.

Here we have it folks, Preacher says. Patience and prayer. This is in our power. This is love, this is hope, a demonstration of faith in the future that is and only is in God's hands. Please join me for a closing prayer.

Shadows descend.

Eli?

We take seat next to Eli, too frightened to reach for hand and not to.

Lord, thank you for this holy day we can come together and be with you. We hand our lives to you Lord. In you we trust. May God protect us, the harvest be good and surrounding. The cancer, the crimson horse. Bless the moss and the smoke, the niece and nephews. I'm calling on angels to protect, Mary, mother, I want to be a good mother. Stars, burning feet and forever, eternity, stone, the stone tilting on mist.

We are dizzy with many.

Heavy in the womb cradle, Christ in heart, rest and roses find wilderness, kingdom, heaven fortress forest, to die and form words again and again and again eyes wide the cross, sin walking to the barn love, love, love Eli the only dream. Oil, shining Gino, twisting vines too long is too long, the blood the fire the thorns gone, by morning light stone rolled away to get a ride to get a ride. The flood Amen our bodies, will stay to the fastest road to take us home, take us home lord. BluBerry take us home. Amen, Amen, AMEN.

Parchment air, wax. Stevven breathes lightness again, separate.

And I'd like to thank Darlene and John, Preacher says, and all the wonderful helpers for preparing us a post-service snack.

Murmurations. Kids stir to snack table. Cellophane crackles off plastic cookies, squeaky clingwrap unclings from deviled eggs.

Stevven still as pillar upholding ceiling, clinging tight to center by which others orbit, tall squinty men with limbs like twobyfours, women in dresses, bellies and breasts like creek stones. Wideface children with meanness blink on pews, snackplates in lap.

Welcome travelers, says pillsburyface, two friendly warts, eyes sparkling purple. I'm Darlene. Where y'all comin from?

Stevven glimpses us double, avoids eyes.

For now we see in a mirror dimly, Darlene says. But then face to face. Now I know in part; then I shall know fully, even as I have been fully known. 1 Corinthians 13:12.

Sinister gray cloud swamps vision. We are eating and not. We are bearpaw, Darlene, and pantyhose.

How many of us have this vision? Stevven asks.

Besides you and me, Darlene says, my husband, the Cooperman family, and Mr. Earl over there by the piano.

And a bear, yes? Where is the bear?

God works in mysterious ways.

You think this mind mixing thing is a power bestowed by your God?

The Lord tells us that we have many spiritual gifts, Darlene says, lays hand on Eli. And that these gifts we must handle with care and should always be tested—she pauses for smile—You two boys look worse for wear. Where you coming from?

Nana's house, Eli says.

Nana's house, hmm. How about we get something for you to eat. It's okay, we can teach you how to use this gift with time. Where are you staying? Have you eaten? I can count your ribs, poor thing. Wait here.

Darlene steps into line and scoops foods onto two paper plates. Stevven watches Eli, Eli watches Stevven.

Stevvenmouth opens, closes. We need to leave, they say. My mind was just gangbanged by a bunch of baptists. And a bear—they look around, fever building, body shivering—Where's BluBerry?

Darlene excuses way around congregation back to Stevven and Eli. Settle down, she says, lays food plate on Stevven lap. Plenty to share.

Darlene tucks Elihair behind ear. What's your name, hun?

Eli.

Eli, what are you doin with all that hair? Ain't you got a mama to cut it?

Eli shrugs.

What happened to your mama?

We ran away because the police were coming.

The police? She was in trouble with the police?

Stop interrogating them, Stevven says, sets snackplate on pew. I left BluBerry outside.

They were coming to get us and she wouldn't move and Stevven took me away, Eli says.

Stevven stops as if hit by tree.

And Stevven won't listen. And I don't know where Gino is or Cullo or anyone. I don't know where they go. And I don't know when they come back or how to find them because we are walking everywhere and I don't know where we are and and—Elivoice strains, breaks into tears.

Oh, hun, come here, Darlene says, wraps Eli in. Cry about it, it's okay.

Stevven burns red, toes writhing inside shoes. They fight visions, total corporeal collapse. Elitears shake them down to pew, weaken muscles, immunities.

Where was all this last night? Stevven says sideways. There was a time for this kind of talk.

Don't attack the poor thing, Darlene says, squeezes Eli in tighter. Tell me all about it, hun.

And they, they—Eli sputters, sucks in tears—they can see things that I can't see and hear things and won't share.

I know, I know, Darlene says.

Church goers mill about scene awkwardly. One hand touches Darlene, offers paper napkins.

Yes, thank you, Darlene says, brings paper to Eliface. Blow.

Eli blows nose into paper napkin.

Poor thing. The Lord loves you and will take care of you.

Don't tell them things like that, Stevven says.

Eli wails.

Don't you interfere with nothing, Darlene says to Stevven. Be nice.

Eli sobs.

We are heavy bear paws pilfering in lap. We are yawning, aching farmerspine. We are four hundred unimportant generations old.

I need to go poo, Eli says.

The bathroom is right over here, Darlene says. I'll show you, hun.

Stevven sputters.

Darlene lays gel fingernails and plastic bracelets on Elishoulders, walks them down aisle.

Stevven looks back to church doors, shut against BluBerry somewhere under antagonizing sun, maybe sideways or dying by deer.

Preacher meets Eli and Darlene in center aisle, spreads warm intones, hands on Eli. Stevven watches, ears ringing, words escaping. Preacher smiles, makes way for passage. Darlene flips on bathroom light, closes door behind Eli.

Darlene turns back towards Stevven, crinkles sympathetic purple vein eyes.

Stevvenhands tremble, find paper snacking plate, cheese cube. They eat distant from food.

Darlene eases into pew, exhales, perfumes air with vanilla, bergamot. I think there is a reason the Lord brought you here today, she says.

How do you keep the parasite in check?

I beg your pardon?

The parasite, the thing that bridges us.

You mean the spiritual gift?

God, the parasite.

Please don't blasphemy His name.

I don't know if the fear is mine or yours.

Sweetie, I have nothing to fear for I have given my heart to Christ.

Stevven eats more, instant potato salty. Churchfellows look and say hello or look disdainfully. Stevven guzzles cookie.

They think we're freeloaders, Stevven says.

Who do you believe you are? Darlene asks.

I don't know. I still believe in a place, just over the hill. Where things could be a little better. Where we can finally stop and stay a while.

What you don't like about the place you coming from?

Stevven shakes head. The city is killing people, they say. I know I've made it harder for myself, for others since the riots. I just, I just wanted to grow a garden— Stevven gazes into hands—I've spent my whole life preparing how to leave, always leave, when the corps and landlords chase me out, but Mary, Gino, and so many others... I've never been alone in all this.

Darlene puts motherly hand on Stevven wrist. Stevven looks at Darlene.

After June, I stopped selling my body to the causes too large to change a fucking thing. BluBerry. June thought BluBerry could solve world hunger. But

BluBerry is holding on like the rest of us. I thought BluBerry was the last place of everything that was good and that could be good. But Eli—

Darlene squeezes Stevven into deep, plush hug. Stevven cries.

Hush hush, it's all gonna be fine. It's all gonna be just fine. Now, here comes your little brother now.

Eli scoots in, sits next to Darlene.

Preacher John reminds us here there is power in prayer, Darlene says, takes Eli under arm.

Gino prays, Eli says.

Is Gino your daddy?

Gino is an Earther. He prays a lot.

Was he Christian?

No, Eli says. I think he prayed to weather and beasts and growing things.

Well I think we might be able to show you one better, Darlene says. Bow your head with me, like this.

Please—Stevven loses control.

Bow your head like this, Darlene says.

We bow head, close eyes. Colors and sounds and memories shape, collect, unite.

Lord, thank you for bringing your lovely children to the church. Thank you for keeping them safe on their journey. We are so grateful here at Battle Creek to receive them. I pray that you open their hearts to receive your good Word, your son, Jesus Christ, and to be saved from eternal damnation, the fire, the gnawing teeth of hell. The solstice, June's favorite, has passed. Another year without her. Will we celebrate the anniversary of the missing. Jon Paw, yes, and little Susan and Gino and all the rest. Don't touch, don't touch me, I'm scared the blue world is large and blue, and the stars will be red at the descent. Poptarts, shoes, and Barbara be good. Barrels of flame bring the light, the horse shit, and the virgin pine virgin signs, wasteful letters, doom charity. Father, mother, parent, Eli forgive me! Forgive the going of flesh and time. Unforgiven.

Get out! Stevven roars up.

Drop your chains! Darlene cries. Come to Christ!

Stevven wheels over pew, crawls over feet, barrels outside church, bruises heart in profane bodily resistance. They fall into BluBerry. Hot sun panic. They draw BluBerry from steaming sun onto parking lot shoulder. Between truck and tree shades, on gravel and dirt, they sit, respire.

BLACKBERRY BRIDGES, SMOOTHS CEREBRUM, RESOLVES words into breath.

We are twelve paws, berry seeds rolling across gums. Church and leaves age into forest, then bursts new like fresh paint. We breathe together, tottering places, making margins whole between inhale, exhale. Photosynthesizers move through us, about us, through crucifix and people. We are bear, we are Stevven, bodily. To wait is to be nonplace, unalive. To stay is to abandon time and become.

CHURCHDOORS TURN IN.

Eli steps into sun, squints at Stevven over gravel sea.

Stevven stands, sniffles. They walk across to Eli.

They wrap arms, speak this way only.

THERE, NOW, ALL BETTER, DARLENE says, exits church. Kids, I'd like you to meet John, my husband.

Large sweaty white man frowns into sun, tweaks nose at Stevven and Eli.

We would like to offer you all a ride back home, Darlene says. And say hello to your folks.

Stevven looks at Eli. Eli nods.

We're going to Sewanee, Stevven says.

Darlene head tics back, hand to heart. She wideeyes John.

John clears throat. I ain't gettin no two toes near the stink of that place, he says.

What, why? Stevven asks.

Oh you poor darlings, Darlene says. I should have guessed.

Course they ain't gonna raise their children right, the commies—John nods at Stevven—Look at the stink eye on that one. Honey, there ain't no hope of saving that one.

Darlene yanks John back into churchshade.

He has the gift, and Eli—Darlene whispers—He has a biblical name. It is a sign.

But look at him, he's Chinese. Don't you wanna wait for—

Darlenepurse hits John. All children are God's children—Darlene leans and smiles at Eli—Don't you mind him, darlin, you're beautiful and perfect.

Eli smiles. Stevven coughs and spits on gravel. Their mom is Japanese, Stevven says.

Darlene breaks scold at John—What was that?

I said Eli's mom is Japanese, not Chinese. And we're not up for adoption, Stevven says.

Darlene chortles. Oh no, of course not—

Thank you for your kindness, Stevven says. The prayer. The bathroom.

They're just freeloading, John says, takes Darlene underarm. Taking advantage of your good heart. The commies train them.

I—I don't believe—

John steers Darlene around Stevven and Eli. She struggles to pivot head back, speak to them. Eli follows her. Stevven follows Eli. They arrive at truck. John opens door for Darlene, lifts her in.

Shoo, John says to Eli, shuts door.

Wait, Eli says, crosses to BluBerry, returns as John loads into driverside.

Darlene rolls down passenger window, tears smearing mascara down doughy face. She dabs face with tissue.

I, I want to apologize for my husband, Darlene says. Oh, what's this?

BluBerry, Eli says, slips leaf into Darlene hand.

Oh, how sweet, Darlene says, blubbers. Oh now I guess it's my turn to cry— Darlene whips around to John as he starts engine—Now just wait a minute. I'm getting out of this truck.

No you ain't, John says, reverses truck.

They growl out parking lot, away, Southbound towards interstate 156. Stevven and Eli listen to engine roll down mountain.

Eli furrows eyes at Stevven. Commies?

Communists. From each according to their ability, to each according to their needs.

Are we commies?

Not sure—Stevven coughs, coughs, coughs.

Eli meets them on ground.

I'm okay, Stevven says, slurps air, drips mucus onto ground. Tell me what you need.

I'm okay.

Food, water, rest? Got your fill of hugs and kisses? Stevven leans towards Eli, snot stringing.

No! Eli laughs, jumps away. Gross!

I'm going to get you! Stevven rocks up and chases Eli once around camper van, stops, leans against hot paint and steel, hacks up fluids.

Better save our energy, Stevven says, dizzy.

They sit down together on gravel in vanshade. They pass water skin. They sift through rocks, pick out small fossils and glass, paint them in sunlight.

People leave in couples and families from church, gossip about Stevven and Eli, throw suspicious eyes, pack into cars, drive home.

Hey!—scrunchy old person in oily breeches rounds van—What do you think you're doing? Scram, get!

Stevven and Eli pick up BluBerry, cross to parking lot edge, stop before highway, scuttling heat. Hateful gaze chases them.

Go on, git!

Eli sets ammonite fossil piece in BluBerry soil.

I'm ready, they say.

MANY STEPS UP HIGHWAY, ACROSS water, rock and mud. Stevven stops, breath lagging. They break. BluBerry drops. Leaves meet ground.

Eli and Stevven pack BluBerry in together.

What's that? Eli says softly.

Stevvenface scrunches. I can't hear anything, they say.

I think it's water, Eli says. Think you can make it?

Stevven heaves, pulls on BluBerry straps, wrists sore. Feet trundle down rocks after Eli. They slip off trail onto rocky creek embankment, waterfall rising, striding towards them. Waterfall begins high over Stevvenhead, sparkles down like bridal veil, trumpets into turquoise pool, yellow rocks.

They drop BluBerry too soon. Gun jumps out, undresses, eats sand. Eli squats down with Stevven creekside, picks up tea towel, oilstains rainbow.

You're sleepy, Eli says.

Blue schists glisten, steal Stevven gaze from sandy muzzle. Jerky brown branches catch creek froth, boil coolly. Sun burns holes through vision, black holes, heat death, stars.

Shoe leaves Stevvenfoot.

Eli?

Eli takes off other Stevvenshoe.

I don't want to get too comfortable, Stevven says.

It's okay, Eli says. We're close.

Eli unvelcroes, sets Elishoes neatly next to Stevvenshoes.

Stevven splashes face with water, focuses, unfocuses on water, reflections flowing down, away.

Woah, Eli says, stoops downcreek.

Don't go far, Stevven says.

What are these? Eli says.

Stevven lies onto side, lays head into twiggy sands. Describe them to me, they say, brightness, coolness running through feet.

Like little gold umbrellas, Eli says.

Are they flat, small?

No.

Can you see what's under them without touching them?

Little canyons, Eli says.

Stevven smiles into coolhot dark. Chanterelles, they say.

There are lots of them, Eli says. Hello.

Who are you saying hello to? Stevven asks.

A person, Eli says. Hair like Gino's.

Stevven wakes up into bigbright, draws gun from wet sand.

Stranger in red bandanna stops downslope twenty feet from Eli, strong, feminine, mountain lion eyes.

I am a friend, Bandanna says, three large mesh bags stacking on back.

We are tiring. We draw Stevven down.

You must be the sharpshooter I heard earlier, Bandanna says. No need to fight over the Chanterelles. There is enough for all of us—Bandanna slowly steps back.

Can you help us find Sewanee? Eli asks.

Bandanna turns eyes between Stevven and Eli. What do you want at Sewanee?

To get BluBerry home, Eli says. We're almost there.

Stevven? BluBerry? Bandanna chews on names, lights up. We've been expecting you.

Keep your hands up! Stevven voices like splinters, slumps into sand.

Gun falls into wet. Rivulets streamline into muzzle. Eli runs over to Stevven, supports head. Bandanna drops bags, takes two steps down slope. Buttons on denim overalls sparkle as they kneel over Stevven.

I'm a nurse, Bandanna says. May I touch your face?

June?

No, my name is Tasha.

Stevvenhead drops into Tashahands.

Good Seed, Tasha says, feels cool sticky hands under Stevvenchin, pulls eyelid diagonal. We should get you back to camp.

Arms under Stevven. Upslope. Feet, cool dirt, creek pulling away.

BluBerry is still back there, Stevven says, ebbs.

They'll be okay, Tasha says.

We need to get BluBerry, Stevven repeats.

We'll come back for them later. You look like you're in more trouble than they are. What happened?

We have to—choke—bring BluBerry, Stevven says.

Salts sting cheeks. Head rolls, roils, boulder, bullfrog. Feet swell into trail, unalone. Red watercolor, television noise. Life like spirals.

HILL RISES, CRESTS. TREES SPREAD, road, gravel, truck. Eli and Tasha rest Stevven against forest service sign with cryptic red, alien signature.

BluBerry, Stevven blubbers, snots.

They pack Stevven into truck, middle seat. Doors shut on both sides, rock hawk feathers, little purple light prisms hanging on mirror. Bubble trembles in compass on centerdash. Stevven raps scratchy compass face, needle lost.

Have some electrolytes, Tasha says, hands Stevven jar. Stevven drinks, vinegar jolts.

Yow!

Pickled radish juice, Tasha says, turns ignition.

Stevven passes jar to Eli.

Yuck!

Eli caps jar as truck rocks over gravel.

Just focus on the road, Tasha says.

The road makes me sick, Stevven says, lies back.

How long ago did you eat the blackberries? Tasha asks.

I don't know.

How much did you have?

I ate as much as I could.

Have you been hallucinating?

Yes. No. I'm not sure.

Shortness of breath?

Just...so tired.

Try to keep your eyes open.

The road makes me dizzy. BluBerry is still back there.

Here, watch something, Tasha says, digs phone out center console, hands to Stevven. Have you seen the Fox story? You're a hit. I think you'd get a kick out of it if anything Tam says about you is true—Tasha reads wide Stevveneyes—On second thought, maybe we should wait until—

Stevven works foggy gaze into focus on video bubbling on screen, presses play.

Tashamouth twists. For the record, they say, I don't believe anything they are saying about you. None of us do.

Fox News logo whips in, out. Host Neil Shullack tells them good evening and culture in crisis.

Newscaster quakes in small Stevvenhand. Eli adds steady hand, leans in, watches.

We have quite the reel for you tonight, Neil says, brought to us by special reporter Barbara Betner. You're looking great despite all the trouble in the field.

It's Barbara! Eli says.

Thanks for having me, Neil, she says. I'm really excited to be here. I'm recovering. Shout out to Stacy's Salon! Couldn't feel myself without her work!

Barbara, your docu covering cult leader Stevven Pane has over 50 million views and counting. Did you know that your reporting was going to reach so many people?

I could have only hoped this would reach so many people, that I could help make the country more aware of those threatening our way of life today.

We're all curious, Barbara, how were you able to gain the trust of this person to get so close?

I just showed an interest, Neil. Egomaniacs need attention. I would visit with the disguise I was writing a story to recruit people for her, that I found her project meaningful.

Reels cycle: Stevven fishes out salad from garbage, Stevven takes money from Eli in shoes store, Stevven talks down to Mary.

How did you continue knowing that she would attack you at any time? Neil asks.

The story. It was too important not to tell. We thought the ecofascist movement died out with the riots, but really, it had found its new leader at the furthest edges of society.

Let's watch some highlights, Neil says, morphs into DonnaApartment. This scene at Adrianna's party. We can really see her insanity here. Tell me, how did she even get into such an exclusive venue?

What's interesting is that Stevven and Adrianna were doing campaign work together before we understood their connection to the ecofascist movement. Pleasure Activist Adrianna Cee Aniefuna-Butler is currently under investigation for her ties to Stevven's terrorist-cult network. We thought their connection was severed some years ago when Stevven went off the grid. Apparently plant liberation and pleasure liberation are all related to the active ecofascism movement, which is of course, at its heart, communism.

I just feel sick to my stomach watching her.

Me too, Neil.

She looks like she wants to bite you. Look, look at how she swats at the camera like that! Ha!

Camera changes to POV footage in Charleston outskirts.

Here we are walking into Roman's district, Barbara says. The homeless people under the bridge verbally harassed us. Oh, Neil. I don't know if I can watch the next part.

How did you feel when you saw that person walking towards you in the dark, weapon in hand?

I knew I couldn't risk my safety, or anyone else's, any longer, and I called the police. I was terrified. I thought I was going to die. Oh, I hate my voice on camera.

Tell me about the victim of this scene, Mary Saito.

Stevven shoved Mary right in front of the taser fire, you can see here. She is just a flower, so innocent, so sweet. She was an easy target for Stevven.

Let's see how she's doing now, Neil says.

Maryface yellow, exhaust. She stares offscreen.

How are you doing today, Mary? Nurse says.

Mary stares past, ghosts.

Eli stares into phone video, face videoblue, gaping.

Can you tell us about where Stevven is going? Nurse asks. Then we'll have a better chance at finding Eli.

Wetness trails down Elicheek.

Maryface cuts away to replay: Stevven hurls Mary into taser.

Mary's in the safe arms of law enforcement, Barbara says. But she is too scared to say more about Stevven.

Advertisement wheels over interview: *Mass Shooting Insurance by Progressive. Name your own price // Oscars 2097 Hosted by Archie 49er // Feel like you're in the wrong splint? Take this FREE quiz now to match to the splint that's right for you! // Bring back bottled water. With Eden.*

And we're back, Neil says. For those of you tuning in, we are diving deeper into the underground ecofascist movement through cult leader Stevven Pane, in an exclusive interview with guest reporter Barbara Betner.

Reels fill screen.

This shot of Stevven dragging Eli away from his mother, Neil says, shakes head sadly. This shot is horrific.

Thanks, Barbara says.

Now we're watching from a surveyor drone, Stevven crossing over the airport fence. She's harassing airport personnel. Where's Gino and Eli?

We suspect Gino wasn't able to climb over. He is earthing, which means he has glued all sorts of plants and dirt all over his body and can't move very well.

Psychotic. Tell us more about Gino, Neil says.

Here's his file, Barbara says, displays live mugshot of young Gino Bearpaw, *domestic terrorist*. He's a total ecofascist. It's no doubt Stevven acquired him to carry out more socialist projects. He's not prone to frequent violent outbursts like Stevven, but he's a ticking bomb. A big ticket criminal.

Neil scoffs. The things people do to their own bodies tell you just how much they hate the world.

He reeked, Barbara says. Even worse than Stevven.

And Eli couldn't come over the fence?

I don't think he wanted to.

I thought Stevven had him in her control.

Stevven has a particularly unique relationship with the child.

You mean—

Yes, Neil. I mean the worst.

Footage: Stevven spoons Eli. They nap together on mattress at Apartment. Quiet moment. Moonlight streams in.

Shot changes to Al. He sits at boat wheel, elbows on chair arms, hands in lap.

I don't agree with much of Stevven's lifestyle, Al says. Come to think of it, I don't know what they did all day. They were very private.

Did you see any inappropriate behavior between Stevven and Eli? interviewer asks.

My buddy says he seen them on the roof running around naked sometimes.

Sickening, Neil says. God protect that poor child. I heard that you were interested in talking with another person who had close contact with Stevven.

Yes, Nora Jones. She was found dead, locked in her own apartment room just two days after Stevven left the apartment. We know Stevven had something to do with it.

Barbara, we all want to know: Where is she now?

We were able to track Stevven trespassing into the airport property, through a passageway that has since been repaired and reinforced. Soon after she assaulted the airport employee, we accidentally flew the drone too close to the private home of someone living in Ladson County, and he shot it down before we could send out another. I didn't have the resources I have now from all the lovely sponsors to catch up with Stevven.

Sponsors reel over screen.

Where is Stevven going? Neil asks. What is she planning to do with this child?

We only have some vague ideas. Sometimes I wonder, Neil, if she even knows.

Barbarahead and Neilhead blink away to Apartment, calm sea.

Crack! Apartment detonates. Water erupts, swallows, drowns. BluBerry tumbles in air, crashes into shallow water reeds.

W ARM. SKIN.

WHITE. SHEET, WOOL BLANKET.

Dust rides breath in bluegray light. Soft ceiling.

Sticky fingers touch eyelids, brush grog. Spit films, flakes off cheeks.

Bird babble, house sparrows. Chirrup, chirrup. Chirrup, deliverance inside feathers and rivering windpipes. Muscle and bone squeezes and trembles, speaks, songs, sounding home, season.

Chirrup. Chirrup.

Eli? Stevvenvoice migrates, placing.

Gaze glides to cream window, blinds full in late morning light. Click, scruff, rodents scratch up trees outside.

Stevvenfoot drops from mattress, knocks wicker basket, poultice and rags. Raggedy clothes wan next to dead candle, washpan on desk, water pitcher. All soft. Tender.

Stevven wraps toes around early century dormstyle desk, presses wood edges into feeling, closes eyes, remembering.

MY SISTER'S GOT A SPOT in Charleston, June says.

Hand on Junechest. Heartbeat. Soft coniferous eyes seeding thought into ceiling. She turns to Stevven like magnolia.

I want you to come with me, she says.

Stevvenhand twitches, eyes descend.

You want to sell your soul to Agrigen? Stevven asks.

I wish you wouldn't say it like that. We talked about this.

They're not going to let you use their labs for anything but evil.

BluBerry is too important to leave behind.

So stay behind with BluBerry and me, Stevven says, strokes Junehand.

I need the cell culture equipment, she says.

Stevven sits back on elbow. Apply for another grant, they say.

I leave in a month, she says, rolls to standing.

Warmth leaves with her.

There is so much good we can do here, Stevven says.

Can you not hear how selfish you are? she says, glares over shoulder.

I believe in your vision. In BluBerry. I do.

It's about thinking bigger, bigger than ourselves. I'm talking about feeding kids. Healthy kids, happy future.

There's work here. It's not an ultimatum.

It's just a with or without you, babe.

ROBIN SKIPS ON WINDOW PANE, wakes Stevven.

Clean shawl drapes deskchair.

Postfever fingers clutch at fabric, hold tight. Breath draws belly up, down. They roll onto side, flesh sliding raw like mud around pecan shell lungs. Slow, sandhourglass waking, then fluttering.

Uaaagh—Stevven sounds, summons claybed body—Uaaaagh—Unleashes noises from deep like ancient ribbons—Uuuuahaaa!

They grapple seat, steady on deskchair, gather shawl in waking fistfuls. They slide shawl over shoulders, clasp soft fibers over chest. Southern pine, twisting mildew, summer.

They wiggle feet onto carpet. Back crows, knees quake, second life.

JUNE KNITS SOCK AROUND BEECH tree outside Wilkins Hall, knees bronze in afternoon light. Lab notebooks stack in Kentucky grass beside yarn. She crochets with friends, invites Stevven to join.

Will it bother the ants? Stevven asks, points to insects trailing over tree sock.

No, June says, threads green yarn into purple. They'll adjust, see?

But what's the point? The tree is beautiful without the yarn.

June smiles at Stevven. Just as I am without your arms around me.

Stevven sifts through spiny beech seeds, cheeks flushing.

Want to try? June says, offers crochet hook.

June teaches them while more beech seeds drop, slow and sweet in afternoon sun.

I still don't get the point, Stevven says, redoes violet chain over treescar.

We're all just out here trying to create something new that isn't babies, June says. If you're not feeling it you can leave, you know.

They laugh together, Junelaugh luscious.

I'm feeling it, now, Stevven says, works in yellow yarn.


STEVVEN DRAWS UP SHAWL, WALKS shakily to door.

Eli?

Noisy unvoice things fold around Stevvenhead, grief and then joy like wind. Stevven feathers current, glides through heavy door. They fly down hallway, old university dorm hallway reeking Osage orange pollen. They catch on stair railing, as if and truly before great cliff.

Stevven? says blossom voice, sweet acoustic signature, child, world.

Stevven drops like tree limb without realization midstair, collapses into joy.

Eli bounds up stairs. They pivot landing, catch Stevven. Small, warm arms wrap around Stevvenneck, close like rain.

You're squishing me! Eli says.

Stevven relaxes into tears.

I'm glad you're awake, Eli says.

Stevven laughs, touches ravenblack braids with flower.

Your hair, Stevven says.

Paintbrush flowers. Meeka did it for me.

Meeka?

My best friend! We're playing Raccoon, Mouse, and Hawk outside. Come play with us!

I was so so scared when I woke up and you weren't there, Stevven says. I was so worried I lost you. Then I saw the bandages, my fresh underwear, and felt the touch of all the people who helped me. And I knew we made it.

That's good. You can play Monkey. Or Toad. There are lots of toads here.

Stevven cries.

Are you sad? Elifingers grow to Stevvenface, smear salts, trace smile.

I'm very happy, Stevven says.

Eli sits on Stevvenknee. BluBerry braided into the river by the chanterelles, they say. They broke through the pot, made big big humungo roots!—Eli squirrels up onto feet—And they're here, too.

Eli outturns pocket. BluBerryleaves tumble into Stevvenhands.

And here! Eli says, pushes out full, sunsoak childbelly. Lots of BluBerry in here.

Stevven hugs Eli in, inhales soft dirty cotton, green leaf piles. Wet pollens, shells, birdsong.

# ACKNOWLEDGMENTS

Though countless are the critters that troubled this story into being, I thank Alex Kinnaman, Mitra Martin, Lily Raff McCaulou, Jeremy Garrison, and Taryn Everdeen. I thank Paul Trembath, William Marvin, David Haskell, Lynn Badia, and Clifton Raphael. I thank my friends at Parksland Retreat and University of the South, Sewanee. I thank my parents. I thank the stirrers, the unsung rebuilders, and the joyful grievers.

Printed in the USA
CPSIA information can be obtained
at www.ICGtesting.com
JSHW022054121023
50071JS00004B/147